Kris Bock

What We Found

Pig River Press

Pig River Press

Socorro, New Mexico

Copyright © 2012 by Christine Eboch
ISBN: 0615674178
ISBN-13: 978-0615674179

This is a work of fiction. Names, characters, places, and incidents are the product of the author's imagination. Any resemblance to actual persons, living or dead, is entirely coincidental.

What We Found

One

I shouldn't be doing this. I don't do things like this.

And yet I kept walking, following Jay through the woods. I stepped carefully along the narrow path, but my good shoes would be dusty by the time we were done. My gaze flicked up to Jay's long legs in faded jeans. His butt had been voted the best in our high school. It wasn't the only reason I'd had a crush on him as a sophomore, but it definitely played a part.

Six years later, it was hard to believe I was really walking through the woods with him. Though we'd grown up together in a town of only 8,000 people, we'd rarely spoken. He was two grades ahead of me, but even if we'd been in the same year, I wouldn't have traveled in his circles. I'd seen him around school or at the pizza parlor, I'd watched his basketball games, I'd felt sorry for him when I heard his dreams of playing college ball fell through.

Since I'd graduated, I'd only seen him around town when I came back to visit. We might smile and say "Hey" as we passed, the way acquaintances did. Yet a week after I'd moved back home, I was taking a long lunch to follow Jay into the woods. I felt like a giddy high school girl again.

I had to remind myself that I was twenty-two, an adult, with a brand-new college degree – with honors. I'd worked hard to get the Hospitality Degree that had landed me one of the few good jobs in the only place in town worth working. I'd come back to my hometown for my new job at the Mountain Inn and Resort and for my brother, not for Jay. And I was old enough to realize that we probably didn't have much in common.

But when my high school crush noticed me for the first time and offered to show me the view from the plateau, how could I resist? I didn't expect to start a beautiful relationship, but it was nice to imagine I'd turned into the type of woman who could attract a cool guy's attention.

My heart was beating a little too quickly and I had to wipe my palms on my slacks. Despite the leafy shade, the air hung heavy and hot, the first really warm day of the year. It had hit 87 down in Albuquerque the day I moved, but summer came later in the central New Mexico mountains, at an elevation of almost 7,000 feet.

We entered a small clearing. Sunlight broke through the trees, dappling the long yellow grass. It was nice to be back in the mountains, back in these woods where I'd walked so often, after four years in a big city. I'd missed the green.

A bird rustled nearby. Jay turned and smiled at me. I smiled back, but my face felt stiff as I remembered his reputation with girls. At the time I'd envied those girls, with all the naïveté of a shy teenager who never got asked to go for walks in the woods with boys. Now I wasn't sure what to do with myself. He'd said he wanted to show me the view and point out the changes since I'd been gone. But in high school, a "walk in the woods" wasn't about the scenery.

I was being silly. We'd grown up since then. And we hardly had time to get into trouble. He couldn't possibly assume we were sneaking out for a quickie after chatting for half an hour in the employee lunchroom. I'd told him I only had a few minutes.

"Come on, let's go through here." He pushed into the trees to the side of the clearing, rather than going forward on the established path that looped around the plateau and eventually back toward the resort. The view should be straight ahead.

I glanced back down the path, but the bright green of the golf course had disappeared around a bend. Still, we were just a few minutes from work. Maybe he knew another path, a smaller game trail.

It was easier to go along than to ask questions. If he had something more in mind than admiring the view, I could stop him later. But no need to cause a fuss yet.

A minute later he stopped in a smaller clearing, where a fallen log had cleared a space among the other trees. A nearby bank sloped down to a ditch that might carry a trickle of water later in the season, after the rains. I kept my smile in place and waited to see what he would do.

He swung toward me and reached out with one hand. I jerked back. My arm bumped against a tree and I felt the bark catch my sleeve. I looked down to free it, my face hot.

"Nervous?" Jay asked with a smile in his voice.

I shrugged and avoided his gaze. "You startled me."

"Ah, sweet little Audra. Not so little anymore, and surely not so innocent?" He brushed his fingers over my hair where it draped over my shoulder just above my breast. I tensed but couldn't move back without hitting trees.

He reached in his pocket and pulled out a small plastic baggie. He unrolled it and pulled out a handmade cigarette – probably a joint. Some of the other rumors about him came back, rumors I'd forgotten. He grinned the cocky basketball-star smile that had melted so many hearts, but it didn't look quite the same now. For the first time I noticed the hollows under his eyes and the faint lines on his weathered skin. Could he really be just twenty-five? Had we all aged so much? Or had the years been harder on him?

He did work outside, which could account for some of the weathering. I was glad I always used moisturizer with sunscreen.

He lit up, took a puff, and held out the joint. I shook my head and struggled to keep a polite half-smile in place. He frowned and kept his arm extended. "Come on, you need to loosen up."

My hand twitched, as if it wanted to follow his command of its own accord. I hated conflict. But I didn't do drugs, and I wasn't about to start. If I got fired from my job in the first week, I'd have a hard time finding anything else in town. I'd been away for four years, only visiting once a month, and I wasn't about to make Ricky deal with Mom on his own any longer.

"Thanks, but no. I, uh, have some mild asthma and smoke makes me cough." I'd found excuses like that more effective than a simple no thanks, which could lead to derision and pressure.

He shrugged and turned away, taking another puff. The smoke drifted toward me, confirming that this was no ordinary cigarette. I edged toward the ditch bank to get away from the smell. As an excuse for backing away, I leaned over to sniff the clusters of yellow blossoms on a gangly wildflower.

I almost gagged.

Could that stench really be coming from those pretty little flowers? I straightened, trying to breathe shallowly through my mouth and hide my disgust so Jay wouldn't think I was disapproving of him.

Once I'd noticed it, the smell seemed strong all around me. Jay sat on the log and smoked. I paced the small open space, trying not to gag. It smelled of garbage, something rotten, decaying, dead. I wanted to get out of there. I wanted to turn back and run through the woods, back to my small office where I could focus on my work. This was a mistake. I'd never belonged with Jay and never would.

My friend Katie's voice sounded in my head. *Stop it! You're channeling your mother again. Not all men are monsters.*

He grinned up at me. "Come on, have a seat."

I stared into his face as my stomach churned. How could he stand being in this place? Couldn't he smell it? Or did his little cloud of pot block out everything else?

I managed a smile. "Can we go now? I don't want to get in trouble my first week."

He made a sound that might have been a short laugh or might've been a grunt of annoyance. "What's the big deal? My dad's the manager. I'll put in a good word for you."

But his dad wasn't my direct boss, and having Jay ask his dad to tell my boss to go easy on me wouldn't build the reputation I wanted.

He gave a smile that I would have found charming when I was fifteen. "Come on, sit down next to me."

I hesitated. I should tell him I was leaving. Just walk away. But I couldn't make the words come out. He might get angry, and as he'd said, his father was the manager.

I didn't want to go back to the office smelling of marijuana. He had the joint in his right hand, so I finally sat on his left a couple of feet away. Once he finished his joint, I'd insist we leave.

He edged closer and put his arm around me. His right hand – fortunately empty – came up to my face. I hoped he hadn't dropped the joint into the dry grass. Fire danger was at its usual early-summer high.

He leaned in and his lips touched mine. I flinched.

Jay leaned back. "What is wrong with you?"

My face heated. "I'm sorry. It's only ..." I searched for an excuse that wouldn't insult him. I glanced toward the ditch. "Something stinks here. It's making me sick."

He sniffed the air. "You're right. Smells like something died."

When he stood, I jumped up too. But instead of heading back for the main path, he walked closer to the ditch. It figured, a man notices something dead and instead of getting away from it he wants to poke around closer. I sighed.

Jay sniffed and then made a face. He pushed past a low-hanging branch and took a couple of steps down the ditch bank. I guess I have my share of morbid curiosity, because I edged closer.

Jay made a choking sound. He stumbled backward, turned, and bumped me hard as he pushed past.

"What is it?" I demanded

He leaned over the log, hands on his thighs, taking deep breaths. I looked toward the ditch, then back at Jay. What could have caused this reaction? Something dead, but larger and grosser than he'd imagined? I pictured a deer with maggots crawling all over it.

I shuddered. Whatever it was, I didn't want to see it.

"Jay? Are you all right?"

He straightened, still breathing heavily. "We have to get out of here. It's a body. I think – I think it's a body."

I stared at him, the words slowly sinking in. "You mean ... a *human* body?"

He didn't answer. I glanced toward the ditch and whatever it hid. "Are you sure?"

He shook his head. His skin looked gray, and his eyes seemed to stare at something no longer there. He lifted a hand and curled it into a fist over his chest. "There was ... a hand."

I swallowed hard and pressed my arm over my stomach. "We need to call someone." But if we reported a body and it turned out to be an animal, we'd look like fools. "We have to know for sure."

Jay made no move. I said again, "We have to know."

I walked slowly toward the ditch. I ducked under the branch. The smell rose up to gag me and I put a hand over my nose and mouth. My face turned away, refusing to see. I had to force myself to turn my head, to keep my eyes squinted open.

No.

It was a body. A woman's body.

The smell choked me and my vision blurred. Behind me, I heard Jay's harsh breathing. I should have listened to my instincts.

I shouldn't be here.

Two

I staggered back to Jay. My face felt strange, my lips pulled back in a weird grimace. "We have to call someone. Nine-one-one. The police." I fumbled in my pocket for my phone.

My hand trembled as I lifted the phone toward my ear. Jay grabbed my wrist. "No."

"What do you mean? We just found a body! We have to report it!"

He plucked the phone out of my hand. "We're not telling anyone. We were never here."

My hands dropped to my sides. "But – but – we can't just – we have to – Jay, this is serious!"

"Exactly." He pushed me toward the main path. "This is serious and we don't want to be involved in it. Let somebody else find it."

"Jay, that's ridiculous." I tried to squirm out of his grasp, but he outweighed me, and with the trees close on either side I had little choice but to keep going forward.

When we hit the main path I wrenched away and turned to face him. "Jay, give me my phone. We don't have to stay here if it bothers you that much. But we need to report this. That person's been missing ..." I gulped. "... for a while. People must be wondering what happened to ..."

The image flashed through my mind, much as I wanted to erase it. The body was hardly recognizable but long hair and the tattered remnants of a flowered jacket suggested a woman. "Her. I think it was a woman. She might have gotten lost or injured while hiking. Caught in a storm. Attacked by a mountain lion."

My stomach roiled. I pressed an arm across it and bent over. Probably not a mountain lion. It would have destroyed the body, scattered the bones. I wanted to throw up but couldn't.

I straightened. "Whatever happened, people need to know about it. She must have family wondering where she is. There's no guarantee someone else will stumble over that soon, not where it is."

He grabbed my upper arms and leaned in so I winced at the smell of pot on his breath. "Listen to me. I have marijuana in my pocket. Do you think I want to bring the police out here?"

"So hide it, get rid of it! Anyway, they're not going to search you."

He leaned closer and spoke slowly. "We are not going to do anything. Let it go. This isn't our responsibility."

He pushed me down the path toward the resort. I stumbled ahead of him, hardly aware of where I was stepping. My body felt stiff and clumsy, and the forest seemed to spin around me. My foot caught on something, and I went down on one knee. Jay hauled me up again.

It had to be a dream. A nightmare. Things like this didn't happen.

I shook my head. Of course they happened. Every year a few people died or disappeared in the wilderness. One of my high school classmates had gotten drunk and walked off a cliff. Hunters had accidents. Tourists went hiking unprepared, not realizing that this luxurious ski and golf resort backed up to miles of unmarked wilderness.

But I'd never had to see it before.

We broke out of the woods at the edge of the golf course. The walk had seemed to take forever and yet to take no time at all. Golfers played in the distance, cheerful spots of color against the green grass. Jay nudged me and I turned to skirt the fairway. In another couple of minutes we would be back in the resort. Did Jay really expect me to go to my office and pretend nothing had happened? The horror had to be written all over my face.

I tried a smile. My cheeks twitched in a spasm.

This was absurd. I had to make Jay understand how important this was. In another minute we'd have no privacy. I tried to ignore my stuttering heart as I turned to face Jay.

Before I could speak, he growled, "Don't start. You're an outsider now. You don't have friends here. You don't know what's really going on. So keep quiet. Leave this alone."

I stared, my mouth open but no words coming out. Jay darted a glance toward the buildings. "I'm going back to the greenhouse. Get back to work and *keep your mouth shut!*"

My mouth snapped shut so hard my teeth rattled. Jay stormed away. I didn't watch him go; I stared straight ahead until my vision blurred.

Finally I shook my head and blinked rapidly, bringing the world back into focus. Brilliant blue sky. Unnaturally green grass. In front of me everything was clean, tidy, sanitized for your protection. But behind, the forest grew untamed, with shadows that now seemed threatening. At the resort, people went about their business, their work or play, with no idea of the thing that lay out there in the woods.

I gulped back a sob. Not a thing. A person. As terrible as that was, it was important, too. Someone had died in those woods. Probably a woman or teenage girl. I hoped she had died quickly, without pain or fear. Had she been caught in a storm last winter? Gone into the ditch for a little shelter from the wind? They said freezing wasn't so bad at the end.

Or had she died violently? I didn't want to believe it possible, didn't want to think about it. But someone needed to find out for sure. Someone needed to bring her home.

Jay disappeared into the greenhouse behind the resort. I crossed the fairway to the main building and went down the hall to my office, my mind still back in the woods. I sat behind my desk and stared ahead. I needed to do something, but I couldn't make myself move. I only managed to blink when my eyes got so dry they stung.

I don't know how long I sat there, staring at nothing. The knock on the doorframe took a moment to register. I turned my head and forced a smile. My face felt stiff, but the smile stayed in place as my boss entered.

"Oh, good, you're back. The preliminary write-up for the Sullivan wedding looks good, but I want to go over a few things." Eslinda stepped closer. At barely five feet tall, she didn't have to duck her head much to peer into my face, even though I was seated. "Are you all right? You look pale."

I swallowed, trying to get rid of the taste of death. "I have a headache. I stepped outside for some fresh air, but it didn't help." I couldn't believe I was lying to my boss. But how could I tell her the truth, that I'd taken a long lunch because a boy had flirted with me in the lunchroom, and he took me into the woods to smoke marijuana? Even without the dead body there were details I didn't want to explain. I had to do something, but until I could think clearly I didn't want to say anything I couldn't take back.

Her round face crinkled with sympathy. "I have some headache medicine in my office. I have pretty much any over-the-counter medicine you could possibly need, in fact. There's a first-aid kit on my file cabinet, behind the philodendron. I keep it well stocked. The first-aid kit, that is, not the philodendron."

My smile trembled. I didn't want her to be nice to me. And I didn't want her to get too close, in case she noticed the smell of pot – or the stench of death. "That's all right. I already took something."

"Maybe you should go home for the afternoon."

I wanted to get away, as far away as possible. But I couldn't walk away from what I'd seen, and once I left it would be that much harder to come back. "No, that's all right. I'm sure it will fade quickly."

She backed toward the door, keeping her voice soft. "You just take it easy for a while then. We can go over that plan later. I'm going to close your door so no one disturbs you."

I stared at the door as it softly shut behind her. "Thank you," I whispered. I was lucky to have a boss like Eslinda. She'd been patient and encouraging, and I could only hope to reach her level of efficiency by the time I took over for her. Though only in her fifties, she was retiring to travel with her husband. He was older and had diabetes. "We don't know how long we have," she'd told me. "We want to enjoy ourselves now, while we can."

I thought again of the woman in the woods. Her time was up. I hoped she was enjoying herself in Heaven, because she'd get nothing else from this world.

Except maybe people to mourn her. If she had family or friends, they must be wondering what had happened to her. I could give them the answer. I could make sure she had a proper burial.

I had to tell.

Three

I paced the small room. Obviously Jay wasn't going to back me up on this. Fine.

Maybe I could make an anonymous phone call. But how would I explain exactly where the body was? What if they couldn't find it? Would they even take me seriously?

How did one make an anonymous call, anyway? Even if I blocked the number, the phone company had to know where the call came from. I couldn't use the phone at the front desk without people seeing me. Maybe I could sneak into another office after hours, but the person who worked there might get blamed. An unused hotel room? I didn't have keys to the rooms.

They made disposable, prepaid phones. But I couldn't buy one anyplace in town without a chance the clerk would remember me. I'd have to drive to a bigger city, and where would I get time for that trip? Albuquerque and Las Cruces were both over two hours away.

I'd never considered how difficult something like this would be. Any option seemed risky, and if they somehow traced the call, that might make matters worse. They'd think I had something to hide.

I shook my head. I'd have to identify myself. But I'd pretend I found the body on my own. It had obviously been there for weeks – maybe months – so the specifics of how we found it hardly mattered. The main thing was to notify the police so they could identify the person and how she died. I could go out there on my own, later, and pretend I'd just found it, keeping Jay out of it altogether. I didn't understand why he was so paranoid, but let him keep his secrets. I didn't particularly want to talk about us being out there together anyway.

I grabbed the edge of my desk, lightheaded, and took a few deep breaths. I could do this. It was the right thing to do.

The dizzy feeling subsided. With that decision, the world settled back into its proper place around me. I couldn't imagine how Jay thought we could just forget what we'd seen. The image kept flashing in my mind and the smell seemed to linger on my skin.

Reporting the body wouldn't make the memory go away. But it might help me live with myself.

If I were really honest, really strong, I'd tell Jay first what I planned. He probably deserved to know, so he could prepare his reaction. But he'd try to talk me out of it, and I wasn't sure I was strong enough to resist. Katie, my college roommate, had told me I had daddy issues, and that was why I couldn't stand up to a man. I'd pointed out that I'd never really had a dad. She said that was the issue.

I missed her. Katie had been my rock from the first week at the University of New Mexico, when we met as dorm mates. A wave of loneliness swept over me. I wished I could call her, get her advice. But she was somewhere in South America with the Peace Corps. We thought she would be having adventures, while I returned to my sleepy hometown and a quiet life of work, with nothing more stressful than dealing with my mother.

I wouldn't call my situation an adventure. But my hometown no longer felt so sleepy.

I wanted the day to be over. I couldn't work. But I couldn't slip out of work again, especially not after what I'd told Eslinda. It would seem most natural to wait until five, and then go for a walk in the woods before heading home.

"She's not going anywhere," I whispered. "She's been there a long time. A few more hours won't make a difference." And yet adrenaline flooded my body, demanding action.

I had to get out of that tiny room. I lunged for the door, but once my hand hit the knob I froze. My body didn't want to turn the knob, open the door. Anything might be out there.

"Don't be ridiculous," I hissed. "You're in no danger here."

I forced myself to turn the doorknob. I opened the door slowly and peered into the hall. Empty, though I could hear the murmur of distant voices over my own ragged breathing.

I crept down the hall like a hunted creature. When I had to pass an open office doorway, I kept my eyes straight ahead and barely breathed, fighting the urge to run. I headed for the restroom for something to do, but when I reached the door, I hesitated again. Why was I suddenly afraid to enter a room, as if some horror might lurk within? How long would this last?

I made myself push the door open. The room was empty, and my sigh of relief echoed. Still, I found myself checking every stall before I entered one. I had to know that no ... *thing* ... waited for discovery.

Even peeing was difficult, as if I couldn't get my body to relax on command. After, I washed my hands for a long time. I splashed water on my face and rinsed out my mouth. I even ran a damp paper towel over my clothes and hair. I wanted to strip off my clothes and take a shower, to get rid of the lingering stench of decay and Jay's marijuana.

Why did he have to smoke that stuff? Even if nothing else had happened, he'd put my reputation at risk, if someone had smelled the smoke on me.

I pushed aside the sense of betrayal. He didn't care about me, but why should he? We barely knew each other. My teenage fantasies about him had been all wrong, or else he had changed. It didn't matter. His cruelty and indifference weren't about me.

I took a deep breath. I had to remember that. This wasn't about me. Jay hadn't betrayed me, because he didn't owe me anything. But he had betrayed her – the woman in the woods – by refusing to acknowledge her.

His behavior had been so strange. Had he known her? Could he have recognized that face?

I shuddered and placed a hand over my nose and mouth, as if the stench still rose around me. Not her face, not anymore, but maybe he recognized the jacket. But wouldn't that make him want to help more?

I tried to bring to mind his words after we'd found the body. I couldn't recall exactly. Something about how I didn't know what was going on around here. The whole memory felt hazy, like trying to remember a dream after waking up. Except for the one image that burned all too clearly in my mind, the details blurred.

I hugged myself. Jay couldn't be involved in her death, could he? That was too outrageous. By what bizarre twist of logic would he have led me to that spot, contrived to find the body, and then refused to report it? I had a vague notion that killers sometimes pretended to find their victims, thinking it would make them less suspicious or something. But then to hide the discovery?

Unless Jay expected me to report the body after all.

I was being ridiculous. Jay didn't know me well enough to know what I would do. And I didn't think he was smart enough for that kind of manipulation. He was just a coward who, as he'd said, didn't want to get involved.

Besides, she had probably died of exposure after getting lost, or after getting drunk and passing out. Maybe she'd OD'd. Maybe she'd committed suicide. Maybe she'd been jogging and a mountain lion attacked her. She wasn't dressed like a jogger, but ...

I had to stop thinking about it. The police would find out.

I left the restroom and turned toward the lunchroom for a cup of coffee. Two steps from the doorway, I heard the shuffle of movement within. I turned and fled back to my office.

I sat at my desk and started doodling on a piece of blank paper, the meaningless swirls and curlicues that had filled the edges of my notebooks in school. The minutes ticked past as I waited, trying not to think, not to remember.

I glanced down at the paper. Among the random squiggles a form took shape – someone lying on her back, one hand curled on her chest. Her head was turned to one side, dark hair half hiding the empty space where the lower part of her face should have been.

I stared at the drawing for a second. What was wrong with her face?

I shook my head, as if I could fling the thought out of my mind. I crumpled the paper and tossed it in the wastebasket. Then I pulled it out again and spent several minutes carefully tearing it into tiny pieces, destroying the image.

Five o'clock finally came. I grabbed my purse and headed for the door. My hands were trembling again, my legs numb with the flood of anxiety. I'd go back to the woods, I'd call ...

I stopped in my doorway. Jay still had my phone.

Should I go and demand it from him? It would be reasonable to want it back. But would he guess what I intended? Would seeing him make it harder to do what I needed to do?

Someone was coming down the hall. I pulled my face into a smile as I glanced up.

"Hi, Audra," Nascha said. "A few of us are heading to the Cactus Club. Thursdays are Ladies Nights, so two-dollar margaritas during Happy Hour, if you're into that kind of thing. Want to come?"

I shook my head. "Not this time. But thanks." Had my voice been too loud? Too soft? It seemed to echo from a distance.

She waited while I locked my door and we continued down the hall together. I liked Nascha. She was a few years older than I was, but still in her twenties, with a beauty that clearly showed her Navajo heritage. She was quiet but friendly, with a confidence I lacked. I'd hoped we could be friends. But I couldn't think of a single thing to say to her.

She turned toward the front of the resort and the parking lot. I hung back and when she paused to glance back at me, I finally forced myself to speak. "Uh, I'm going out the back. Take a little walk before I head home. Too much sitting today." I managed a chuckle that sounded false to my ears.

Nascha gave me an odd look. "All right. See you tomorrow."

Several heads turned in the lobby as her graceful figure strolled past. I wanted to catch up with her, head to the bar for a casual drink and some girl chat. I hoped she wouldn't think me unfriendly, when I so desperately needed friends.

I blinked away tears and turned toward the back of the resort.

When I stepped out on the edge of the golf course, I glanced toward the greenhouses a hundred feet away, but I couldn't face Jay again. There were other phones.

I kept to the edge of the golf course until I reached the path Jay and I had taken earlier. Waves of hot and cold washed over me as I stepped into the trees. Thirty feet in, I stopped and glanced back. The narrow strip of golf course still visible at the end of the path glowed like the light at the end of a nightmare tunnel. It pulled at me, but I held my ground. No one could see me now. Good. I wasn't walking all the way down the path again. No way was I going near that body.

But I couldn't call the police yet. I needed to wait long enough that I could have made it all that way and back, just in case anyone had noticed me head into the woods.

How long had it taken me to get to the path? Maybe five minutes. Another ten and the regular office staff should be gone. I couldn't do anything about the people who worked evenings, or the guests, but the less commotion I caused, the better. And this would be easier if Jay was gone for the day, if he didn't find out what I'd done until he heard the story in the morning. As a groundskeeper, he might work irregular hours, though. What would he do if he saw police cars pull up?

Hide, probably.

I paced. A dull ache filled my stomach. I wished I could throw up and be rid of it.

The memory of that smell lingered. I was too far away to smell anything, but still I breathed shallowly. Everything smelled bad, the trees, the musk of the woods behind me, the faint smell of exhaust drifting from the parking lot. Would my nose ever get back to normal?

How much time had passed? It felt endless, but probably no more than a minute or two. Without my phone, I couldn't check.

The woods loomed over me. The afternoon heat pressed in. I gave a sobbing gasp.

I ran out and across the golf course, headed for the men gathered around the nearest tee. I ran as if something was chasing me. My legs burned and I gasped for breath, but I couldn't slow.

Another few minutes wouldn't matter at all. But I ran.

Four

Half an hour later, I paced the larger clearing, where Jay and I had turned off the main path. My hair hung damp against my neck, but despite the heat I hugged myself. I could hear the murmur of soft voices from the police officers with the body. My mind played back over events, starting with the surreal feeling of dialing 911. Those three tones hit me like a punch to the gut. You didn't dial 911 unless it was a real emergency.

The golfers, a group of middle-aged men, had seemed more intrigued than horrified. The one who'd lent me his phone had asked if he should take a look at the body, to confirm what it was. I'd refused to go back there.

The police had arrived ten minutes later, two officers, one probably in his forties and the other younger. I had already forgotten their names.

A branch snapped. I whirled toward the path back to the golf course. A man was coming toward me. He wore some kind of uniform; his long-sleeved shirt had a patch on the shoulder, but the shirt was tan rather than the dark blue of the police uniforms. I drew back to the edge of the clearing, my heart racing, even though logic told me he was probably there in some official capacity.

He stepped into the clearing, a small man in his fifties with gray hair and a mustache. He nodded and gave his name, but by the time he finished his introduction, the only word I remembered was "sheriff." I pointed to the side path with a shaky hand and he left.

I wanted to get out of there. I wanted to start running and not look back. But they'd asked me to stay around to answer questions.

I took a deep breath. I'd done nothing wrong.

But I didn't want to answer any questions.

A few minutes later, one of the officers and the sheriff came back. The scene seemed to blur for a moment, as if they were walking through a haze. The older police officer stopped in front of me while the sheriff hung back a few feet. The officer said, "We'd like to ask you a few questions, ma'am."

I nodded, but my throat felt too tight to speak.

"How exactly did you find the body?"

I swallowed twice and cleared my throat. "Um, I just wanted to go for a little walk. Get some fresh air. Clear my head. I had a headache." I swallowed again. Stop talking so much. Just stick to the basics. "I, uh, wandered into the woods. And then I smelled something." My throat closed up and I dragged in a couple of shallow breaths. The smell of evergreen trees and parched weeds filled my nose, and I told myself I couldn't possibly smell anything else from here.

"I looked around a little. I was curious. And then I saw ... saw ..."

He half smiled. "You saw her looking back at you."

A spasm twisted my stomach and I pressed a hand to it. "I suppose." So it was a woman. "Do you think you'll be able to identify her?"

He nodded. "Finding her is a real breakthrough."

Breakthrough? What did that mean? They were looking for her? A missing person case? "Did you ..." I forced the words out. "Could you tell ... how she died?"

He just looked at me.

I gave a helpless shrug. "I keep hoping it was ... that she didn't suffer. That it was quick and ... some kind of accident."

His face tightened. He gave an almost imperceptible shake of his head.

I gulped. Somehow the thought of violence – human violence – made the death worse. It was one thing to discover an accidental death, to see that the victim had a real burial and to bring closure to a family.

It was entirely different to uncover a crime. This was far from over.

"How close did you go to the body?" he asked.

I hunched my shoulders. "Not very. Just close enough to see what it was."

"Did you stay at the top of the bank or go down?"

I hesitated. I honestly couldn't remember. It was like waking from a dream and only having bits and pieces still clear. But I wouldn't have gone any closer than necessary. "I stayed at the top."

"And then what did you do?"

"I ran back out to the golf course and found someone with a phone and called the police."

"Did you see anyone else?"

I shook my head. I hadn't seen anyone else hanging around suspiciously. I hadn't seen anyone *else*, besides the person I was with.

He looked down. He seemed to be studying my feet. Then he looked up and held my eyes. "You're telling me you came out here alone, and you didn't see anyone else while you were here. Is that what you're saying?"

I swallowed and nodded.

I was lying to the police. Not just the sin of omission, but flat-out lies. How had I been so stupid that I didn't see it coming? I'd assumed all I had to do was point out the body. I hadn't thought beyond that. But his questions sounded suspicious.

Was I being paranoid? Was this always the way the police talked? Or had I missed something?

Footprints. It was dry, not muddy, and I hadn't noticed any footprints, but I hadn't been looking for them. The police probably had some way of identifying footprints even in the hard packed dirt and dry grass.

And hadn't the ground been a little softer on the bank? I thought I recalled my foot slipping a little. Maybe I had gone down the bank farther than I'd thought.

I stared at the officer while the world blurred. I felt as if I was going to pass out. I wanted to pass out, if it would get me away from the questions.

"It's important we find out exactly what happened," the officer said.

I nodded, but I couldn't speak. Details were coming back to me. I had walked down the path behind Jay, but I'd gone back in front of him. That meant his footprints were both under and over mine. If the police had seen that, they knew I hadn't been alone.

What had happened to the joint? Had he taken it with him or left it behind?

The world seemed to spin and my knees felt weak. A hand gripped my arm. I blinked and tried to focus on the officer's face.

"Are you all right? Do you need to sit down?"

I glanced around at the patchy grass and dirt of the clearing. The only clean place to sit was on the log near the body, and I wasn't going back there. "I need to get away from here," I whispered.

The officer and the sheriff exchanged glances. Then the police officer said, "Mike will walk you back to the resort."

I nodded and kept my head down as I edged back to the path. My heart was still hammering, screaming at me to run, but it took all my focus to put one foot in front of the other. I felt like I had the flu. I felt like I was in a dream. On some level I still couldn't believe this had happened.

At least I'd done what I had to do. The woman in the woods would not be lost any longer. I'd done that much right.

I heard the soft rustle of leaves as the sheriff walked behind me. I could feel him looking at me. What did he think? Did he see a quiet, polite young woman? Or did he see a liar and a coward?

I should tell the police the truth. Jay wouldn't like it. Maybe he'd get in trouble. That shouldn't be my problem.

But if I changed my story now, would they believe anything I said? Jay would deny it. I couldn't prove he'd been there. And his father managed the resort, he had friends there, while I was new. If it came down to choosing sides, I didn't think I'd have anyone on mine.

I stepped out onto the golf course. The smell of meat and smoke touched my nose, and my stomach roiled, before I realized it was only dinner smells drifting from the resort's kitchen vent. I turned to the sheriff. "Thank you. I'm all right now. Can I go?"

"They'll want to talk to you again, probably later tonight. They'll call to let you know when."

I nodded. They'd taken my address and phone number earlier, even looked at my driver's license. But Jay still had my phone. I couldn't think of a single good excuse for why they shouldn't call it.

I stared at the sheriff for a moment. Then I turned and walked toward the parking lot. I'd survived one trial, but I faced an obstacle course ahead.

Five

Light glinted off the windows of the greenhouse. Was my phone in there, with Jay? Had he left and taken it with him?

I needed my phone. A visit to the greenhouse was worth a chance. If Jay was there, I didn't have to tell him what I'd done. Just grab my phone and leave. The police hadn't used their sirens, and the way the greenhouse windows were tinted Jay wouldn't be able to see out. He wouldn't know the police were there unless he'd seen them when he was leaving.

I glanced back toward the path. I didn't see the sheriff, so he must've gone back to the body. I changed direction and a minute later opened the door to the greenhouse and a wave of humidity. Light and greenery filled the large room, at least forty feet across and twenty feet deep. I didn't see anyone among the long tables filled with plants, but I heard someone moving to my left. The sounds were coming from big racks of equipment at one end of the room. At the other end, I spotted a closed door in a plain white wall. Maybe an office? Worth a try.

I crept toward the door and paused before it. Was Jay inside? I knocked lightly. No answer. I tried the handle and pulled open the door to reveal an office, small and cluttered with boxes on the floor and piles of paper stacked high on a desk. And next to a computer, my phone.

Finally, something was going right! Relief flooded me as I grabbed it.

I swung toward the door, caught my foot on the desk chair, and stumbled. How did a big guy like Jay maneuver with all the stuff in here? Two four-drawer file cabinets were stuffed so full the doors wouldn't close all the way. Long, plug-in lights – grow lights, maybe? – leaned against the wall next to a golf bag. Boxes were stacked three and four deep, some labeled and some not. Jay might have a green thumb, but he didn't have organizational skills.

I crossed the room and slipped out the door – and found myself face to face with a stranger. He was wearing jeans, a long-sleeved shirt, and gardening gloves. "What are you doing?" he snapped.

I instinctively hid my phone behind my back and then realized that carrying a phone wasn't suspicious but hiding something was. I dropped my hand and gave a casual shrug. "Looking for Jay. I guess he's gone for the day?"

"You just missed him."

I smiled and edged past the guy. "Okay, I'll catch him tomorrow."

When I reached the outside door, I glanced back. He was still staring at me, his face suspicious and grim. I fumbled with the door handle and ran the first few steps away from the building.

I forced myself to slow. The man probably wasn't suspicious at all. Why would he be? I was just suffering from my own guilty feelings.

Halfway to the parking lot, a bench sat beside the building, facing the golf course. I slumped onto it, tipped my head back, and closed my eyes. What a day. I was going to be late for dinner, but I needed to collect myself before I faced going home.

I opened my eyes and looked across the golf course toward the woods. What was going on in there? What clues were the police finding – and how many of them led straight to me and Jay?

A man stepped out of the woods. I jumped, even though he was a couple hundred feet away. He wasn't wearing a uniform, and I didn't think I'd seen him before.

He paused, head bowed, and lifted a hand to cover his face. He stayed like that for a full minute. It was only when he dropped his hand that I noticed his other arm. It ended just above the wrist.

I shivered. So he'd had some kind of accident and lost his hand. Big deal. That shouldn't be creepy. But combined with everything else that had happened, with seeing him suddenly appear from the woods where a dead body lay, it was.

He straightened and strode toward the parking lot. What had he been doing in the woods? Just a random tourist heading that way by chance, or a busybody who'd seen the police and wanted to learn the gossip? Neither possibility explained his reaction.

I got up and followed him. I had no plan, just a strange curiosity about this mystery man. Maybe the woman in the woods and the investigation of her death were none of my business. But I was involved, as much as I'd been involved in anything in my life. If her death wasn't natural – if it might be, as the officer had hinted, murder – I wanted to see it resolved.

My gut told me this guy was involved as well. But how?

I lost sight of him for a minute in the parking lot, but then I heard a door slam. I headed in that direction, past SUVs, minivans, and nice sedans – the typical vehicles of our mainly upscale tourists. Two police cars had pulled into the fifteen-minute parking spaces. A faint, strange sound, like a rusty door closing, drifted through the air.

An engine started. The battered old truck stood out like a janitor at the prom. It was dark blue, splattered with mud and probably decades old, with a cap on the bed. The evening sun glared off the side window, but as I walked slowly past the front I saw a figure inside – the one-handed man. He had his hand on the wheel but his head back, eyes closed.

I paused, studying his face. I guessed he was in his twenties, with short, light brown hair and pleasant features in a mask as still as death.

He opened his eyes and looked straight into mine.

I couldn't move as he held my gaze. My heart thumped against my ribs. He studied me without expression, no smile, no frown, nothing in his face but weariness.

Finally I had to blink, and once the eye contact was broken, I jerked my gaze away and kept moving. I quickly turned between the next two cars, to get out of his view. I'd have to cross behind his truck to reach my car, which might look odd if he was still watching, but I didn't care so long as I got out of there, fast.

I noticed the rusty screeching again. It was coming from his truck. I stumbled to a stop, staring at the back of the truck. What could be making that sound? The tailgate and back window on the cap were closed, hiding the sight inside, but the screech came again and again like someone – something – screaming.

The screams seemed to echo in my head. I couldn't take any more. I turned away with a hand over my mouth to hold back my own scream and hurried to my car.

Six

I pulled up in front of the house and turned off the car. For a minute I just stared at my home, as if seeing it for the first time. The three-bedroom bungalow had seemed so big and beautiful when we moved in twelve years before, after Mom got married. Now the wood siding looked faded, and a lonely stump in the front yard was all that remained of the tall pine that had to be cut down after suffering damage in a heavy snowstorm. The evergreens around the sides of the house were dropping needles on the patchy grass, which needed to be mowed.

I sighed. My escape had been temporary. I'd been so excited and terrified moving to Albuquerque, where the student body at UNM was three times the size of my entire hometown. Mom had warned me of all the dangers there, but despite a few scares, I'd emerged unscathed – only to return home, let my guard down, and stumble on death.

The heat started to build up in the car, and the smell of fried chicken tightened my throat, but I took a moment to rehearse my lines. I wanted to collapse in my room with the lights out and hide from the world, but that wasn't going to happen.

I pushed my hair out of my face, grabbed the grocery bag, and headed up the walk, trying not to let my shoulders slump.

I had a smile in place by the time I entered. Ricky was on the couch, messing around on his phone while the TV murmured about some science topic. He grinned at me, his cheerful face still chubby with baby fat despite a recent growth spurt, and my smile became a little easier. Jay was wrong about one thing. I did have a friend in town, even if it was just my little brother.

I set the bag on the coffee table and sank down next to him, putting my arm around his shoulders. He snuggled against me, affectionate behavior that was probably abnormal for a twelve-year-old boy, but no one had accused Ricky of being average.

Mom stepped into the room. "You're late. It's your turn to make dinner and it's already after six."

"I know. I got delayed at the resort." I was glad I had practiced the words so I could avoid the truth without actually lying. "I picked up dinner on the way home. Didn't you get my text?"

"I got it," Ricky said. "Mom, I told you."

She glared. "I should never have let you get him that phone."

I was careful not to smile. Texting meant I didn't actually have to talk to Mom, but the disadvantage was she could pretend she hadn't gotten the message. Copying Ricky was my backup. I wasn't sure if he'd caught on to that or just thought he was doing Mom a favor by notifying her when a message came in. It was a complicated system, but it worked for me.

She sniffed the air and turned her scowl to the bag on the coffee table. "What is that?"

"Fried chicken. And potato salad and coleslaw."

"Cool!" Ricky leaned forward and peered in the top of the bag. As my mother opened her mouth, I tapped Ricky's back and said quickly, "Take it into the kitchen and set the table." He dashed from the room.

I stood, but Mom blocked my way. "I expect you to fix healthy meals, not bring home junk. Ricky's fat enough as it is."

"He's fine, Mom. He's still growing. An occasional treat won't kill him." I took petty pleasure in the fact that my extra five inches forced her to look up at me. I had inherited my mother's delicate bone structure and bland coloring. So far as I knew, only my height came from the father I'd never met.

Ricky was his father all the way. And that was something our mother couldn't forgive.

We got through dinner somehow. Mom peeled the skin off her chicken, skipped the potato salad, and snapped comments at Ricky about his table manners, which were better than any man or boy I'd ever known. Ricky chattered, seemingly immune to the moods around him, or simply so used to Mom that he thought this was normal. Maybe I should have been grateful that he didn't show more obvious scars from being raised by a woman who hated men. But the scars had to be there, so I was determined to be there too, trying to balance out my mother's influence.

I picked at my food. My stomach rumbled, but somehow hunger wasn't translating into appetite. I had to figure out what I was going to tell them. Part of me wanted to say nothing, but the story would come out eventually. It would be worse if Mom heard it from someone else.

Ricky cleared the table and started washing the dishes. Before Mom could start in on me again, I said, "I need to change," and headed for my room.

I stripped out of my clothes and stuffed them in my laundry bag, grimacing as they touched my other laundry. I wanted to throw out the clothes I'd worn that day, burn them even, so they couldn't taint anything else, but I couldn't afford to lose a good office outfit.

I stood in the room where I'd lived from age eleven to seventeen. I hadn't gotten around to redecorating, so it had the same faded posters of kittens and puppies on the wall, the same pink and gray quilt on the single bed. I wanted to burrow under that quilt and hide. I wanted to run screaming from the house and never return. I was back where I had started. I'd thought I was stronger, that I could make my own life and help Ricky get started on his.

I'd made nothing but mistakes.

I pulled on sweatpants and a T-shirt and forced myself to leave the room before the urge to lie down overwhelmed me.

I stepped into the living room as a news bulletin interrupted the local broadcast. A woman's body had been found at the resort.

She had been identified.

They showed a picture of her. Not as I'd seen her, but as she had been in life. And then I recognized her.

I'd never met her, but I'd seen the "Missing" fliers around town. The newscaster reminded me of the details:

Bethany Moore, twenty-seven, missing for almost a month. I remembered glancing at the poster in the bank window, feeling vague sympathy for the family and hoping the woman had only run away. I hadn't paid too much attention, because of course I'd never see her myself. Those things just didn't happen.

Her body had been found by "a resort employee" in the woods. She'd been identified by her brother. I let out a shaky breath. They hadn't named me.

They cut from a shot of the woods across the golf course to the sober face of the newscaster. "Ms. Moore's disappearance has been under investigation for several weeks. Police have already interviewed several people associated with the case, including her ex-boyfriend, Thomas Bain. Ms. Moore had filed a restraining order against Mr. Bain two years ago. He admits to being in contact with her recently, but claims an alibi for the weekend she disappeared. There were also rumors of other boyfriends and drug use. The death is being investigated as a homicide."

Mom was shaking her head. "Poor girl. That man must have killed her."

"Which man?" I asked. "The ex-boyfriend?"

"You can't trust men. Let this be a lesson to you, Audra. Men are no good."

I glanced at Ricky, whose attention seemed to be focused on the TV, but how could he not be affected by comments like that? "Not all men are the same."

"They'll find some way to destroy your life. Trick you, abandon you, lie to you."

"I found her." Anything to interrupt the rant.

"What do you mean?"

"I found the body. I was the resort employee." For once I'd rendered her speechless. They both stared at me. I wanted to explain how horrible it had been, I wanted sympathy, but I also didn't want to say another word about it.

"And you're just now telling us?" Mom demanded.

I sighed. "I didn't want to … spoil dinner."

"A woman is murdered and you're worried about dinner?" She shook her head. "What happened? How did she die?"

"I don't know. I couldn't tell." I rose. "Look, it was awful, and I don't really want to talk about it. The police are going to interview me later tonight. They said I'm not supposed to talk to anybody before then." I didn't remember them saying any such thing, but it sounded reasonable. "I'm going to go lie down for a while."

I left them staring after me. All in all, I'd gotten off easier than I'd expected. I could only hope Mom didn't keep up her litany of the evils of men to Ricky. He'd heard it all before, but that didn't mean he couldn't be damaged further.

I collapsed on my bed, determined to speak to no one before the police called. Fifteen minutes later, a knock came at my door. "Audra, there's a man here to see you." Mom's tone of voice would have been more appropriate for a man-eating lion. Unfortunately, in this case she was right. The door opened and Jay pushed past her. At least I had the satisfaction of seeing him close the door in Mom's outraged face.

"You little bitch. You called the cops. I knew I shouldn't have trusted you."

I sat up, swallowing hard. "I didn't realize trust had anything to do with our relationship." I swung my legs off the bed, but he leaned over me before I could get up.

"Do you realize the trouble you've caused?"

I forced myself to look into his face. "I didn't tell them about you."

He straightened and crossed his arms. "But you will. That's the kind of idiotic goody-two-shoes you are."

"I didn't tell," I snapped. "But Jay ... it really would be better if you told them yourself. There may be ... evidence. I think they're suspicious. If we tell the truth—"

"Of course they're suspicious! Because you couldn't keep your mouth shut!" He leaned over me again, close enough that I flinched. At least his breath didn't stink of marijuana. "But you'd better keep it shut now. You'd better keep me out of this."

I pushed myself back to sit against the wall. "Look, Jay, we did something important today. We uncovered a murder. Now that they have her body, maybe they'll be able to figure out who killed her. It's ... heroic! You could be a hero."

"I don't want to be a hero. I want to be left alone."

Yeah, me too, but that didn't look likely to happen.

"Getting involved is dangerous. There's a killer out there, and once he finds out you exposed him ..." He let the implication hang as he stepped back. I scrambled off the bed but he was still blocking the door, and anyway I didn't want to bring the conversation out where Mom or Ricky might overhear.

Jay stared at me as if trying to read my thoughts. "Rodrigo said you were snooping around the office. I don't know what game you're playing, but you'd better stay out of my business."

"I don't want anything to do with your business! I just want—" My throat closed up and I couldn't go on, not even to explain I'd only been getting my phone.

"You just keep your mouth shut. Or else." He stormed out of the room.

I flopped back on my bed with a shaky sigh. As threats go, his was pretty weak. At least that's what I told myself as I lay trembling.

Seven

The police came by to interview me at midnight. The two officers were different from the ones I'd already met. They were state police, I think, the ones who were already investigating Bethany Moore's disappearance. One was tall, at least six and a half feet, and lanky, with dark blond hair. He wore a button-up shirt and tan pants, with a black gun holster strapped to his hip. He looked about thirty. The other was a few years older, average height, black hair and eyes, muscular in a black T-shirt and jeans. They were both good looking, like actors off a TV set. Maybe not leading-man handsome, but definitely sexy enough for a sidekick.

It didn't make it any easier to describe what happened. It didn't make it any easier to lie.

Mom and Ricky had gone to bed, and I met the officers at the door before they could ring the bell. But Mom came out anyway, of course. The tall officer took one look at her and said he'd interview me in his car. I don't know if that was standard procedure or if he had extraordinary deductive reasoning skills, but I was glad I didn't have to tell my story in front of Mom. The other officer stayed inside to photograph the shoes I'd been wearing. No doubt he got treated to Mom's theories on the death.

I sat in the front passenger seat of the officer's car, not a black-and-white but a nice midsize car. The scent of the leather seats mixed with the officer's spicy aftershave, a foreign, masculine scent. I clenched my hands in my lap and tried to control my breathing.

We sat in the dark and he recorded our conversation as he took me through the experience again. He wanted to know exactly what I'd done. What I'd seen. What she had looked like, with her green skin and half-missing face.

I got through it somehow. My conscience nagged at me to tell the truth, the whole truth, but I'd promised Jay I'd keep him out of it. I thought I should tell anyway, but I couldn't quite decide, and once I said the first thing about Jay there would be no going back. What would he do to me then?

I tried to skirt reality while avoiding outright lies. I took my time before answering and sometimes didn't answer exactly the question he'd asked. I hoped the tremor in my voice would convince him I was confused because I was upset. I could honestly say I wasn't sure about my every move, since the memory was blurred by shock. Still, if the officer had been able to hear the words in my head, he'd have gotten an entirely different story.

He finally walked me back to my door and said goodnight. I was trembling, but I'd managed not to cry. He shook my hand. For a moment I looked into his eyes, but I couldn't read anything there.

Mom stood in the living room, arms folded across her terrycloth robe, and watched through the thin curtains as the headlights backed out of our driveway. "They seemed halfway competent. At least that Hispanic one listened to me."

I winced. What had she told him about me? She didn't know anything – I had to remember that – but I still imagined the officer could have learned a lot about me with a few pointed questions. Would Mom have portrayed me as honest and reliable, or incompetent and ungrateful? She hadn't been pleased with me that day.

She turned from the window, shaking her head. "Though I don't know why they haven't arrested the ex-boyfriend already."

If she'd been focused on the sins of men, maybe my reputation had come through unscathed. "They have to have proof."

She snorted and headed for her bedroom. For Mom, the fact that a man was involved was proof enough.

I stood in the living room, staring at nothing. I couldn't predict what would happen next. But one thought steadied me. I'd done something important that day. I'd exposed a murder. Now that they had her body, maybe they'd be able to figure out who killed her.

I considered making a cup of tea, something to soothe my queasy stomach and delay the moment of sleep – and possible nightmares. But suddenly I could barely stand up. I stumbled toward my room.

As I pushed through the door, something moved on my bed.

I gasped and jerked back, banging into the doorframe.

"Audra! It's me."

A sound like a whimper came from my throat. I clung to the doorframe as my legs threatened to collapse. My brain recognized the voice, but it couldn't control my body's reaction.

My bedside lamp flicked on. Ricky, sitting cross-legged near my pillow, grinned at me. "I'm sorry I scared you. I didn't want Mom to know I was in here."

I closed the door and staggered the three steps to the narrow bed. "Ricky. What are you doing here? Everything's all right. Go to bed."

"But I want to help!"

I rubbed my hands over my face. Half my brain was already asleep and the other half wanted to join it. "Help with what?"

"Help investigate! Help you find out what happened to that woman."

"What?" I shook my head and sat on the end of the bed. "No. That's the police's job. I told them what I know. I'm done."

"But they have a lot of cases, hundreds, probably. Those guys aren't even local. They could use our help. They don't know what's really going on here, in our town."

His words created an odd echo of something Jay had said. "What do you mean? What's going on here?"

"I hear stuff in school, you know, who's selling drugs or who got knocked around by her dad or whatever. Stuff the police don't know."

I remembered hearing rumors like that in school as well. I hadn't always understood all the slang and innuendo, but Ricky, curious boy, would have figured it out. "But that stuff doesn't have anything to do with this."

"Maybe it does! You have to keep an open mind when you're investigating. You have to look and listen. I can do that at school and around town. You can do that at the resort. Then we can put together what we learn and figure it out."

It was too much. Too much pressure, too much risk, simply asking too much. "That's crazy! I don't know anything! I don't know what I'm doing or—" I broke off, trying to hold back the tears.

Ricky got up. He stood beside the bed and smiled gently down at me. "You're tired. We can talk about it tomorrow. You'll see what a chance this is."

I shouldn't have given him the complete collection of Sherlock Holmes stories for his tenth birthday. It had seemed like a good idea at the time, since he'd read every *Encyclopedia Brown*, *The Three Investigators*, and *Hardy Boys*. It looked as if I'd pay for it now.

He left, closing the door quietly behind him. I dragged myself across the bed, crawled under the covers, and flipped off the light. Let the nightmares come. They couldn't be worse than real life.

Eight

I did not want to go to work the next morning.

Unfortunately, I hadn't built up any sick days yet, and I was in enough trouble without lying to my boss again. I was awake and restless at six, so even after spending extra time on my makeup to hide the dark circles under my eyes, I got out of the house early. I couldn't face breakfast, I didn't want to talk to Ricky about "the case" in front of Mom, and I didn't really want to talk to Mom at all.

I was half an hour early as I neared the driveway to the resort. I slowed, prepared to turn – then hit the gas and kept on driving. I imagined heading out of town, just driving forever.

The thought was too tempting. When I got to the next turnoff, I jerked the wheel right. Otherwise I might have kept going until I ran out of gas.

I realized I'd turned onto a dirt road that circled around the plateau through the forest – the same woods where we'd found the body, but about a mile away. I didn't want to go anywhere near there! Was everything in my life leading me that way?

I bumped over a rock that threw me against the door. My wheel hit a rut and the car skidded toward the trees. I hit the brakes, jerked forward against my seatbelt, and slowed to a crawl, jolted out of my stupor.

The path was narrow, used more by ATVs than by cars. I'd have a hard time turning around. I debated backing up the hundred feet or so I'd already come, but somehow I just kept driving. My mind and body wouldn't sync up.

A minute later the path widened. I told myself to hit the brakes and finally did so, my movements jerky like a doll controlled by a child. I put the car in park, fumbled with the door handle, and got out. I leaned against the car with the door open to the beep-beep-beep warning me about my keys in the ignition, and breathed in the morning air, the scent of trees and earth and wildflowers. But no death. This place was clean.

I tipped my head back, closed my eyes, and said a prayer for Bethany Moore. I hoped she'd found some peace.

Something rustled in the bushes, and I flinched. But the sound had been small, a bird or lizard. I drew in a deep breath and blew it out slowly. How long would it take before standing in the woods no longer filled me with fear? A month? A year?

Had this changed me forever?

I wanted to dive back in the car and lock the doors. Instead, I stepped away. The trees thinned near the cliff edge, and I focused on the patches of blue sky beyond. In a few steps, I could see down a couple hundred feet to the farmlands and scrub desert below the mountains that made it possible to have skiing and other winter sports in central New Mexico.

At the edge of my field of view, cars moved along the main road into town. People were going about their business as if this were a normal day. For most of them, it was.

Nothing had changed, really, in the larger scheme. People died every day, some violently. It only made a difference when it touched you.

If this experience did change me forever, maybe that was good. Maybe I'd care more about strangers. Maybe I'd value life more. Maybe I'd choose to live differently, though I couldn't yet say how.

A dark blue truck with a cap on the bed turned off the road and drove through the fields. A tremor ran up my spine. Was that the truck I'd seen in the parking lot yesterday, with the one-handed man?

The truck passed between farm fields and on into the undeveloped public land where ranchers grazed their cattle. It pulled off to the side of the road and someone got out. He went to the back of the truck and opened the window and tailgate.

I took a step closer to the drop-off and peered down. Why would somebody stop there, alongside the road, a mile or more from any building?

He did something at the back of the truck; I couldn't see what. And then he walked away from the road, into empty land, carrying an object like a suitcase.

He walked a few hundred feet and put down the suitcase. At that distance, I couldn't tell if he was doing anything besides standing there. I wished I had binoculars.

He made some kind of gesture with his arm, and then he was still. Had he signaled to someone? I scanned the land all around but couldn't see another person or vehicle in range.

I got the impression he was looking up. Had he signaled to someone in a plane? I scanned the sky. Nothing. And then – a tiny dark speck.

I squinted, trying to keep it in view. It came closer in a lazy arc. A hawk or falcon, catching the morning thermals.

I frowned down at the man far below. His behavior was odd and struck me as somehow suspicious, but I couldn't see what standing in a field had to do with a month-old murder in the woods above. Could he be dumping evidence from the suitcase? Why there, why now? And even if he was, what could I do about it? I'd feel stupid trying to explain this to the police when I didn't really know anything, not even who the man was. If I wanted to talk to the police again, I had more relevant things to tell them.

I shook my head and turned back to my car. If I didn't get moving, I'd be late to work. But I carried with me that image, of a lone man standing in the desert, looking up at the sky.

I still got to the resort a few minutes before eight. The lobby was busy with checkouts. A bellhop pushing a cart loaded with luggage gave me a long sideways glance. One of the receptionists leaned over to whisper something to the other, her eyes on me. The customer she was helping turned to scan the room. I ducked my head and hurried past.

When I reached the hall to the offices, I slowed. Maybe I was just imagining the looks. My name hadn't been mentioned on the news. People might have seen me with the police, though, and the small-town grapevine worked quickly.

I couldn't do anything except pretend everything was normal and focus on work. I needed to check with Eslinda on the tasks for the day, but her door was closed. Should I knock, or check back later? Then I heard a murmur of voices behind the door. She wasn't alone.

"Audra!" someone hissed from across the hall. Nascha waved me closer from her doorway. "The police are in there with Eslinda. They're asking her questions about yesterday, about the body. Rumors are flying."

She looked past me at the door, and I was glad for the chance to control my expression.

But what was the point in trying to keep my involvement a secret? Nascha would hear the truth – at least the part I'd already admitted – soon enough. If I denied it now, or even avoided the subject, I'd break the fragile thread of our possible friendship.

"I found her."

Her eyes flicked to my face and then away. "Finding death is a terrible thing. I'm sorry."

"Thank you."

She glanced at Eslinda's door. "We'd better not talk about this now." She backed into her office. "Today won't be easy. Don't try to handle everything alone."

I nodded, though I wasn't sure how much choice I had.

I left the door to my office open to show I had nothing to hide. Another lie. I stared at the paperwork on my desk, ignored from the previous day. If I could bury myself in wedding planning, maybe I could forget the family that was planning a funeral.

Eslinda came into my office an hour later. She closed the door behind her and sat across from my desk. For a moment we just looked at each other.

"I've been talking to the police," she said. "I'm so sorry."

My heart jolted. What had she told them?

"They say you found that body in the woods. That must've been terrible."

Oh. "Yes, it was."

"And after you were already feeling so bad yesterday afternoon!" She shook her head. "You poor girl."

Was she testing me? Hinting at suspicions?

She sighed. "I don't know what to say. I went to school with her mother. I didn't know her well – Bethany, that is, I knew her mother fairly well back in those days. Anyway, it's such a tragedy. And after what happened to her brother, too."

I stared at her, my own thoughts churning. In a town of 8,000 people, it wasn't surprising that she would know the victim's family. I wanted to ask about them, but I wasn't sure of the questions. And I wasn't sure I wanted to know anything that would make them more real, or more tragic.

She sighed again. "Do you want to take the day off? Or would you rather work? When I'm upset, sometimes that's better. Working, I mean."

"Um, work. I need to keep busy." Otherwise I might run through the hotel screaming. I might blurt out Jay's secret. I might destroy my reputation and my career.

She nodded and kept me busy for the next few hours. By lunchtime my stomach was snarling. I'd forgotten to pack a lunch and didn't want to deal with the hotel restaurant, but the break room had a vending machine.

The conversation stopped when I entered the break room, and four sets of curious eyes gazed at me from around the table. A woman I only knew on sight watched me walk across the room. "The police are interviewing Jay right now! I had to tell them I saw him coming back from the direction of the woods after lunch."

I kept my back to them as I put coins into the vending machine. Had she seen us together? Had they found evidence at the scene?

Someone else spoke. "You don't really think he had anything to do with it?"

"No." She sounded disappointed. "That girl was into drugs, so I bet she got on the wrong side of her dealer."

"And who is that supposed to be?" someone asked.

"If I knew, do you think I'd go around bad-mouthing him? *I* don't want to get on his bad side."

The mixed smells of clam chowder, microwaved burrito, and vinegary salad dressing churned my stomach, and I breathed shallowly through my mouth. The vending machine treats blurred together as a memory of the ditch filled my vision.

Another woman said, "I heard she slept around a lot, maybe even did some prostitution. That's dangerous business." I glanced over my shoulder as the motherly-looking woman with white hair went on. "It could've been one of her johns. Or her pimp." The words sounded funny coming out of her mouth.

The youngest woman said, "What if it's a serial killer?"

"Here?"

"Why not? You won't catch me going into those woods again!"

The one man in the group spoke up. "It's only a serial killer if he kills more than once. This is the first murder here in two years, it said so in the paper."

"He could've killed people somewhere else!" the girl said. "He might be a traveling serial killer."

"Then he's long gone," the man said.

"He could be staying here for a while." She really wanted it to be a serial killer. It was almost funny. Almost.

I stared at the choices in the vending machine without really seeing them. I knew it was just gossip, but what if one of them were right?

The first woman spoke again. "It's hard to believe it could be anyone in our town." I thought I could feel her staring at my back. "But these things do happen. Aren't most murders committed by somebody the victim knows?"

I punched a button at random and a bag of pork rinds dropped down. I shoved in more coins and managed to find the button for granola bars. I scooped up my lunch and swung around, my gaze on the door.

The first woman said, "Hey! You found it, right? You found the body."

I paused at the door. "Yes, I found her. I found Bethany Moore."

I headed for my office before they could ask more questions. Was that all you became after death? Fodder for gossip? Entertainment over lunch? The body? *It*?

Not if I could help it. It was too late to save Bethany Moore, but I'd do everything in my power to see her killer brought to justice.

Nine

I turned into my office, lost in thought, and almost bumped into the tall detective who had interviewed me the night before. He grabbed my arm to steady me. "Ms. Needham, how are you?"

I made myself look him in the eyes. "Fine." What did he want? What did he know?

"I'd like to go over your story again. Is now a good time?"

What had Jay told him? I needed to know that before I said anything else. I needed to see him. "No. I have something I have to do for a few minutes. Can you come by my office in about half an hour?"

"That would be fine. Maybe we'll grab some lunch while we wait."

We? Only then did I notice the second detective, leaning against the windowsill. I twitched, a slight movement but surely noticeable to the man whose hand was still on my arm. I forced a pleasant smile. "The restaurant here is very good."

"Is that why you're eating pork rinds for lunch?"

I would have sworn his eyes had been on my face the whole time, never glancing down toward my hand hanging at my side. I tried to think of a joking comment, but the moment for a natural response passed. I shrugged. "I'll see you in a little while." I edged past him, around my desk, and picked up the phone. I held it to my ear as they left the room.

I didn't want to call Jay. As much as I dreaded seeing him in person, I didn't think I could be convincing on the phone.

I gave them a minute, then peeked into the hallway. No one in sight. But what if they were hiding to spy on me if I left? I should have pretended I needed to go somewhere, rather than pretending I needed to make a phone call. It's a good thing I had never dreamed of being a master criminal, since I obviously wasn't cut out for it.

I pressed my fingers to my temples. I was over-thinking everything. Even if Jay had told the truth already, the police didn't have any reason to suspect me of involvement in the murder. And they probably had better ways to keep track of people than lurking in the hallways. A phone tap, maybe. All the more reason to see Jay in person.

I hurried down the hallway, trying to look as if I had an important appointment or something. What did that look like, anyway? I didn't know how to act natural anymore. It would be suspicious to glance around, showing I was worried about being watched. I kept my gaze ahead and frowned thoughtfully.

I took the back exit and walked alongside the golf course to the greenhouse, trying not to glance across the fairway to the woods. I paused with my hand on the greenhouse door and closed my eyes. I was already trembling slightly from nerves. I was hardly ready to confront someone I found intimidating at the best of times. But what choice did I have?

I would give Jay one last chance to come clean on his own, if he hadn't already. And then ...

I wouldn't think about then. Surely he had to understand by now how important the truth was, and how risky it was to keep pretending. Probably he had already told the truth when the police confronted him. I was just confirming, and getting permission to do the same.

I nodded once and pushed through the door.

A voice broke off as I entered. "We can't, now that they're—"

I blinked, adjusting to the dimmer, greener light as I breathed in the musty scent of damp earth and growing things. Jay and the other groundskeeper – Roberto? No, Rodrigo – turned toward me from the other side of a long table filled with young shrubs.

I tried to ignore the scowls. "Jay. I need to talk to you."

He stared for a moment, then jerked his head toward his office. I trailed after him, eyes down and hands fisted at my sides. He didn't look like someone who had come to terms with an unpleasant situation.

He stomped into the office, turned, and leaned against the desk with his arms folded. I shut the door and stood just inside it. My shallow breathing seemed to echo in the small room as I glanced around, looking anywhere but at Jay.

He didn't speak, just stared. I rubbed my lips together, swallowed a couple of times, and finally forced words out. "I heard the police interviewed you."

He snorted. "You're dang right they did. Thanks to you."

I finally looked at him. "I didn't say anything about you!"

"Yeah, well, no thanks for that favor. People saw us together." He kicked at his chair. "The cops saved that bit of information until after I'd sworn I hadn't been near you or the woods all day."

"I'm sorry," I whispered.

"It's a little late for that now."

I leaned against the door and forced myself to breathe. I couldn't back down now. "That's right. They know so much, we might as well tell the truth. It will be easier that way."

He pushed off the desk, took two steps, and loomed over me. "Easier for who?"

He smelled of breath mints, cigarettes, and dirt. Dirt where living things decayed and new life grew. "Easier for Bethany Moore. Easier for the police to find her killer. Don't you want that?"

He hesitated, and then jerked one shoulder in a shrug. "Sure. I hope they find the guy who did that." His face scrunched in disgust, and I realized he must have the image of her body seared in his mind as well. "The dude who did that ought to be put away. But it has nothing to do with me. I don't want the police poking in my business."

I braced myself against the door and met his gaze. My voice trembled, but I got the words out. "They're in your business already. I'm going to tell the truth. You'll be better off if you do the same."

He slammed a hand against the door beside my head. "I can make your life miserable."

I turned my face away. It took all my effort to whisper. "You think it isn't already?"

We stayed frozen like that for half a minute. I couldn't bring myself to look at his face, just inches from mine. I felt his breath on my cheek and wished I didn't have to breathe the same air.

Finally he dropped his arm and backed up a step. "Come on. You've already lied to the police. You don't want to change your story now." His tone was wheedling. I pressed against the door and watched him warily. I didn't trust this mood any more than the last one.

"Just let it ride," he coaxed. "No one can *prove* we were together. It doesn't matter whether I was there or not. The police will find the killer, and everyone will forget about this."

"Maybe you're right. Maybe it doesn't matter." I edged sideways and fumbled for the door handle. When I was partway through, I added, "But maybe it does. And if there's any chance it will help the police find a killer, I'm telling the truth."

I pulled the door shut and scurried away as Jay's curse rumbled behind me. Rodrigo was in the center aisle, fifteen feet away. He lunged toward me, but I darted to the next aisle and ran for the door. I didn't know what Rodrigo wanted, probably to hold me so Jay could finish yelling at me, but I wasn't going to wait to find out.

I rushed outside, blinking against the bright sun. I kept glancing over my shoulder as I hurried toward the lodge, but no one came out after me. By the time I got to the bench alongside the building, I was shaking so hard I could barely walk. I grabbed for the bench and slumped into it.

My heart stuttered in my chest. A thin film of sweat turned my forehead clammy. A drop ran down one temple but I couldn't find the energy to brush it away.

"You're all right," I whispered. "You did fine." Katie had made me practice talking to men – any man – so I could get over my shyness and anxiety. A few years before, even small talk would have sent me into panic mode. At least this time, I had a good excuse for my nerves.

I shifted to a more comfortable position on the bench and leaned back with my eyes closed. I should reward myself for getting through that. I hadn't been to the ice cream parlor since I'd moved home. I'd get a waffle cone with caramel swirl and eat the whole thing where Mom couldn't watch and criticize my diet.

But not yet. First I had to get through the police interview and the rest of the day.

I imagined telling the tall, good-looking officer that I'd lied to him. What would they do to me?

If I could get through that, I might earn a whole hot fudge sundae.

I'd stopped shaking, but I couldn't bring myself to get up yet. I rubbed my fingers over my forehead and temple, trying to ease the lurking tension. In a minute, I'd face the police. I just needed to gear up for it.

Thwack! A sound like a loud clap exploded near my head. I jumped and almost tumbled off the bench.

I looked around wildly, but I didn't see anyone within a hundred feet. What had made that sound? I looked up. Nothing. I glanced back over my shoulder.

A fresh ding marred the stucco wall, about a foot from my head. And then I spotted the golf ball shining white against the green grass beside the bench.

I pressed a hand to my chest. That had been close. I knew it wasn't entirely safe to linger near a golf course, but this spot wasn't in the danger zone, or they wouldn't have put a bench there. Still, it was astonishing how far off track some shots went. And a golf ball to the head could do serious damage, even kill.

I pushed myself up off the bench and scanned the course for the golfer responsible. He should have yelled, "Fore!" He should be hurrying to apologize. What kind of bozo doesn't even apologize after nearly braining someone with a golf ball?

I saw three men walking toward a distant tee. But they must have just finished putting, and anyway, they wouldn't have been shooting in this direction. A golf cart was crossing the fairway a couple hundred yards distant, but they were heading in the wrong direction as well. Maybe they were fleeing, embarrassed by their close call.

I looked back at the mark in the wall. It was a deep, round hole. That golf ball hadn't hit at a glancing blow from down the fairway. It had hit almost straight on.

I looked across the fairway. The ball had come from the direction of the woods. No one was over there. No one that I could see.

My legs threatened to give out. But I didn't sit again. I turned and ran for the lodge.

Ten

I paused just inside the door to catch my breath and let my eyes adjust to the dimmer light. Had that really happened? Was it an accident, random chance ... or something worse? A threat. An attack.

I shook my head. This couldn't be happening. How had my life turned into this?

I pressed a hand to my forehead, imagining a golf ball flying at my face. Should I tell the police about this? Or would it sound paranoid, or pathetic, as if I was making up stories to prove I wasn't involved?

I needed time to think. But I must have already used up a good chunk of my half hour. I hadn't even eaten, and despite my anxiety the ache in my belly told me if I didn't get food soon, the trembling and waves of lightheadedness would only get worse.

I hurried toward my office. If I could just get a few minutes to eat my granola bar and settle my nerves, I might make it through the afternoon.

My office was already occupied. But not by the police.

A man was seated behind my desk, shuffling through my papers. I blinked a couple of times before recognizing him as the general manager, one of several people who had interviewed me for the job. I stood with one hand on the door jamb, staring. What now?

He looked up. "Miss Needham, there you are. I've been waiting for you."

I couldn't think of a response. Even a greeting seemed beyond my powers.

He leaned back in my chair. "This is painful for me. I understand that you have been starting rumors about my son."

His son? Oh. Jay. Right, this was Mr. Preppard.

I shook my head. "I haven't said anything about your son."

"You're new here. Maybe you don't know how we do things. We try to be discreet."

"But—"

"Finding that thing so close to resort property is bad enough. Bad for business." He made a face. "The police asking questions. Our name associated with a murder. It's distasteful. But I suppose it can't be helped."

"It's not like I—"

"But I won't have you involving my son."

"I didn't ... he ... that is ..." Finally he seemed inclined to let me finish a sentence, and I couldn't get one out.

He stood and came around the desk. He didn't look much like Jay. More like an aging businessman with a potbelly and thinning hair. But like Jay, he stood too close. He smelled of stale grease and cigarettes. "Your job is on the line, Miss Needham. What you do outside of work is your business. But don't involve the resort, or my son."

I could only stare as he brushed past me. I staggered the last few feet to my desk. Sitting in the chair where that man had just been made my skin crawl, but I didn't trust myself to stay upright without help.

I sat staring at the door. Had my boss's boss really just threatened me? Shut up or lose your job? Maybe Jay and his father had a lot more in common than appearances would lead one to believe.

A sharp pain cramped my stomach. One thing at a time. I needed food.

The bag of pork rinds sat on my desk, open and half empty. No wonder Mr. Preppard had a potbelly. I picked up the bag with two fingers and dropped it in the trash.

Fortunately he hadn't touched the granola bar. I washed it down with the half cup of cold coffee left over from that morning.

My stomach still grumbled, but my nerves slowly settled. I leaned back and debated the next step. I was in a lot of trouble, no matter what I did. If I told the truth, the police might not believe me, especially if Jay refused to back my story. I'd have at least two enemies at the resort, Jay and his father. Assuming I managed to keep my job, they could make my life difficult.

Despite what I'd told Jay, I knew my life wasn't so bad that it couldn't get a lot worse. This was the only place in town I wanted to work, the only place that paid well and had a good chance for advancement. If I lost my job among nasty rumors, I'd have trouble getting *any* job in town. For myself, I wouldn't mind moving away. But I didn't want to abandon Ricky.

If I told the truth, I could lose my job. If I didn't, the police might uncover the truth anyway, and I might face criminal charges. Either choice could ruin my life. I had to make the choice I could live with.

Someone rapped on my open door. I looked up and the tall police officer smiled. "Ms. Needham, are you ready for us?"

I guess there comes a time in every life where you have to make a choice, to back down or take a stand. I straightened my back. "I'm ready."

And I told them everything.

Eleven

By the time they left, I felt like a crepe paper streamer that got dragged around on the bottom of someone's shoe at the end of a wedding. They had seemed to believe me, though the officer scolded me about how important it was for them to know everything, in order to investigate properly. Well, now they knew everything I knew. We'd gone over it at least three times. I forced myself to explain, as clearly as I could remember, exactly what Jay had said. No more protecting him. I mentioned the golf ball, but I didn't make too big a deal of it. The tall officer said they'd take a look around the bench, but I doubted anything would come of it.

I leaned back, eyes closed, until Eslinda and Nascha bustled into my office. I managed to lift my head and tried to focus.

Eslinda hurried forward. "Are you all right?"

I blinked at her, trying to make sense of the question.

She leaned down and gave me a quick hug. "You poor girl! You've had an awful couple of days, haven't you?" As always, she smelled of cucumbers and mint. Since I'd never seen her eat either of those things, I assumed she used some kind of lotion or shampoo with the scent. I found it oddly comforting.

I rubbed my hands over my face, worrying only vaguely that I was smearing the makeup I'd taken such pains to apply that morning. "It hasn't been great."

"Yesterday must have been terrible," Eslinda said. "And to have to go through it all over again today!" She pressed a hand to her large chest. "I tell you, I got nervous talking to the police, and I didn't have anything to do with it. Oh! I didn't mean that you had anything to do with it, except by the most unfortunate accident."

I looked from her to Nascha, who hadn't yet spoken, but who gave me a sympathetic smile. I pushed myself a little straighter in my chair and took a deep breath. "That's not entirely true." I met Eslinda's gaze. "I did something really stupid yesterday. I lied to you."

Her lips twitched. "Oh, honey, if that's the worst thing that happened yesterday, we could all be grateful." She leaned against my desk. I felt as if I should give up my chair but couldn't bring myself to rise.

"I think I'd better explain." I glanced at the door, and Nascha moved to close it.

My story should have been polished to a fine sheen after my time with the police, but I was so tired I'm not sure I made much sense. Still, they listened with occasional murmurs of sympathy and sounds of shock at Jay's behavior.

"I should have called the police right away," I said. "I'm sorry."

Eslinda rubbed my arm. "That was pretty foolish. But I can understand. You certainly aren't the first girl who's been talked into something stupid by a man, and Jay put you in an awful position."

"It may be even worse now. His father threatened to fire me if I involved Jay, and I just told the police everything."

Eslinda drew herself up like an offended quail. "How dare he! You're my employee, not his. I'm the only one who can fire you."

That didn't exactly put me at ease.

She pushed away from the desk. "I'm going to give him a piece of my mind. Don't you worry about Lewis Preppard." She stormed to the door but turned back with a motherly smile. "You should get out of here. Nascha, go buy Audra a drink or something."

"You heard the boss," Nascha said. "You want a drink?"

"But it's only ..." I glanced at the clock. Huh, after four. How time flies when the day sucks. And realistically, I wouldn't get any work done in the next hour. I hauled myself out of the chair. "If I drink alcohol, I'll be asleep in five minutes. But I'll give you—" I almost said "my right arm," but that brought back the memory of the one-handed man. "—anything for an ice cream sundae."

"Even better, since I don't drink, but I do eat ice cream."

She drove. I gazed idly out the window as we passed slowly down Center Street looking for parking. A man stepped out of the hardware store. I recognized him even before I checked for his missing hand. When I glanced at his face, our eyes met and held for a long moment as we drove past. A shiver slid down my spine.

"Nascha, do you know who that was?"

She began to back into a space by a meter. "Who?"

I resisted the urge to turn around in my seat. "The man who just came out of the hardware store."

She craned to look in the rearview mirror. "I don't think so. Why?"

"He was in the woods yesterday. After the police got there." I shrugged. "It's probably nothing."

She gazed at me. "But you think he's connected."

"I'd just like to know who he is. I saw him in the parking lot and his truck was making a strange sound." I shook my head. "Not the truck itself, something inside it."

She checked the rearview mirror again. "He's still looking this way. Okay, now he's turning away. Was it a blue truck?"

"Yes." This time I couldn't resist twisting around. The man was opening his truck's door. He tossed a small bag inside and closed the door, then crossed the street. Nascha and I watched him until he was hidden by parked cars, then we looked at each other.

"You heard something strange in his truck?"

I nodded. "In the back. Kind of like screaming, but inhuman somehow."

She frowned. "Let's take a look."

We got out of the car. I was glad to be on the sidewalk side, better hidden from the one-handed man. Nascha joined me and we strolled the short distance to the blue truck, acting casual.

We glanced around. No one seemed to be paying much attention to us. I stepped behind the truck and shaded my eyes to peer through the tinted window. Nascha did the same.

It took a moment for the shapes to make sense. Cages. Two wire cages, a couple of feet in each direction. They were empty. Behind them some darker lumps appeared to be tote bags and a toolbox.

We stepped back and stared at each other. Nascha said, "He must keep animals of some kind."

"But what? That wasn't a dog I heard. A cat?" I hesitated and shook my head. I'd heard cats yowl, but I didn't think that was the sound from yesterday. Besides, why would anyone be carrying cats around in cages in the back of his truck?

"Rabbits?" Nascha said.

"Rabbits don't sound like that! I didn't think they even made noise."

"They can scream when attacked." She looked back at the truck window, her face troubled. "If he had rabbits and some other animal threatening them ... But why?" She shook her head. "I grew up in Santa Fe. I'm a city girl. This is not my area of expertise."

She glanced down the street toward her car. "Oh, I forgot to put money in the meter, and they're checking! I'm not usually here this early in the day." She hurried back to her car.

I took one last look in the back window. Those cages were not big enough for a person. Definitely not. Whatever they were used for, they were not used to transport screaming women into the woods. But instead of solving a mystery, I'd increased the questions.

I stepped back, studying the dried mud splattered halfway up the sides. The truck obviously went off road in all kinds of weather. I wondered if you could look up license plates online or if you had to have official access to some database. I memorized the number just in case.

I stepped back onto the sidewalk. Someone spoke from beside the truck. "Hello."

My gaze swung to the one-handed man. I jerked back in shock and stumbled off the curb. I almost fell out into the street, barely catching myself on the bumper of his truck and the hood of the car behind.

I held myself there, gasping. He stepped around the truck. "Are you all right?"

I pushed myself up. The hot metal of the truck hurt my hand, but I wasn't sure of my ability to stand without help at that moment so I held on. At least he didn't offer to help. If he'd gotten close enough to touch me I would have leapt into the street without a thought for traffic.

I scrambled for some excuse for my presence. The only reason I wasn't babbling was that I was breathing too hard to speak.

The man gazed at me solemnly. "You found Bethany."

"I ... yes." I was too startled to say anything but the truth.

"Thank you."

What an odd thing to say. His mouth carried a hint of a smile, but his eyes were so bleak my heart ached even as it slowed its furious pumping.

"I remember you," he said.

I couldn't think of an answer. Of course he remembered me from yesterday. We'd just established that he recognized me.

His lips curved a fraction more. "You had a locker down the hall from me." I must have still looked blank, because he added, "In high school."

Understanding dawned. His smile became more natural than I'd seen it yet. "You don't remember me."

I struggled for something – anything – to say, so I wouldn't look like a complete idiot. "I'm ... sorry?"

"No surprise. You were a grade ahead. And I was kind of a geek."

That was hard to believe. At a glance he was nondescript, but on closer examination, he had a lean, tough build, though his clothes hung a little too loose. I would have believed he was a wrestler in high school, but geek didn't come to mind. He was kind of cute in a boy-next-door way, with close-cropped brown hair and those sad gray eyes that probably would have had Eslinda all motherly.

But there was something about the way he stood, something lurking under the surface of those eyes, that warned against getting too close. He reminded me a bit of a stray dog, thin and abused and tragic, but still tough and wary, the kind you wanted to feed but were afraid to touch because you couldn't quite trust it not to bite.

My quick examination ranged over his faded jeans, hiking boots, and the long-sleeved gray T-shirt he had pinned up over his missing hand. I was pretty sure I would have remembered someone missing a hand in high school.

He lifted the arm in question. "I didn't have this then. It came later."

I felt myself blushing. I hadn't meant to stare. I was dying to know how he had lost it, but of course I couldn't ask. I tried to think of something else to say, but questions crowded my mind. What was Bethany to him? He was younger than me, or maybe the same age since boys sometimes started school later. Surely he was too young to be one of Bethany's rumored boyfriends.

I could ask. Surely it was a natural question in the circumstances. Not whether he was her boyfriend, but how he knew her.

I glanced around, anywhere but at him. Nascha stood about twenty feet away, watching us. She raised her eyebrows as if asking whether she should interrupt. It was tempting to ask for rescue, but that would end the conversation before I'd gotten any answers.

I turned back to the man and said in a rush, "How do you know Bethany Moore?"

His eyes closed for a moment. "She's my sister."

Someone had mentioned a brother – Eslinda – she'd said something had happened to him. I hadn't wanted to ask what, but had vaguely assumed he'd also died. But maybe this was that brother. I forced myself not to look down toward his hand.

"I'm sorry you had to see that," he said.

What? His hand? Or – my gaze wanted to shift toward the back window of the truck, but I made myself look at his face.

His mouth twisted unhappily. "That can't have been easy for you. Especially without warning." He added very softly, "She was pretty, once."

He was talking about seeing the body. And he had been in the woods while the police were there. To see her, too? I cringed as the memory rose in my mind. It had been hard enough for a stranger. I couldn't imagine seeing someone I'd loved in such a condition. And he offered *me* comfort! "I'm so sorry," I said. "Sorry for your loss." That sounded pathetic and clichéd.

"You did us a favor. Now we know." His face hardened and his gaze shifted to the distance. "Maybe now we can do something about it," he muttered, more to himself than to me. He met my eyes again. "Anyway, thank you. Your friend's waiting. Maybe I'll see you around."

"I guess so." I started to walk away, but spun back. "Wait! I don't know your name."

"Kyle. Kyle Moore."

I nodded. "I'm Audra Needham."

He smiled. "I know."

Twelve

He got into his truck and I joined Nascha. As we headed down the street, she asked, "What do you think about that drink now?"

I blew out a breath. "That was definitely more than I bargained for. But it's all right. Everything makes sense now, I think." I hadn't actually had time to figure it out. I paused by the ice cream parlor entrance and glanced back as the truck pulled away. "It's her brother. Bethany Moore's brother."

"Oh, of course. He was there yesterday to identify the body."

"How do you know that?"

"It was in the newspaper that her brother identified the body. I forgot until now."

"But that doesn't explain the cages in his truck, or the strange screaming." I shook it off. "That poor man, to have to identify his sister's body. It was bad enough for me to see it from a distance. If it were someone I knew and cared about ..."

"Assuming, of course, they cared for each other."

I stared at her. She shrugged and added, "Not all families are happy."

I knew that well enough. "Did the newspaper article mention me?"

"Not by name. They just said a female employee of the resort found the body. But I imagine it's no secret now, at least at the lodge."

"So the whole town won't know until tomorrow, maybe." I pulled open the door. "I really need that ice cream."

We settled in chairs by the window. Nascha finished her sorbet and watched me plow through my caramel sundae. When I finally leaned back, she said, "Feeling better?"

"Yeah, I needed that. Well, I needed food. I *wanted* ice cream. And I want to never have another day like today or yesterday."

"At least those officers were pleasant to look at."

I nodded absently.

"I'm not sure which I prefer," she added. "The one was so tall and had very nice green eyes. But the other had more of a sense of humor, I think. I liked the way he smiled." Nascha looked at me, clearly waiting.

"Oh ... no, really, you can't think ... I couldn't ..." I shook my head emphatically, even if I couldn't explain what I was so emphatic about. "They've been very nice. Nicer than I deserve. But I wouldn't know what to do with men like that."

She grinned, suddenly much less serious – and more wicked – than I'd ever seen her. "I have a few ideas."

I smiled reluctantly. "I just mean they're so, well, competent. And older. Intimidating. I'd feel like a shy, awkward teenager with a crush on a teacher or something."

"You wouldn't feel equal."

I nodded. "It's hard, isn't it? I don't want to be like my mother, how she is now. Maybe she was different with my father; she was only sixteen. He was here for the winter, teaching skiing, and left before he found out she was pregnant. Or maybe when he found out. But I've seen Mom with other boyfriends, and she dominates. Everything has to be her way."

Nascha leaned her elbows on the table. "Has she ever married?"

"Yes, she married Ricky's – my brother's – father. It lasted less than three years. He left when Ricky was a baby." I sighed and poked my spoon at the melted swirls of vanilla and caramel in the bottom of the bowl. "And I can't really blame him. He was a nice guy, but Mom made his life miserable."

"You were fond of him?"

"Yes. I was ten when they started dating, and I very much wanted a father. I tried to be the perfect daughter. He was always kind to me, but ..." Memories I'd tried to forget lurked in the shadows of my mind. My stomach churned.

"Audra." Nascha touched my arm. "Are you all right? Did he try something?"

"No! Oh no, he didn't do anything wrong. It was my mother." I rubbed my hands over my face. Tears pricked my eyes and I couldn't believe how easily the pain came back. But it was better to acknowledge it and move on. "I matured early. Physically, that is. I realize now I was incredibly naïve in high school. Anyway, by thirteen I'd shot up to five foot ten and gotten a figure, such as it is. I think my mother was jealous."

"I don't think I like your mother very much."

I gave a watery chuckle. "When I'm feeling generous, I can feel sorry for her." I straightened. "But she started picking at Richard for everything. And me, too. Making snide innuendos. I guess she finally found his breaking point. He walked out. I haven't seen him since. She won't even let him see Ricky."

"If he really wanted to, he could fight for that right."

I sighed. "Yes. And that hurts, too. He was nice, but weak. Mom is strong, but such a perfectionist she's often cruel. I don't want to be like either of them."

She patted my arm again. "You aren't. From what I've seen, you're already better than either of them."

"Thank you." The ache started to recede.

"But I can understand why you don't want a handsome, dominant police officer." She gave her wicked grin. "So then you won't mind if I take both of them."

I laughed. "You're just trying to cheer me up."

"Is it working?"

"It is, thanks." Tears wanted to well up again, but I blinked them back. "I wasn't usually this weepy. "And thanks for, well, putting up with me. You and Eslinda. You didn't have to ..." I broke off.

She scowled at me. "Am I going to have to buy you another sundae?" I managed a weak laugh and her voice grew gentle. "Audra, you're not the villain here. We're on your side."

"I'm glad. It makes a difference." I checked the time and sighed. "I should get going."

Nascha rose. "At least it's Friday."

"Is it? I guess it is."

"You'll be at the festival tomorrow?"

I groaned. Even though Eslinda and I had been talking about it that morning, I'd forgotten. Working in event planning meant I often had to work evenings and weekends. The summer festival would attract tourists and locals alike, and I had to help keep the crowds happy and under control.

"I'll be there." We bussed the table and headed for the door.

I really needed a quiet evening and a good night's rest. But I still had to deal with my mother and Ricky, the amateur detective. And I couldn't even bear to think about what the next day would bring. Telling my story to the police didn't end things. I shuddered as I wondered how Jay would react to the police questioning him again. And what about his father? Could Eslinda really control him?

I'd answered one or two questions, but far more remained. I wondered if I'd see Kyle Moore again. Nearly the whole town came out for the festival, but he probably wouldn't attend so soon after his sister's body had been found. His image rose in my mind, compassionate but guarded, with his sad eyes and hesitant smile. I wondered how long it would be before he could smile all the way, and what he'd look like then. I wondered about his hand, the cages in his truck, how it felt to lose a sibling, and whether he had anyone standing by him the way I had Nascha, Eslinda, and Ricky.

A shiver tickled my spine, but this time I wasn't sure if it was fear or something else.

Thirteen

At least it was Mom's turn to cook. Her meals were guaranteed to be healthy but bland, and I didn't have much appetite after the ice cream sundae. Ricky, on the other hand, had become quite a chef. Mom thought men should do their fair share in the kitchen, so Ricky had been responsible for dinner two or three times a week since he was ten, as I had been. I didn't disagree with her logic, especially after meeting men, and women, in college who didn't know how to boil spaghetti. Self-sufficiency was good for either gender. Ricky had taken it beyond mere competence to genuine skill and enthusiasm. I wouldn't want to feel too full for one of his meals.

I played with my food, waiting for someone to ask about my day. I wasn't sure what I wanted them to know, and I was too tired to think of subtle comments to skirt the truth. Maybe, having come clean with the police and my boss, it was time to tell my mother the truth as well. But I imagined her reaction to hearing I'd lied to cover up for a man, and I cringed.

She talked about her day. She didn't ask about mine. Ricky shot me a couple of meaningful glances but didn't bring up the murder. He'd apparently already learned what I hadn't figured out until I was thirteen or fourteen – if you didn't bring up topics in front of Mom, she wouldn't forbid you to do things. If she didn't forbid you to do something, you wouldn't have to lie or sneak around, and risk getting caught. And you always got caught.

After Ricky and I had washed and dried the dishes – our chore regardless of who cooked – we joined Mom for the rest of the local six o'clock news. Of course they were talking about the murder case.

"Police have questioned Thomas Bain. Mr. Bain, forty-two, had an on-and-off relationship with the twenty-seven-year-old victim for three years."

Mom snorted a comment about old lechers preying on younger women. Considering that he was barely older than she was, her comment about "old" men had a bit of unintended irony.

I tuned her out and listened to the newscaster. "According to Mr. Bain, the relationship ended a year ago and he has seen little of her since. However, he admits to contacting Ms. Moore the day before her disappearance, as phone records show."

"What did I tell you?" Mom said.

"I'm glad they have a suspect," I said.

I tried to catch what the newscaster was saying while they showed a video of a man going into the police station. Was that Thomas Bain? He looked ... harmless. An average guy, not too big, with brown hair and ordinary features.

"Mr. Bain claims his daughter can provide an alibi for the night Ms. Moore disappeared. Sources say the police are also questioning the daughter, eighteen-year-old Lia Bain."

Ricky nudged me. "But it could be someone else! It's never the obvious suspect."

I nudged him back. "In your books, maybe. I expect in real life it's often the obvious suspect." I wondered about the daughter, though. She could hardly be called unbiased, but would a teenage girl lie to protect her father if he'd killed someone?

I glanced at Mom without turning my head. Despite our differences, I couldn't imagine turning her in for a crime. Of course, I couldn't imagine her committing murder, either.

Ricky leaned close so his whisper tickled my ear. "You wouldn't want the real killer to go free. We should help investigate. The police don't solve a lot of cases, you know."

Mom leaned forward to glare back at both of us. "Audra, stay out of this. Both of you! That man is dangerous and probably crazy."

"He's also in jail. I can't exactly stay out of it at this point, but I don't want to be any more involved than I have to be."

She jabbed her finger at me. "They didn't say he'd been arrested, just that they were questioning him. He could be loose by now! And in a town this size, he'd have no trouble finding out where you live and work."

I clenched my hands in my lap and hoped my voice remained steady. "Why should he care about me? I just found the body – found *her*. It was an accident."

She looked back at the screen, where they were showing a map of the woods with the location where Bethany Moore was found. Where *I* found her. It was still hard to believe I'd become a part of all this.

Mom shook her head. "A man who would do something like that – kill a woman, leave her in the woods for weeks and pretend nothing had happened – he's not normal. Not sane. There's no telling what he might do."

I couldn't think of an answer to that. I knew Mom exaggerated the evils of men, but this time she might be right.

The TV shot returned to the newscaster. "The body was identified by Kyle Moore, the victim's brother, who returned home just over a year ago after losing his hand in Afghanistan." They showed a picture of Kyle in fatigues, his hair even shorter than it was now. He looked younger, healthier, and a whole lot happier. Poor guy. No wonder he looked so bleak, after everything he'd been through. I was a wreck after two days of a murder investigation. I couldn't even imagine going to war, losing a hand, and then having to deal with a missing sister.

'So that boy's involved, too," Mom said.

"Who, her brother? You don't have to make him sound guilty of something. It's hardly his fault that he's related to her."

Mom frowned at the TV, even though the newscaster had gone on to another story. "He had some problems when he came back from the Middle East."

"Well, yeah, he lost his hand!"

"No, not that – mental stuff. He was troubled, from what I heard."

I'm not sure why, but I had the urge to defend this man I barely knew. "It would be pretty surprising if someone wasn't troubled after fighting in a foreign country, getting injured, and losing his hand."

"Maybe so. He served his country, and that's an honorable thing. But soldiers can't always adjust to civilian life. They have high rates of domestic abuse."

I was having trouble following her. "Is he married?"

Mom stood. "I'm just saying that's not a family you want to know. I've heard things about them all. They draw trouble."

"It sounds more like bad luck to me."

She fisted her hands on her hips. "Women don't get murdered by their ex-boyfriends because of bad luck. It's bad choices. Now I'm going to go read." She strode out of the room, her classic way of making sure she had the last word.

I pondered what she'd said. I was sure her arguments didn't hang together, but without recording the whole thing and playing it back piece by piece, I wasn't sure I could figure out where the holes were and where she had a point.

It didn't matter. I wasn't planning on getting involved with any of them.

Ricky twisted to face me. "So, how are we going to help solve this? Do you want to hear my ideas?"

I gave a weak laugh. Normally I'd be glad to see that he wasn't crushed under Mom's thumb, but for once I wished he'd obey her. "I'm sure the police have it under control. I don't see what we can do. We'd only get in the way."

"No, see, we have the inside track! We can talk to people and they won't be so careful like they are with the police. We can spy on people, too. They won't notice us the way they would the police."

I almost snarled a refusal. But his face shone with excitement and I didn't like to be too harsh. Plus, if I refused to help, I was pretty sure he'd just investigate on his own. If he was going to be spying on people, I wanted to know where and when.

I glanced at the TV, trying to think of a way to appease Ricky while letting him think he was helping. The newscaster was mentioning the summer festival the next day. I had to be there anyway.

I turned to Ricky and smiled. "Okay, how about this? Come with me to the summer festival tomorrow. Everyone will be there, so it's a great place to listen in on conversations. And I bet people will be talking about the murder."

He bounced with excitement, seeming much younger than twelve. "I can listen, and no one will pay attention because I'm a kid!"

"Exactly. But you have to be a very careful detective and make sure no one knows what you're doing. And promise me you will not follow anyone or leave for any reason, without telling me first!"

"Okay. This is going to be great!"

Yeah. Great.

He opened his mouth to speak, but my phone rang. A perfect excuse to end the conversation before Ricky got even more carried away. Hmm, maybe I'm more like my mother than I like to admit.

I shook off the thought – I wasn't trying to get the last word in an argument, just keep my brother out of trouble – and stood. "I'd better get this." I checked the display as I headed for my room. It was a blocked number, which normally I wouldn't answer, but I felt obligated to follow through on my excuse. "Hello?"

"Audra Needham?"

"Yes?"

"You'll pay for causing trouble," a low voice growled. "From now on, mind your own business." The call disconnected.

I stared at the phone. The blood seemed to have left my head and was pulsing through my limbs. Had I really just received a threatening phone call? Who would do such a thing?

Unfortunately, I had too many suspects, too many people who resented my accidental involvement in this crime. Jay. His father. Bethany's ex-boyfriend and potential killer, Thomas Bain.

I shook my head. Surely someone suspected of a murder would have the sense to keep quiet. Why draw attention to yourself by threatening people? He might be annoyed that I stumbled onto the scene of his crime, but there wasn't anything he could do about that.

Unless he was insane and out for revenge, as both Jay and my mother had hinted.

I tossed the phone, which suddenly felt tainted by association. It bounced on my bed. I rubbed my hands over my face and up into my hair, gripping my hair until my scalp hurt. Suddenly I understood that cliché about pulling one's hair out. I wanted to pull the thoughts out of my head, so I could fling them away, or at least line them up nice and orderly where they might start to make sense.

I took a deep breath and slowly lowered myself to the bed, away from the phone. Most likely the call came from Jay. My number was unlisted and it was an Albuquerque number, not local, but Jay could have gotten it from my employment records or from the phone itself, when he had it. A prank call was the kind of childish thing he might do. But he couldn't really hurt me.

I remembered the close call with the golf ball and trembled.

Nonsense. Jay was simply a spoiled child who refused to grow up. It was easier to think of him that way. His father might be angry at me, too, but at least I had Eslinda on my side. Even if she couldn't protect my job, I could survive a job loss. It wouldn't be easy. It might take me away from Ricky again. I didn't want to leave him to Mom's untender mercies; I hated to think how he might turn out growing up with only her influence. But it was survivable.

All this was survivable – the police questioning, the gossip at work, the animosity from Jay and his father and Rodrigo. It was merely an ... an inconvenience.

Not like what happened to Bethany Moore. I could survive the inconveniences if it helped bring her killer to justice and bring closure to her family.

Closure. What a weak word. Could anything really take the pain from Kyle Moore's eyes at this point?

The phone rang again. I jerked back as if it had turned into a rattlesnake.

On the third ring, I leaned forward enough to see the display. My phone didn't recognize the number, but it was local and unblocked. It might be the police with more questions.

I reached for the phone, drew my hand back, and finally grabbed it on the last ring before voicemail. I hit answer but couldn't get words through my tight throat.

"Audra? Are you there? It's Nascha."

I sank back. "Oh. Hi."

"Have you heard?"

"Huh?"

"The police stopped Jay on the way home from work! Apparently he rolled through a stop sign, and they used it as an excuse to search his vehicle." She paused dramatically before adding, "They found drugs."

"Oh?" I wasn't exactly the best conversationalist, but Nascha carried on.

"Pot. They took him to the police station. His dad had to go down to bail him out."

At least they were having a worse week than I was. "Wait, are they at the police station now?" That would screw my theory about the phone call. You didn't use your one phone call on petty harassment.

"I don't know. I heard the news from one of the girls. I suppose he may be out now. Why?"

I closed my eyes with a sigh. "I guess it doesn't matter." If Jay had been unable to make the phone call, I didn't really want to know it. I liked that theory better than the alternative. And even if it wasn't him, he could've had Rodrigo do it.

"Anyway, I thought you'd want to know."

"Thanks. I guess."

"You guess?" After a long pause, she added, "Are you all right?"

I stretched out on the bed with my eyes closed. "Sure. It's just ... confusing."

"Surely you don't feel sorry for him? I'm glad he got in trouble after what he did to you. He deserves it."

"I don't feel sorry for him. I'm just not sure what it means. He's already so angry at me, him and his father. What will they do now?"

She didn't answer for a long time. I could almost hear her considering and discarding possible comments. Finally she said, "Whatever they try, we'll handle it. Eslinda and I have your back."

I smiled for what felt like the first time in ages. "Thanks." I yawned. "And now I think I'll go to bed. I don't care how early it is, I need some rest."

"Good idea. I'll see you tomorrow."

Yes, tomorrow. At the festival. Where all I had to do was make sure everything ran smoothly, withstand gossip, avoid anyone who might want to hurt or threaten me, and make sure my little brother didn't get too close to a murderer.

I couldn't wait.

Fourteen

Getting extra sleep turned out to be a bad idea. Extra sleep meant extra time to dream.

I dreamed of Bethany Moore.

I woke several times in the night, once crying, once struggling with the blanket. I lay awake, staring into the darkness, heart racing, trying to convince myself that everything was all right and the faint creaks and groans I heard were the same house sounds I'd always known. I thought about getting up, making some tea, watching TV – anything to push back the horrors of the night – but I couldn't bring myself to leave the cocoon of my bed. And every time I fell back to sleep, I saw her again.

I did not feel rested in the morning.

I wore my dressiest shorts, a scooped-neck shirt, and comfortable tennis shoes. I'd be outside and on my feet a lot. I gazed at my face in the mirror. I didn't think I was capable of the makeup job that would cover up those signs of fatigue. Anyway, SPF thirty sunscreen was more important. Fortunately I had a little natural tan to my skin, but not enough to prevent sunburn after a full day in the sun.

I tossed the sunscreen to Ricky as I passed through the living room, where he was watching cartoons. I grabbed a wide-brimmed straw hat and a shoulder bag from the coat closet and transferred the standard contents of my purse into the bag. I added the spray bug repellent in case the mosquitoes and gnats got bad.

In the kitchen, I filled two water bottles. Mom said, "What do you want for breakfast?"

I felt queasy after the rough night and my stomach gave a spasm at the thought of food. "I'll grab something over there."

"Make sure it's something healthy."

"Sure," I grumbled as I left the room. "I'll get some yogurt on a stick."

I ignored Mom's gasp behind me and Ricky's giggle. "Let's go." I added the sunscreen to the shoulder bag when Ricky finished with it, handed him a ball cap, and headed out the door.

Ricky settled into the passenger seat with a broad grin that just made my mood darker. "How should we start?" he asked.

"By finding breakfast." I had to shake off this mood. It wasn't fair to Ricky, and it wouldn't help me do my job. I forced a smile. "It might take a while to find yogurt on a stick."

He laughed. "Forget that. I want fry bread!"

I stopped myself from asking if he'd already eaten breakfast. I kept myself from commenting on the nutritional qualities of deep-fried dough. My mother's voice might speak in my head, but that didn't mean I had to let her out. "Sounds great."

I turned in at the resort, pulled around to the overflow parking lot, and parked in the back corner to save the better spaces for the public. The grounds around the building were already bustling, even though the festival didn't officially start for half an hour. As we got out of the car, I could smell hot grease in the air. The frying vats were already at work.

We crossed the parking lot and the smells got stronger. Frying potatoes, meat. Somebody was putting together breakfast burritos already. My stomach rumbled, and I thought I might manage breakfast after all. A full stomach would make it easier to get through the day.

I smiled at Ricky. "All right, breakfast first. You can have your fry bread if you want. I'm going for a well-balanced meal with all four major food groups – tortillas, meat, cheese, and green chile."

He practically skipped. "Me too! I want a breakfast burrito first. Chicharrones, eggs, cheese, and chile."

Fried pork fat for breakfast, yum. Of course, I was considering ordering bacon in mine. Something about the smell of fried food, which could be so overwhelming in an enclosed kitchen, got the appetite going on a cool, fresh morning outside.

The breakfast burrito place was doing a brisk business among the workers setting up and a few early attendees claiming shady spots under the trees near the bandstand. A group of shaggy musicians walked by with instrument cases.

I knew the schedule by heart. Some easy-going folk music to start the day, with a mariachi band and dancers a little later, before it got too hot for the poor girls in their heavy skirts. Then a juggler, and at midday a local rock band that was mainly popular because the various members counted half the town among their relatives. In the afternoon, a talented bluegrass quartet that worked cheap because their style of music wasn't in great demand in New Mexico, a magician who was mediocre but managed to entertain the children, and the high school jazz quartet.

Evening would bring back yet another mariachi band and some of the audience would join the dancing. A folk-rock band, also very danceable, would finish off the night. All through the day, vendors would sell food, charities would hand out flyers and ask people to sign petitions, and children would play on the giant inflatable waterslide. An ambulance was standing by to treat heatstroke and any heart attacks brought on by the overabundance of deep-fried foods.

It was going to be a long day.

I'd attended the event often enough in the past, but then I'd been able to hang out for a couple of hours and leave. At least I didn't have specific duties, other than keep an eye on things and pitch in if something went wrong. Eslinda was still in charge; I was in training.

I was nibbling at my hash brown, bacon, and cheese burrito, and keeping an eye out for Eslinda so I could report in, when Ricky whispered, "You talk to the resort people, since you know them. I'll walk around and see if anyone's talking about the murder. Do you think Thomas or Lia Bain will be here today? I found pictures online so I know what they look like. Oh, we should watch the woods! They say criminals return to the scene of the crime."

For a moment I'd put it out of my mind, focusing only on my job. Now I couldn't make myself look toward the woods. I managed to swallow the bite in my mouth. "Ricky, I do not want you to go into those woods. Do you understand me? Not for any reason."

He shrugged, avoiding my gaze.

I had to find a way to keep Ricky busy and out of trouble. "Why don't you grab a spot under the trees?" I gestured that way without turning my head. The cluster of trees at the end of the golf course had a great view of the bandstand. Beyond that lay the woods. "Those people have parked there for the day, and they don't have anything to do but gossip. I bet you'll hear lots of interesting stuff."

"Okay. I found a tape recorder app for my phone, so I can record anything good."

"Be discrete," I warned. At least a twelve-year-old boy playing on his phone shouldn't raise any alarms. "If you see or hear anything suspicious, call me. Stay by the trees so I'll know where to find you."

"Got it!" He ran off and my heart constricted as I watched him. I wished he weren't so interested in mysteries. I wished I could lock him away from all danger. But danger had a way of finding you even when you were minding your own business.

I closed my eyes for a moment. The image of Bethany Moore lying in the ditch rose up in my mind. I opened my eyes but even bright sun and bustling crowds couldn't erase the vision. I could no longer tell if the ache in my stomach came from hunger or emotion. But I didn't think I could choke down any more of my burrito. I looked around for a trashcan. I knew we had fifteen extras set up for the event.

I turned around and almost ran into someone. I stumbled back, dropping my burrito.

Jay stepped forward, looming over me.

Fifteen

Before I could turn and dart away, Jay grabbed my arm. "Hey, bitch. Ruin anyone's life today?"

I struggled to breathe. I told myself he couldn't hurt me – not here, in the middle of everyone. I forced words out. "It's not my fault."

"Is that what you think? Well I think it is your fault. And I'll make sure everyone else knows it." His lips stretched in what might pass for a smile in some alternate world where smiling was a bad thing. "I'll tell them you're jealous."

"Jealous?" That made no sense.

He leaned closer. "Jealous because I didn't want you. Spreading rumors because I turned you down."

That was so ridiculous I let out a short laugh, though it sounded more like a croak. I clenched my fists, trying to still my trembling. "Sure, everyone will believe that. Except the police. They'll probably pay more attention to the evidence in your car."

His grip tightened on my arm. "You could have planted that." His eyes shifted toward the man at his side – his father – then back to me. "You did plant it."

"Is that your story?" My voice wavered, but I met his eyes. "Good luck with that." I wanted to storm off, but I wasn't sure I could pull away and didn't want to get into a public arm wrestling match.

His father edged closer. "I warned you about causing trouble for my son. He's told me how you had a crush on him all through high school. If I'd known you applied here to get close to him, I never would have agreed to the hiring."

I stared at him. It was like I'd entered some alternate reality where people spouted nonsense and assumed you'd understand.

"Don't think your job is safe just because Eslinda has taken a liking to you. She won't be around much longer." He nodded in satisfaction and Jay gave me a triumphant smile.

"Audra!" a voice called. I went weak with relief as I turned to see Nascha and Eslinda.

Jay released my arm as the women hurried up to us. "Hey Nascha," he said with an easy smile as he looked her up and down. She looked cool and elegant in pale linen slacks and a butter-yellow shirt. Her dark hair swung loose over her shoulders. "You look great. How's it going?" Was he actually flirting with her? Right after bullying me?

"Fine." She shifted her body toward me, subtly excluding him. "Audra, we've been looking for you. We have some things to discuss."

"I wanted to be here earlier," Eslinda said, "but my car was vandalized. Someone threw a huge rock at the front window! The rock was still sitting in the middle and it's all cracked. The window, not the rock."

Jay grinned. "Really? That's too bad."

His father looked at him, his expression confused and a bit troubled. He turned back to Eslinda with false cheerfulness. "I'm sure you have plenty to do here. We'll let you get to it." He jerked his head in a gesture for Jay to follow him, and they walked away.

I would have leaned against something had there been anything to lean against. My legs felt weak and my arm still throbbed from where Jay had gripped it.

"Are you all right?" Nascha asked.

I nodded. I had yet to process everything Jay and his father had said. Two things were clear, though. My job might not be as safe as Eslinda had suggested, and Jay was planning a smear campaign. Would anyone believe his rumors?

They might. He was well known in the community and at the resort, which could work for me or against me, depending on how other people saw him. The bit about me having a crush in high school was true. Would any of our classmates remember that? Would they believe I had come back home desperate to see him and had turned into a crazy stalker when he didn't want me? Would anyone think that possible of me?

I wasn't sure anyone knew me well enough to say for sure.

Something wet touched the back of my knee and I leapt half a foot. A dog had been enjoying the remains of my burrito and apparently wanted to thank me by licking my legs. Eslinda leaned forward and rubbed the dog's ears. "Ooh, aren't you a sweet boy!" Eslinda was wearing a white cotton dress with colorful embroidery around the neck and hem. The straight cut evened out her various bulges, and it ended above the knee, showing off pleasantly rounded calves.

"That's a nice dress," I said.

She straightened, beaming at me. "I got it in Mexico. They understand large women there."

I tried to put everything else out of my mind and focus on my job. "What did you want to talk about? Should I be doing something?"

"No, except be handy if I need you. We were only trying to get you out of the Preppard clutches."

She was like a plump, Hispanic fairy godmother, and I wanted to hug her. Instead I just said, "Thank you."

"I need to check out a few things. You girls will be all right?"

"Sure." I decided not to tell her about Lewis Preppard's threat. It would upset her, and if he was right, she wouldn't be able to do anything about it anyway. The way things were going, maybe I'd be glad to leave the resort, regardless of the consequences.

Eslinda bustled off. Nascha and I walked slowly through the growing crowd. "Are you all right, really?" she asked.

I shrugged. "As good as can be expected, I guess." I thought about the nightmares. If I told Nascha, she'd sympathize. But she probably wouldn't really understand. I'd always been an outsider, standing on the edge of life looking in. Now I felt more cut off than ever. Few people could imagine what it was like to find a murder victim. Few people wanted to. I didn't want to burden anyone else, or deal with platitudes from someone who didn't know what it was like. I wished I could talk about my feelings with someone who truly understood, but the one person who had shared the experience with me was not an option.

"They're trying to intimidate you," Nascha said. "If you don't let them scare you, they can't hurt you."

I made a vague noise. I wasn't convinced of that. "Jay isn't going to make it easy for me. I got a stupid prank phone call last night. I figured it was Jay, since he'd be able to get my number." I came to a sudden halt. "Nascha, how did you know my phone number?"

"I saw it on your résumé. They passed it around to all of us before your interview."

I stood still as the crowds brushed past us. "But – that was a month ago. Why would you memorize my number then?"

She shrugged. "I remember numbers."

"For months?"

She frowned, considering. "As far as I know, forever. They just stick with me. You want to order a pizza, make a doctor's appointment, or get the ski report? I know the number."

Wow. I couldn't remember a phone number from the time I looked it up until I picked up my phone. I had to have the number right in front of me and go over it piece by piece. "Do you have a photographic memory?"

"Not for anything but numbers. It's handy in my job."

Yes, it would be, since she handled purchasing for a resort that had daily deliveries of everything from salmon fillets to golf tees. It hardly seemed fair that she should be beautiful and elegant, and have a mind like that.

I sighed. "It's a good thing you're so nice." When she shot me a puzzled look, I added, "Because otherwise I'd hate you. At least now I can keep my jealousy to a sullen grumble."

She laughed and linked her arm through mine. "Come on, I'll buy you a coffee."

"Thanks again for coming to my rescue."

"We women have to stick together. Especially when there are so many crazy men out there."

"Funny, that sounds like something my mother would say."

Nascha wrinkled her nose. "I'm not sure I like being compared to your mother. I'm not saying all men are bad. But when things this bad happen, there's usually a bad man involved. Jay is one. Whoever killed that woman is another, assuming Jay didn't do it. Either way, you can bet it was a man."

"Probably, though I guess it could be a woman."

"I took a Women's Studies class in college on women who kill. The numbers aren't large, but when it happens, women almost always kill a husband or lover, usually in self-defense. Or else they kill their children."

"That's horrible!" I'd heard one or two news stories along those lines, but I didn't think it was common.

"Often that's an attempt at protection, in a twisted way. An abused woman kills her children and herself, to protect them all from the abuser. Though some women have killed their children in order to get a new man who doesn't want a woman with baggage. One way or another, there's nearly always a man involved somehow. If a woman tries to kill another woman, it's usually jealousy over a man."

I made a face. "I'm not sure I want to know all this."

"The point is, with women, the victim is almost always someone very close to the killer, so it's easier to track down the criminal. Women don't kill strangers. But men kill for many reasons. For jealousy, for control, for revenge, out of drunken anger, even for fun. That makes it much harder to find out the truth."

The truth. Where was it in all this muddle? Would we ever know? Ricky still thought investigating crimes was fun and easy, but many murders never got solved.

Ricky. I'd meant to keep a closer eye on him. I studied the area around the trees and spotted him standing at the back of the crowd, turned in my direction. He lifted his hand and I waved.

He frantically motioned me over. At that distance I couldn't see his expression, but the way he was wriggling like a fish on a line, he'd attract attention quickly. "I need to talk to my brother," I told Nascha. "I'll catch up with you later, okay?"

I headed for Ricky. With one last wave, he trotted away from the group of people. Where was he going? Not toward the woods! I broke into a run, my heart racing even though logic told me the woods held no particular dangers today.

He darted around a small building used for equipment storage. I jogged up to it and found him waiting on the other side, where the building screened us from the crowd. I tried not to look at the woods fifteen feet away.

Ricky started talking before I closed the gap between us. "You would not believe the stuff I heard! I don't know if I got it on tape recorder, though, they might've been too far away. But everyone's talking about the murder." He frowned down at the phone in his hand.

I tried to keep my expression calm. "What are they saying?"

"One lady said there have been five other missing women around the state in the last year, and one unsolved murder of a woman whose body was found in the desert. At least, they think that was murder. It was hard to tell because she'd been there so long."

My stomach churned and I had to concentrate on my breathing. But to Ricky, it was just a series of clues to plug into the equation. It wasn't real.

"So this lady? She says her cousin's with the sheriff's office, and the reason the state police are involved is because maybe all these cases are connected. Maybe it's a serial killer who moves around."

Huh. So the girl from the lunchroom might get her wish after all.

"Maybe it was a resort guest!" Ricky went on. "What do you think? Maybe some guy is staying at different hotels and killing women wherever he goes. We should find out if any of the missing women worked at hotels."

"Wait, Bethany Moore didn't work at the resort. Did she?" I didn't recall hearing anything about her job.

Ricky shrugged. "Pretty much everyone in town does at some point, right? Anyway, it doesn't all have to be hotel employees. Just someone around the hotel, playing golf, eating in the restaurant, whatever." He frowned. "That's hard to track, though. If we're lucky, we'll find a more obvious connection."

"Sure, that would be nice," I said weakly.

I had to get him to calm down. I tried to think clearly about the serial killer angle. "Look, Ricky, if it's a serial killer, I don't think there's much we can do." The thought cheered me up.

"We know the night she disappeared, so you could check on the hotel guests at that time."

"And do what? That would be hundreds of names. We can't investigate them all." I tried to let him down easy. "Your idea was that we could help with the investigation because we're local. But if it's somebody who moves around, we can't help."

"That's just one possibility! Some people think it has to do with drugs."

"Yeah, I've heard that one." I wished I had someplace to sit down. "Look, why don't you keep listening. Make notes and we can talk about it all later."

"Yeah, okay." He was quiet for a moment. "You don't sound like you really want to find the killer."

"Of course I want to find him! Or rather, I want him to be found. But I—"

I broke off as someone stepped around the building behind Ricky. He was an average-looking man, maybe in his forties. I didn't think I'd met him, but something tugged at my memory.

I gasped and stepped back. It was Thomas Bain.

Sixteen

"Ricky, come here. Now," I said.

Ricky glanced back and started to turn, but Thomas Bain placed a hand on his shoulder. "Don't run away. I just want to talk to you." He looked past Ricky and met my eyes. "You're the girl who found Bethany's body, right?"

I couldn't speak. Couldn't move. I might be facing a murderer. Spots danced before my eyes and the ground seemed to shift.

Thomas Bain moved forward, guiding Ricky along. "I want to thank you."

Thank me? I fought back the waves of dizziness and nausea and tried to focus on the man. He looked perfectly ordinary. He was a few inches taller than Ricky, maybe five foot eight. Average build, not particularly muscular. Brown hair, brown eyes without any glimmer of evil in them, a bit of stubble as if he hadn't shaved that morning. He looked tired.

I wouldn't have noticed him on the street.

I still wanted to get away.

Ricky was fumbling with his phone, holding it close to his body where Bain might not notice. I hoped he was calling the police.

Bain smiled slightly. "I know what you must think of me. But I didn't have anything to do with Bethany's death." He dropped his gaze and shook his head. "Poor girl. I cared about her, but she was so troubled. The drugs, the sleeping around – we couldn't make it work."

I couldn't think of a single thing to say. Ricky, however, didn't have that problem. "You're a lot older than she was. She was, like, twenty-three when you started dating, and you were almost forty? My mom would say men go for younger women because they want someone they can control."

Yep, that sounded like Mom. But what on earth was Ricky doing? We needed to get away, not risk making the man mad.

Bain patted Ricky's shoulder. "I suppose some women would see it that way. You'll understand, when you're older." His eyes met mine again. "If you didn't know her, you can't possibly understand how lovely she was, how full of life."

My stomach twisted as I thought of Bethany as I'd seen her.

"She was young," Bain went on, "but if you'd known her, you wouldn't blame me." He gave a short laugh. "Maybe it was a midlife crisis. I was lonely, feeling old. I wanted to touch something young and beautiful again."

"So why did you stop going out with her?" Ricky asked.

Bain turned his head toward my brother. "I loved her, but she was only interested in having fun. There were other men." His voice shifted on that sentence, but he sounded more hurt than angry. "And drugs. She had to have her drugs." His voice dropped. "I'm afraid that's what killed her."

I almost felt sorry for him. He could have been telling the truth. But my body was shaking with the urge to run, and as long as he had Ricky, I couldn't. I finally forced words out of my throat. "If she'd died of an overdose, the police wouldn't be calling it murder."

He gazed at me across the short space, and I thought I saw the shine of tears in his eyes. "I didn't mean an accident. I meant the people she got involved with."

I glanced at the phone Ricky still held at waist level. He hadn't spoken into it. Had he called for help? If he had, how would they find us? The phone had a GPS, but tracking it might take time.

The faint murmur of voices drifted on the breeze. The band was tuning up with brief bursts of random notes. Maybe I could draw Bain out into the open, where we'd be visible by the crowd.

I took a step backward. "That's an interesting theory. Do you know any of those people by name?" I edged back another step.

Bain said, "I told the police everything I know." He stayed where he was, and so did Ricky.

Maybe if Ricky got the hint, he'd break away from Bain and run to me. I took another step back.

I sensed movement behind me a moment before I backed into a solid body.

I yelped and leapt forward, spinning around. My hat tipped forward over my eyes. I saw legs in faded jeans, a sliver of white T-shirt, and an arm that ended at the wrist. I pushed my hat back and gazed at Kyle Moore.

The look in his eyes made me take another step back. It was a killing look. My heart hammered, even though he hadn't glanced at me. All his attention was on Thomas Bain.

"Kyle," Bain said softly. "How are you doing?"

I edged closer to the building, out of the way, as Kyle stalked Thomas Bain. That's what his movement brought to mind, a hunter stalking prey. I could believe he'd been a soldier. "What do you think?"

I glanced from Kyle to Bain like someone watching a tennis match. Bain looked perfectly calm, though he dropped his hand from Ricky's shoulder and shifted to the side as if preparing for an attack – or to run. At least he wasn't using my brother as a shield.

"I think you must be hurting as much as I am," Bain said. "Bethany wouldn't want us to be at odds."

Kyle gave a harsh laugh. "Bethany would have—" He broke off and pressed his lips together for a moment. "What Bethany would have wanted doesn't matter anymore. But Audra matters. Stay away from her."

I stared at him, feeling a flush of warmth.

Bain said, "I don't mean any harm. I never did. Audra." He waited until I looked at him. "You take care of yourself." With a little wave and a half smile, he sidled around the side of the building.

Kyle scowled after him, his fist clenched. He obviously had a leading suspect in Bethany's death. Was there history to back him up, or was his grief causing him to latch onto the one person who'd been mentioned by name?

Ricky checked around the side of the building. "He's gone."

I hurried to Ricky and gave him a quick hug. He wriggled away and studied Kyle. "You're Kyle Moore. Bethany's brother." He had an odd expression. I wondered if he was realizing for the first time that this case involved real people with powerful emotions, and not just pictures with names.

I glanced down at Ricky's phone, which seemed to be running a stopwatch. "What's that? I thought maybe you called the police."

Ricky gave me a warning look. I stared back, baffled. He shifted his eyes to Kyle and back to me.

I sighed. "Ricky, would you please just tell me?

He made an annoyed sound and touched the screen. The timer stopped. "I was recording the conversation. I hoped Mr. Bain might say something suspicious, but I don't think he did."

I took a step back to better stare at him. "You were recording that? Not trying to get help? Ricky!"

He glanced at Kyle and whispered, "I thought we might get evidence."

I realized he didn't want Kyle to know about the recording, and in fact had still been recording after Bain left. Did he think Kyle might say something suspicious? Or did he just not want Kyle to know we were investigating?

I flashed back to the moment before Bain had stepped around the corner. Ricky and I were arguing about investigating Bethany's murder. He must have heard us, and now he would think we were seriously trying to find a murderer. I groaned inwardly.

"Should I follow him?" Ricky whispered.

"No! You should keep away from him."

Ricky glanced at Kyle again and nodded. "Okay. I'll just go back and ... listen to the music." He turned so he could give me a thumbs up without Kyle seeing, and then scurried around the building.

"Ricky—" I sighed.

"That's your brother?"

"Yeah, lucky me," I muttered.

"Are you all right?" He stepped closer, and I felt my heart, which hadn't yet settled down, speed up again.

"Fine." I hunted for anything to say. "Why are you here? I would have thought – I mean, after—" My face heated. So much for not babbling like an idiot.

"I'm keeping an eye on things."

That was vague. He stopped two feet away. I studied his chest, the lean muscles visible under the thin white T-shirt. He raised his arm toward me, and my gaze dropped to the stump at his wrist, the skin shiny and scarred over the end.

He froze, then dropped his arm.

My face heated and I stared at his chest. Did he think I would be grossed out if he came near me with his injury? He'd lost his hand fighting for our country. The last thing he should feel was shame. I tried to think of something to do or say to make the moment better, but it stretched out, awkward.

Finally he spoke. "Audra, what are you and your brother up to?"

I blew out an exasperated breath. "I'm not up to anything." I risked a glance at his face. "But Ricky wants to be one of the Hardy Boys."

Lines formed between his eyes. "Audra, you two need to keep away from Thomas Bain. He's dangerous."

"We didn't do it on purpose! He found us here."

Kyle stepped back and looked around the building, maybe trying to spot Bain again. I took the opportunity to study his face in profile. It was hard to believe he was younger than I was. But unlike Jay, who seemed to have aged through hard living, Kyle's face held the strength that came from surviving a hard life.

The rest of his words sank in. "You think Bain did it."

He looked back at me. "Yes. I know what he did to Bethany before."

I couldn't look away from his gaze. "You mean he hurt her?"

"More than once. She wouldn't keep away from him. I couldn't do anything from overseas. Not that she ever listened to her kid brother. She replied to my e-mails sometimes, and she sounded all right. But it's easy to lie in e-mail. I heard the truth from other people." He put his hand over his eyes. "By the time I got back, she'd stopped seeing him. I'd like to think she could've gotten clean. She deserved the chance. I would have helped her." He sighed. "Maybe if I'd been here all along, I could have."

I took a step closer. I remembered the way I'd left Ricky behind when I went to college, and I thought I understood some of the things he wasn't saying. "Sometimes you have to get out. For your own survival. It doesn't mean you don't care about the people you leave behind."

He looked into my eyes for a long time. I couldn't remember ever holding a man's gaze like that. I could feel the slow thud of my heart. I caught his scent, something unusual but strangely familiar and comfortable. I wanted to get even closer but my body held back.

He dropped his gaze first."Get out there and keep an eye on your brother. You'd better go first. You don't want to be seen with me."

Why not?

I think I do.

The words drifted through my head, but I couldn't speak them aloud. I pulled my gaze away from his face. As I passed by him, I recognized part of his smell – eucalyptus, like the ointment athletes sometimes use for sore muscles. Did he have hidden injuries as well?

I felt him watching me as I walked away.

Seventeen

I made sure Ricky was back under the trees. I'd need to have a stern talk with him, but first I wanted to sort out everything in my own mind. Eslinda was on stage introducing the band. I saw Nascha with another girl from the resort, one who worked the reception desk. I searched for her name ... Jenny? No, Gina. I joined them with a smile that felt stiff.

"There you are!" Nascha said. "Is everything all right?"

I nodded. I really wanted to talk to her privately, but I didn't know how to get rid of Gina. I blurted out, "I saw Kyle Moore."

Nascha looked interested. Gina gasped. She was a few years older than I was, maybe close to Bethany's age. I wasn't sure if she'd grown up in town or moved here for the job. Could she have known Bethany and her family?

"He's not here for the festival." I didn't want people to think Kyle wasn't properly mourning his sister. "He was only passing by."

After a moment's hesitation, Gina asked, "Are you ... friends?"

I shrugged. "Not exactly."

"Why?" Nascha demanded of Gina.

Gina glanced around, looking uneasy. "It's nothing, really."

But it was obviously something. I wanted to walk away and refuse to hear what she had to say. I also needed to know. I waited as the band started up with a cheerful fiddle tune.

Gina bit her lip and looked from Nascha to me. "It probably doesn't matter. Unless you're thinking of getting involved with him."

I waited for her to explain, but she didn't. I wanted to shake her. I couldn't claim I was planning to get involved with Kyle, but if I didn't learn the big secret, my own imagination would take over. Had he lost his hand not in heroically fighting for his country, but in something that had resulted in a dishonorable discharge? Had he joined the military because of some trouble in town? Was there something nasty in his past, something to do with Bethany? I had enough trouble making conversation without those kinds of questions rushing through my head. "You'd better tell me."

Nascha gave me a quick look. Did she think I *was* planning to get involved with Kyle? I felt my face heat but kept my gaze on Gina.

She glanced around again and finally leaned close and lowered her voice. "It's just he has a drug problem. I feel sorry for him, and you can hardly blame him after everything he's been through. But you don't want to get involved with someone like that." She grimaced. "Trust me, it's not worth it. You can't save them."

Kyle, a drug addict? It seemed unlikely, after his attitude toward Bethany's problem. But then addiction did tend to run in families, didn't it? A genetic predisposition of some kind. Maybe his comments about Bethany getting clean had been some kind of cover-up, or he'd been wishing she'd been able to do something he couldn't. I tried to shift the puzzle pieces into some order that might fit, but I was missing too many pieces.

"What did he say to you?" Nascha asked.

"What?" I shook myself out of my ponderings. "Oh! Thomas Bain found me first."

This time Gina and Nascha both gasped. "What did he want?" Nascha asked while Gina looked around wildly as if he might be lurking behind her.

"He ... he thanked me."

They both stared. I could hardly believe it either, especially when I remembered how scared I'd been, but if I thought back to what he actually said, that was the truth. "For finding Bethany's body. He said he cared about her and didn't have anything to do with her death."

Nascha grimaced. "He'd hardly tell you otherwise."

"No." But when I really thought about it, he hadn't done anything wrong or threatening. If anything, Kyle was the one who'd looked dangerous. I couldn't blame him under the circumstances, and my instinct was to trust Kyle and avoid Thomas Bain.

But could I trust my instincts? How much were they influenced by expectations? Between the fear of men instilled by Mom, and my own shyness, I hadn't spent a lot of time with men, even as friends. My instincts hadn't been tested much. Jay hadn't set off the alarm bells as quickly as he should have. Maybe I couldn't rely on my instincts at all.

A headache throbbed behind my eyes. I fished in my shoulder bag for sunglasses. Nascha and Gina were talking about the murder, but I'd had enough. "I'm going to get that coffee now. I could use the caffeine."

Nascha touched my arm lightly. "Try to stay out of trouble. No wonder you looked so odd when you walked up."

I suspected that had more to do with my confused feelings about Kyle than with Thomas Bain, but I let it go. I joined a long line of people waiting for coffee. I inhaled the scent of it, dark and earthy but soothing in its familiarity. The world hadn't changed that much. Whatever else happened, people still waited for their morning coffee fix. It wasn't much to hold onto, but even a cup of coffee was better than nothing.

I tried to sort through everything that had happened in the last few days. It felt more like weeks or months. There were too many pieces all jumbled together. Thomas Bain, Kyle, drug addiction, Jay and his father – wait, Jay smoked pot. Was that a connection to Bethany?

The line shuffled forward. I frowned at the back of the man in front of me and tried to tune out the chatter nearby. I didn't associate marijuana with violence. Usually it was meth that turned people crazy. But if Jay smoked pot, maybe he did other drugs, too. Anyway, it was a possible link.

And a link to Kyle? I hoped not. I liked him. Maybe some of that was pity, or respect because he'd been injured in service of his country, or flattery because he remembered me from high school. For whatever reason, I wanted to think the best of him.

Someone cleared their throat behind me and I realized the line had moved forward again. I closed the gap. Maybe I should follow Ricky's lead and make some lists or charts or something, like a real investigator. Possible suspects, pros and cons for each, links between people and so forth. I might not solve the case, but at least I could sort through some of the jumble in my head.

I finally got my coffee and wandered away from the booth. I checked on Ricky again – still settled under the tree, now chatting with another boy his age. I hoped they were talking about normal boy things like video games and how much they hated their teacher – or even about girls – and that Ricky wasn't letting the whole world know that he was tracking a murderer.

The band had picked up the pace in a toe-tapping folk tune. Eslinda was with the sound technician. I walked past some food booths and wrinkled my nose at the smell of hamburgers and dill pickles. It was only ten AM. I looked around for Nascha and Gina, though I wasn't sure I wanted to join them again yet.

And then I saw Jay. He was standing with a slim, dark-haired girl who was shaking her head. Another of his amorous attempts? Surely he wouldn't try to get her off into the woods. Even he couldn't think that would sound romantic anymore.

I edged closer, staying out of Jay's line of vision. The girl was pretty, but young. Maybe still in high school even. She was looking up at Jay intently as he bent over her. Should I warn her somehow? Jay hated me so much already that I could hardly make it worse. But what could I do? Just walk up and tell her Jay was a jerk?

I didn't think I could get up the nerve for that. Possibilities floated through my mind, things I'd seen on TV or in movies. Playing the part of an offended girlfriend. Accusing him of giving me some sexually transmitted disease.

I giggled at the thought, but I didn't think I could manage that either. Besides, it would look like evidence that I really was jealous and stalking Jay.

I edged closer, pretending to watch the band, my back to Jay. If I could hear what they were saying, I might know if the girl was in trouble. And if she wasn't in immediate trouble, maybe I could speak to her privately before she did something stupid, like I had.

They were talking softly. A family crowded past me and I got out of their way, using that as an excuse to back closer. I could still only hear murmurs. I kept my gaze on the bandstand and backed up a little more, casually, I hoped.

Suddenly I could hear Jay quite well. "And here she is now – we were just talking about you."

I glanced over my shoulder to find him looking at me. I turned slowly as the girl moved up beside him, her eyes narrowed and lips tight.

Jay gestured to me. "That's Audra."

The girl took a step forward. "So you're the one who's trying to ruin my father."

Eighteen

They hadn't shown her picture on TV, but this had to be Thomas Bain's daughter. She didn't look much like her father. She had long dark hair and thin, arched eyebrows over heavily made-up eyes. She was slim, petite even, but a low-cut black tank top showed off impressive cleavage. She said, "You got no business dragging my dad into this."

She stepped closer, hands on hips. I had at least half a foot on her, but I felt the urge to back away from that ferocious glare. "I never said—"

"He didn't hurt nobody! That bitch got herself in trouble and now my dad is paying for it. She took his money, made him miserable, broke his heart. Now this." For a moment her jaw trembled. She whispered, "I'm glad she's dead."

She turned and stormed off as I stood there with my mouth open. Jay swaggered the last two steps toward me, smirking. "Are we having fun yet?"

I started shaking and clenched my fists at my sides, struggling for control. I'd never been the focus of so much anger. Casual cruelty, yes, the humiliations that go along with being a weaker member of the schoolyard pack, and the thousand pricks and stings my mother administered on a daily basis. But most people barely noticed me. Now I had Jay, his father, and this girl I'd never met spewing poison on me.

I'd never said anything about Thomas Bain. How could I, when I'd never heard of him before the news reports? But Jay must have told Lia Bain that I'd accused her father. He was circling around me, leaning too close, trying to intimidate me.

He draped an arm across my shoulders and opened his mouth. Before he could speak, I shook him off and whipped around to face him. "How dare you! I've done nothing wrong and you keep trying to get me in trouble."

His eyes widened and his head jerked back.

I let my anger boil over and carry my voice with it. It felt good. "I don't know what you had to do with the murder. I was assuming you're just acting like an ass because you didn't want to get caught with the pot." I stomped closer and poked my finger at his chest. "But if you had anything to do with killing Bethany Moore, I'm going to find out about it, and I'll see you in jail!"

He stared at me with his mouth half open. My chest tightened and my throat closed up. I stalked off through the crowd before he could go on the offensive again, or I ruined my rant with tears. I wove among the food stalls, dodging people, trying to get away.

I finally found myself alone behind the little storage building. I sank to the ground, leaning against the building with my knees drawn up. I wrapped my arms around my legs and rested my forehead on my knees, letting my hat fall to the ground. Tears slipped past my closed eyelids.

How had everything gotten so complicated? It should have been straightforward. You found evidence of a crime, you reported it, the police took over. Done. So how had I become embroiled in such a mess?

And what did it mean for Bethany? It didn't sound as if she was that great in life. I had a feeling I wouldn't have liked her at all. But that didn't mean she deserved to die. And it didn't mean she deserved to have people talk about her death as if it was an inconvenience, important only as it affected them.

I lifted my head and wiped at my eyes. Bethany Moore deserved justice, no matter what she had done. Was I the only one who saw that?

I dug in my shoulder bag for a tissue and blotted my face. I was being foolish. Of course I wasn't the only one. The police were working on the case. I hadn't seen or heard anything from them since my last interview, but surely they were doing whatever police do when they investigate a murder.

I remembered Ricky saying something about the police failing to solve a lot of cases. You did hear about a lot of unsolved murders. They didn't have enough clues, or they couldn't find proof, and then the police got too busy with something else.

I didn't think I could stand it, never knowing what had really happened to Bethany Moore.

I tipped my head back against the building. Movement at the corner of my eye caught my attention and I flinched. Who had come after me now?

I tensed to spring up, but then saw it was Ricky and let myself fall back. He stopped a few feet away. "I saw you run past. Are you all right?"

I nodded. "Make sure no one else is around, close enough to listen, okay?"

He circled the building and came back. "Okay! Good thinking. Do you have a new plan?"

I dug out a brush and started pulling it through my hair. "No, nothing specific. But you're right. I'm in this too deep to let it go. If we can, we need to help solve the murder of Bethany Moore. Let's start by figuring out what we know."

I made sure Eslinda had my cell phone number and then took Ricky to my office. With the door closed, we'd have some privacy. I had mixed feelings about encouraging Ricky's involvement, but I couldn't face doing this alone. Besides, maybe he really had learned something from all those detective novels.

We made a list of the people who might be involved or who had acted strange lately. Thomas Bain topped the list, of course. But there was also Lia Bain, who had provided his alibi. If he was guilty, she must be involved as well.

Jay was next on the list. I still had a hard time imagining why a murderer would bring me to the body and then get angry about reporting it, but I couldn't fathom how his mind worked in any area. I had to hope he wasn't the killer, because if he was I'd been stupid to warn him I was coming after him. The one time I can't keep my mouth shut, I have to go threatening someone who could be dangerous.

Lewis Preppard and Rodrigo made the list because of their association with Jay and their threatening behaviors.

Finally, I added Kyle Moore. I didn't like doing it, but he obviously had a strong connection to Bethany and that, plus the rumors of drug addiction and "mental trouble," had to make him a suspect. I couldn't believe he would intentionally kill his own sister, but if he'd supplied her with drugs he might have felt guilty enough about her death that he wouldn't report it. That might cause the haunted look in his eyes.

But if he'd only supplied drugs, the death would've been an accidental overdose. The police had never released a cause of death, but they were calling it murder. Why? Maybe they weren't sure, so they had to investigate it as a murder.

Bethany's image rose up in my mind, her skin greenish-tinged and something missing where her jaw should be. There was a clue there, but I shoved the vision away. I dragged in a breath, smelling the faint lavender scent of my shampoo and green chile on Ricky's breath, and tried to focus on the black names on white paper.

"Put down serial killer," Ricky said.

"Right." I wrote it down. Even if we didn't have a specific suspect, it was worth remembering the possibility. "I heard some other rumors, too." I thought back to the lunchroom and wrote down drug dealer and pimp. I bet Encyclopedia Brown, the kid detective, didn't have cases like this.

I wasn't too surprised that Ricky didn't have to ask me to explain drug dealers or pimps. But I realized he probably got all his information about relationships between men and women from Mom, school, and TV. No doubt he knew the mechanics of sex, but what kind of warped attitudes would he have with Mom drumming "men are evil" into him on one side, and punk classmates bragging about their conquests on the other? I might have to give him "the talk" one day soon. Wouldn't that be fun.

I tried to think of anyone else involved in the case, anyone connected to Jay and the resort and Bethany Moore. Anyone I'd had unusual contact with in the last couple of days. I tapped the pen against the paper a few times and then finally dropped down a few lines and added Eslinda, Nascha, and Gina.

"Isn't that your boss?" Ricky asked. "Who are the other two?"

"Women who work here at the resort. I don't think they had anything to do with the murder, but they all know Jay, and Gina told me something about Kyle Moore. Eslinda knew Bethany's family. Nascha ..."

I trusted Nascha. I really did. It was simply some combination of paranoia and brutal honesty that forced me to list her name. "I don't think she knows the Moores or the Bains, but she's been very interested, asking a lot of questions. But I'm pretty sure she's on my side."

"Maybe those people aren't suspects, but, like, sources of information."

"That's right." I drew a line above their names and wrote Sources. That made me feel less disloyal than adding their names to a list of suspects.

"Put Person Unknown in the suspect list," Ricky said.

"Serial killer and pimp would be people unknown."

"But it could be somebody else, someone other than a serial killer or pimp, that we haven't even thought of yet."

Like another boyfriend, maybe, or someone who had a grudge against Bethany that we hadn't even heard whispered yet. I added Person Unknown to the list above the Sources line. That was an appealing option, since it meant somebody I didn't know and who didn't know me. After all, there were 8,000 people in this town, besides thousands of strangers passing through every year.

Of course, I did know a couple hundred people in town, at least on sight. My mind flashed over familiar faces, former teachers and classmates, the grocery store clerks, waiters and waitresses, doctors and dentists. It was astonishing to think that any one of them might have been involved in this crime or some other. We wouldn't know it unless they were caught and named in the paper.

And I happened to know that the middle school principal and the former mayor had both been convicted of drunk driving, a dentist was under a restraining order from his ex-wife, and a few years ago a police deputy had been fired for improper advances against women he'd stopped for traffic violations. Ordinary people, even those in positions of authority, could lead secret lives.

I leaned back and pushed my hair away from my face. "All right, what do we do now?"

Ricky stood next to me and peered down at the paper. "Let's see what we can find online. We should look into the victim, too, to see if we can learn more about her, or find anyone else she hung out with. Then we can decide who we need to follow or interview or whatever."

"Great." I pushed back my chair and rose. "You can have the computer." I wouldn't think about the following or interviewing part yet.

It turned out that the local paper had the police blotter and other news online, going back years, and they had a policy of naming the accused. Thomas Bain had three traffic violations. Police were called to his house twice after neighbors reported sounds of fighting, but no charges were filed and it didn't name the victim.

Bethany had been taken into custody twice for possession and stopped twice for Drunk and Disorderly. She had three DUIs and four other traffic violations, the most recent driving with a suspended license. An accidental overdose seemed entirely possible, so why were the police calling it murder? We didn't find anything about soliciting, which made the pimp seem less likely, though of course it's possible she was guilty but never caught.

Kyle showed up only under general news, with a brief note that he was being deployed, and slightly longer articles about his injury in the call of duty and his return with an honorable discharge. A roadside bomb had flipped his truck, and though he hadn't been directly injured by the bomb, his hand had been crushed in the accident. If he had a dark, criminal past, it wasn't showing up online. The knots in my stomach loosened.

But Jay didn't have anything on the police blotter either. I guess his booking for possession the night before hadn't shown up yet, or else his dad had pulled some strings to keep it quiet. Lots of articles from a few years before mentioned his basketball career, and that was about it. As far as public info went, he looked as good as Kyle.

A few articles mentioned Jay's father as a spokesman for the resort or in activities involving the Rotary or Lions Club. I didn't know Rodrigo's last name and couldn't think of a good way to get it at that moment. Nothing showed up on Lia Bain.

I studied our notes on the list. "Doesn't it seem like the biggest criminal on here is the victim?"

"Mom would have something to say about that." Ricky pulled the paper over to look at the next name on the list.

"Wait." When he looked up, I added, "I don't feel right about investigating my boss or my friend."

"A real detective has to consider every possibility."

I sighed. "I guess I'm not a real detective. Anyway, I'm tired and hungry." I stretched. "Let's get some lunch."

"All right. Let me clear the search history off your computer."

I sagged back, feeling like someone had punched me in the chest. I hadn't thought about leaving a trail of our investigation where anyone at work might find it. Good thing I had Ricky along.

"The memorial is tomorrow," Ricky said. "I bet we can get some good information there."

Bethany's memorial. I wondered who would attend. Surely not Jay or either of the Bains. Bethany's parents would be there, no doubt. I wondered what they were like, to have raised a daughter like Bethany and a son like Kyle.

Kyle would be there for sure. I felt my face heat. I'd have to talk to him, knowing that I'd listened to rumors and investigated him. Knowing that a good detective would investigate farther. Knowing that he was my best chance of learning more about Bethany Moore.

And not knowing if we were on the same side.

Nineteen

The rest of the afternoon passed without incident. I managed to avoid arguments, harassment, and even sunburn. If I felt queasy, that could easily be blamed on the Indian taco. The fry bread topped with beans and hot red chile didn't bother Ricky, not even when followed by deep-fried Oreos, but I wasn't a twelve-year-old boy.

Nascha and Gina must have gone home early. I didn't see anyone else from our list, except Eslinda who was busy, so I considered myself absolved from investigations for the rest of the day. Eslinda said I could go home early, but Ricky wanted to stay, and I couldn't think of any advantage to being at home.

We sprawled on the grass and listened to the music as darkness fell and the air cooled. The scents of insect repellent, coconut sunscreen, stale perfume, and greasy foods kept me grounded in the festival, so I could almost ignore the dark woods lurking behind us. Someone called three times from a local number I didn't recognize. I ignored it, and they didn't leave a message.

When we finally got home, Ricky staggered off to bed and I dropped down on the sofa next to Mom, who was watching some historical movie with lots of fancy costumes. I stared at it, bleary-eyed, without processing anything.

Mom glanced at me. "You look tired. Why don't you go to bed?"

I shrugged and shook my head. I didn't turn toward her, but I could feel her looking at me. Finally I said, "I haven't been sleeping well. Maybe if I'm tired enough I'll sleep."

She rose and left the room. So much for maternal sympathy.

She returned a minute later and handed me a bottle. "What's this?" I asked.

"Sleeping pills. Just over-the-counter stuff, but it works pretty well when my insomnia is bad."

I hadn't known she had insomnia.

She went on. "I only take one, because the full dose knocks me out completely for about ten hours, and then I'm groggy. But you're bigger than I am, so two might be okay." She turned her attention back to the TV, not waiting for an answer.

I got up. "Thanks. I'll try it."

As I left the room, she called, "Sleep tight."

The pills didn't banish the nightmares entirely, but I slept through the night. Mom had to pound on my door to wake me for church. I hadn't been a regular churchgoer at college, but before that Mom had made us go since Ricky was about five. I don't think she was really that religious, more like church was a way to help ensure Ricky grew up decent. I'd gone with them whenever I visited home, so the plain little church in the refurbished storefront still felt familiar. Maybe I'd find some comfort there.

We arrived as things were starting and sat at the back, so we were first out at the end. Mom suggested skipping coffee hour, which was fortunate because I saw several people eye me curiously and suspected the rumors had gone around about who found Bethany Moore's body.

Ricky made a nice omelet for brunch, with sautéed spinach, garlic, and feta cheese. I kept my church clothes on, since Bethany's memorial was at one o'clock. It didn't register that Mom had done the same, until I was ready to go. She grabbed her purse and stood at the door.

"You're coming?" I asked.

She gave a firm nod. "I want to show my support."

I thought that was one of the nicest things she had ever done for me. Then she added, "I didn't know the girl, but we have to show that we won't tolerate that kind of treatment of women. Whatever she did, it doesn't excuse violence."

Oh. Not support of me, support of Mom's anti-man policy. Oh well, if Jay showed up and started bothering me, I'd sic Mom on him. He wouldn't stand a chance.

The memorial service was at a large church across town, where we pulled into a nearly-full parking lot. I sat in the car, grasping the wheel, as Mom and Ricky got out. I wasn't looking forward to this.

Kyle met us at the door, handsome and somber in a suit. He took my hand. "Thanks for coming." He thought we'd come to honor Bethany or support him, not to spy. I had a hard time meeting his eyes as I introduced Mom and Ricky.

I glanced toward the front of the chapel, a plain room with whitewashed walls and hard wooden benches. "There's no casket."

"The police haven't released her body yet."

"Oh, of course," I mumbled, my cheeks burning. That's why they called this a memorial and not a funeral. I'd expected a closed casket, but still dreaded even being in the same room as the body. This would make the afternoon marginally more bearable.

"We don't know how long it will be," Kyle said. "We thought it better to do something now that it might ... help."

Help what? Help who?

Ricky, good detective that he was, voiced the question. "How will it help?"

Kyle gazed toward the front of the room and spoke softly, so only we could hear. "We didn't know what happened to Bethany for so long. It's been hardest on my mother. She kept hoping. Maybe this will help her come to terms with the fact that Bethany is really gone."

A couple of women came in, already teary, though their short skirts and low-cut tops seemed more appropriate for a bar than a memorial. Friends of Bethany's? Kyle nodded to them but didn't step out to greet them.

"We're also hoping people won't pay so much attention after this," Kyle said, "though of course it will be news until her killer is caught and sentenced. There's a reporter here." He nodded toward a skinny man in a brown suit sitting in the back row. "We had to tell the TV news people they couldn't come inside. I think they shot some footage of people entering the building."

I hadn't noticed them and hoped they'd gone before we arrived.

"We've gotten a lot of phone calls, too," Kyle said. "Most of them offering condolences, but even that gets tiring. Hopefully this will give people a chance to express themselves, and then they'll let us be for a while."

I gave a weak smile. "Good luck."

"It's filling up. You'd better find a seat; there are still some at the front."

I guess I wasn't the only one who preferred hiding quietly at the back. We walked up the center aisle. I saw Eslinda and we exchanged smiles, but that bench was full. The second and third rows had some empty space on each side. Mom turned to the left. Ricky said, "It looks crowded. I'll sit over here," and turned right.

"What's gotten into that boy?" Mom muttered. She settled onto the bench. "Doesn't want to be seen with his mother, I suppose. You were like that at his age. I guess he's turning into a typical teenager despite my best efforts."

I glanced over at Ricky as he plopped onto the bench in the middle of the third row and studied the people around him. He caught my eye and gave a quick nod. I got the message – I was supposed to listen and watch on this side, and he'd take the other. It seemed wrong to play spy games during Bethany's memorial. We should be honoring her memory.

But helping catch her killer would honor her as well. And as Kyle had noted, it wouldn't be over for his family until the murderer had been put away. We were doing the right thing. Weren't we?

Noise erupted at the back of the chapel. I turned and saw Kyle nose to nose with Thomas Bain. The church had gone silent as every head turned toward them, so Kyle's low voice carried over the crowd. "You're not coming in."

Bain spoke louder, as if he didn't care if everyone heard him. "I want to pay my respects. I cared about her, too, you know. But I won't insist if it makes you uncomfortable." He turned and left. Kyle watched him go but didn't stop Lia Bain from slipping up the side aisle and squeezing into an empty spot. Maybe he didn't realize who she was.

As her dark eyes scanned the crowd, I turned and bent forward, pretending to adjust my shoe. Why was she here? Was she planning to cause trouble? Should I warn Kyle, or would that cause more of a disturbance?

A minister came out and began to speak. Kyle, grim-faced, joined the front row. He was too far away for me to whisper in his ear, unless I leaned across several people. I glanced back at Lia. She had her head down and seemed to be keeping quiet. Better to let everything be.

I let the minister's words wash over me as I studied the people in the front row. These were probably the people closest to Bethany, her immediate family members and best friends. A middle-aged couple sat next to Kyle. The man sat up straight and stiff, and from my angle I could see his clenched jaw and flat lips pressed together. The woman hunched, her head down, sniffling into a tissue. Bethany and Kyle's parents?

What was this like for them? I couldn't imagine.

How did one survive the death of a child? A sibling? Of course I knew, in an abstract way, that it was awful, devastating, heartbreaking. But I'd been so wrapped up in my own problems that I hadn't really thought beyond the surface. When Kyle became a soldier, they'd have known he'd be in danger. When he came back, even injured, the relief must have been extraordinary. And then they lost their other child.

And Kyle. He and Bethany might not have been close, with about a six-year age gap, but Ricky and I were ten years apart. I glanced across the aisle at Ricky and my heart squeezed. Losing him was the worst thing I could imagine.

I blinked back tears and tried to concentrate on the preacher's voice. "Then be afraid of the sword for yourselves, for wrath brings the punishment of the sword, so that you may know there is judgment."

I stared at the man. Those were hardly the words of comfort one expected at a funeral. How would the family take it?

The man I thought was Bethany's father nodded. The woman next to him sobbed quietly into her tissue. I couldn't tell if she heard the words or not. Kyle's face was hidden from me.

The man finished in a thunder of righteousness and stepped back from the speaking stand. Kyle rose and passed the man to take his place, without a hug or even a handshake. Kyle's voice was flat as he said, "Please join us in the Great Hall for coffee and share your memories of Bethany in one of the books you'll find on the tables there."

Kyle came back to the front row, glared at his father, and muttered, "That was inspirational."

His father rose. "The girl made her bed and now she has to lie in it. There is no escape from the judgment of God."

Kyle bent over his mother and placed a hand on her shoulder. "Let me take you to a back room where you can rest." He led her out with an arm around her waist.

That was it? No time for people to stand up in front of the group and share their memories? No family members or close friends offering their thoughts? I glanced around the room. A couple of heavily tattooed men in denim and leather checked out the teary women in short skirts and tight tops. Several men in suits and women in drab dresses joined Kyle's father and the preacher, shaking hands and nodding solemnly. Other people whispered together, their expressions more curious than grieving.

Perhaps Kyle's family was concerned about what people would have to say about Bethany. I pictured a fistfight breaking out between her rebel friends and what seemed to be the conservative members of her father's church, while the town gossips watched avidly and the reporter took notes.

We stood to join the exit shuffle. "That was ... odd," Mom said. I nodded, for once completely in agreement. As

I waited for an empty space in the aisle, my gaze met Lia Bain's.

Something flashed in her dark eyes. She spun away and pushed through the crowd.

We mingled for a while. I introduced Mom to Eslinda. I saw Kyle at a distance, but he seemed too busy to interrupt. His father held court in one corner and glared whenever someone with a tattoo or piercings passed by. I didn't see Kyle's mother again.

Ricky drifted from group to group, largely ignored. He spent several minutes talking to an older couple who had been in the front row on his side. I hoped he was learning more than I was. I felt as if I'd learned a few things, but nothing that helped Bethany.

I should be doing more. I tried to tune into the conversations around us while Mom and Eslinda talked about real estate prices. But would people talk about dark secrets in a situation like this? Even if I heard about another boyfriend, or Bethany's drug habit, what good would it do? It all seemed so hopeless.

I looked around for Lia Bain. I still couldn't figure out what she was doing at the memorial. I saw her leaning over one of the pretty journals, her hair hiding her face. She didn't seem to be writing anything, which was good, because I couldn't imagine she'd have anything positive to say.

When she moved away, I casually wandered to the journal and glanced over the comments. "We'll miss you" with several exclamation points and little hearts around it. A comment about Heaven having another angel – I doubted Kyle's father would agree with that. A few Bible quotes that were much more comforting than the ones the preacher had shared.

I doubted Lia had written any of those comments, and I didn't see anything else remotely useful for our supposed investigation. Someone came up beside me and gave me that "Are you done?" look, so I moved away. I had no memories of Bethany that I wanted to share or that anyone else wanted to hear.

Ricky caught my eye and waved me over. He was still with the older couple from the front row. I forced a smile as I joined them, hoping Ricky hadn't been too obvious with his interrogation.

He said, "This is Mrs. Griffin and Mr. Begay. They raise falcons and hawks!"

While I was trying to process that and figure out what it had to do with Bethany's murder, the woman took my hand in a warm clasp. "Call me Nancy." She had gray hair in a long braid down her back and fabulous bone structure that the lines in her face couldn't hide. I guessed she might be seventy.

"And I'm Daniel," the man said. The name Begay was Navajo and his dark skin and eyes confirmed that heritage. His hair was just starting to go gray, so he looked a decade or so younger than the woman. And they had different last names, so maybe they weren't a couple after all.

"I know another Begay," I said. It was a common name, so I didn't assume he knew her, but it was something to say. "My friend Nascha, who works with me at the resort."

"Oh, you know my niece! She's a smart girl."

"Uh ... yes she is." Nascha had never mentioned an uncle in town, but then we hadn't chatted that much about our lives. "I guess she has a great memory for numbers."

He nodded. "Amazing. I've never seen anything like it. She'll remember any number you tell her." So that much was true. Not that I doubted her, exactly, but it was nice to know for sure.

"Audra likes birds, too," Ricky said.

Birds? Oh, right, falcons and hawks. I nodded. Sure, I liked birds, though I still had no idea what this had to do with anything.

An image flashed into my mind – the hawk soaring toward me while Kyle looked up at the sky from below. And then I remembered the cages in the back of his truck. Could that be what he was doing? Maybe he worked with these people, or was like a dog walker for birds of prey. I tried to think of some way to form a reasonable question.

"So we can go tomorrow, right?" Ricky asked.

"Um ..." I hated not knowing what was going on! Ricky should have introduced me as his idiot sister, or claimed I was mute.

Daniel chuckled. "He means to see the birds. He tells me he's always wanted to have a falcon. He's almost old enough to become an apprentice."

I looked at Ricky. "That's great." It was the first I'd heard of it, but that didn't mean it was untrue. Maybe this had nothing to do with Bethany's murder.

"Bring him out after you get off work," Nancy said. "I'll give you a tour."

"Sounds great." I hoped my smile looked natural. "Where exactly?"

She gave me directions to a place outside of town. And then she asked, "So how did you know Bethany?"

No. Oh no, I couldn't tell them that. "Uh, I didn't, really. But ... I went to high school with Kyle."

An odd light came into her eyes, somehow pleased and speculative. "That's nice. He's a wonderful young man."

"He certainly is." I needed to get away before they asked more questions with awkward answers. We'd better go – my mom is ready to leave. Thanks." I pulled Ricky away. "Hawks, huh?"

"That's Bethany's grandparents!" he whispered. "I didn't want to ask too many questions here, but I bet we can learn a lot about her tomorrow."

Great. Bethany's grandparents meant Kyle's grandparents. Would they mention that they'd met a high school friend of his? Maybe not, with everything else going on. They'd shown no sign of recognition at my name, so probably the gossip about who had found Bethany's body hadn't reached them.

I prayed it would stay that way. But as I tried to make sense of the newest puzzle pieces, I felt constriction in my throat, like a noose getting tighter.

Twenty

By Monday morning, I was able to focus enough to get some work done. But at noon, I faced the options of eating alone in my office, dealing with lunchroom gossip, or going outside where I'd have to contend with strong winds, the possibility of flying golf balls, and the memory of what I'd seen in the woods nearby.

Or I could deal with one question, even if it was one of the smaller things.

Nascha came out of her office as I walked down the hallway. "Hey," I said. "Lunch plans?"

"Only that I'm getting some. You?"

"I owe you for the ice cream sundae. How about lunch?"

"You don't have to buy, but sure. I was thinking about the Main Street Café."

"Okay." We walked out of the building together and she drove the short distance. A thousand conversation starters ran through my head, but we didn't talk much until we had ordered and were seated.

"How was the rest of your weekend?" Nascha asked.

Perfect opening. I grabbed it. "I met your uncle."

She frowned for a moment. "Oh, you must mean Uncle Daniel. Great guy. He helped me get my job."

"Really?" I hesitated, but if I didn't clear this up, I'd wonder what was really going on. Then I'd act weird and lose the friendship I was hoping we'd develop. "You didn't mention that you're related to Bethany Moore."

She stared, lips parted, the picture of astonishment.

"I met Daniel at the memorial yesterday. Ricky said he was Bethany's grandfather."

She gave a long "Ahh" and her face cleared. "I guess so. I hadn't realized."

"How could you not realize?" I snapped. "You're like her aunt or something, or at least a second cousin." Kyle's, too. But she'd said she didn't know him.

"First of all, Daniel isn't my uncle the way you mean it. It's an honorary title. He's a friend of the family, an old Army buddy of my father's. I remember his visits when I was a kid, and he did tell my parents to tell me about the position here, but we're not especially close. We met for coffee a couple of times when I first moved down here, but I haven't seen him in, oh, it must be over a year, except a few times in the grocery store. Second, he's been with Nancy about five years, and if they're actually married I never heard about it. We had dinner once, but I never met her kids or grandchildren."

My face was burning and I tried to find the words to an apology.

She said, "I do remember him mentioning that Nancy's grandson had gotten injured overseas." She shook her head. "That was a while back, before he came home. They didn't know how bad the injury was yet. I didn't realize it was Kyle. Wow, small towns."

"Yeah." I cleared my throat. "Look, I'm sorry if I sounded ..."

She crossed her arms. "Suspicious?"

"Right. Sorry. It's just ..." I shrugged helplessly. "Everything has been so weird lately. I don't know what's going on, or who to trust, so when things don't seem to fit right ..."

She sighed. "I suppose you get a break because you've been through a lot lately."

Some of the tension left my shoulders. "Thanks. I really am sorry."

A girl brought over our sandwiches. When she was out of earshot, Nascha said, "I guess the whole situation is confusing. It's been bothering you?"

I started rearranging my meat, cheese, and veggies so they were evenly distributed. "You have no idea. I feel suspicious of everybody and everything. And I did something kind of stupid."

Her eyebrows went up. "Please share."

I glanced around the small room. No one seemed to be listening. "Ricky has this idea that we should investigate – help the police by poking around locally. And Saturday at the festival I got so mad at Jay that I agreed."

"But what can you do?"

"That's part of the problem!" I realized I had raised my voice. I leaned closer to Nascha and whispered, "I have no idea. But now Ricky has arranged it so we're going out to Daniel and Nancy's to see the falcons tomorrow, and I'm afraid Kyle will find out."

"Hmm." She nibbled on a pickle spear. "Is he one of the people you're suspicious about?"

"I guess. Kind of. Maybe." At her smile, I added, "It seems unfair, after everything he's been through. But I've heard rumors of drugs and mental problems, and after what he must have been through, it wouldn't be surprising if he was kind of messed up, right?"

"Post-traumatic stress disorder? Maybe even some brain damage from his accident, or if he was exposed to chemicals." She made a face. "You're right, it seems mean to suggest he might not be the wholesome, all-American hero. But soldiers are people too, and people are messed up."

I paused with my sandwich halfway to my mouth. "You're kind of cynical."

"Or sensible."

I sighed. "Maybe there's no difference."

Ricky walked over to meet me at five, and we headed out to see falcons. Fortunately Mom had taken Ricky at his word and not asked too many questions about our visit. I suppose she thought falconry sounded like a nice sophisticated activity for a teenage boy, not too macho. She even said we should get our own dinner, and she'd go to a meeting.

As I drove out of town, I asked, "So what's this meeting Mom's going to? She didn't say." And I'd been glad enough to get away without questions, so I hadn't asked any.

"It's her dating group."

"Dating?"

"Yeah, mature singles or something. Mom complains about the name because she said it makes them sound old. I guess she's one of the youngest ones there." Ricky was playing on his phone as he talked, hardly paying attention to the conversation.

"How long has she been doing this?"

"Um, a year, maybe?"

"First I've heard about it," I muttered as I turned onto the long dirt road to Nancy and Daniel's place.

Ricky shrugged. "It's only once a month. You haven't been here."

"Has she been going on dates?" Not that I'd mind. She was about to turn forty and was still attractive. It would be good for her to find someone – if she could keep him. More likely, she'd drive him away and get even more bitter.

"A few." Ricky didn't sound traumatized by the whole thing, though he was the one likely to suffer if Mom got a new man in her life.

We came to a wide metal gate. "Get that, would you?" I said. Ricky hopped out, swung the gate open, and then closed it after I pulled the car through. He got back in and we drove the couple hundred feet to the house. I'd have to think about Mom and her boyfriends later.

The house was a sprawling, low stucco building, the kind that had probably started as one or two rooms a hundred years ago and been built on by subsequent owners. A garden in the front grew half wild, but the plants looked healthy and scented the air with spicy smells. A huge, fluffy gray cat lay on its back, crushing some new shoots. It looked at us as we walked up the path, then rolled over and went back to sleep.

I paused before knocking and murmured, "Don't get all crazy with your interrogation. Remember, these people just lost someone they love, and we don't want to make them feel bad."

"Don't worry." Ricky bounced and fidgeted. This was excitement to him. "We'll be sneaky. But you could ask about the family. Pretend you're interested in that guy, her brother. Girls want to know all about the guy they like, right?"

Oh boy. Before I could think how to answer that one, the door opened. Nancy Griffin smiled at us, her gray hair still in a braid but her quiet funeral clothes replaced by a loose, peach-colored linen top and a rainbow skirt over clunky sandals. "Hello, hello! I thought I heard a car."

"Thank you for having us," I said.

"My pleasure. I always like to show off my birds." She called back over her shoulder. "Daniel! We'll do the tour first, then come back for tea." She turned back to me. "Then Kyle can join us. He's not home yet."

"Kyle lives here?" My voice came out squeaky.

"Yes, but he had class this afternoon. He'll be back soon."

So much for keeping this visit secret. My stomach fluttered at the thought of seeing him again. How was I supposed to act? What was I supposed to say, assuming I could manage to say anything? Would he think I was here because I had a crush on him – or would he suspect we were meddling? Which would be worse?

Maybe if we hurried – if we did a quick tour and then I said we had to get home right away – we could avoid seeing Kyle. And if I was very, very lucky, maybe he'd never know I'd been there.

I wasn't feeling lucky.

I followed Nancy and Ricky back through the garden and around the side of the house to another small building. It was stucco, too, with several doorways along one side. A kind of cage made of chain-link fencing ran along the building, so that you had to go inside the cage before you could get to any of the individual doors.

Nancy led us into the chain-link area. "This is so if any of the birds get out of their rooms, they can't fly away." She opened one of the narrow doors to the building. She went in and Ricky followed, but I stood in the doorway to reduce the crowding. The room was about eight feet by eight feet and had a heavy, musky scent of animals and straw.

A beautiful bird sat on a perch. I couldn't identify different kinds of falcons and hawks, but this was clearly a bird of prey, with a sharply hooked beak and long claws on the yellow feet. It was only about a foot high, but the tiny black eyes rimmed with yellow had a fierce look, warning that this was not a cuddly pet.

"This is Lucy," Nancy said. "She's a peregrine falcon, an old girl like me. She was a rescue. Got shot by a hunter. It's illegal, but it happens. She can't fly anymore because of her damaged wing, but she's been a great breeder. She's old for that now, too, but she's an easy-going bird so I can take her on school visits or to other educational events."

"I think I remember you coming to my class in fourth grade!" Ricky said.

The bird turned her head to Ricky and shrieked, her little pink tongue visible in the open mouth. Nancy ran the back of her fingers down the bird's breast. "Yep, that would have been us."

Ricky took a step closer, but he had the sense not to reach for the bird. "Wow! She's amazing."

I edged in beside him. I'd never been this close to a falcon before. She had beautiful coloring, dark brown on the head and back, with a white throat that gave way to a mottled pattern of cream and brown on the breast. I had the urge to reach out and stroke her like Nancy had, but I wasn't sure the bird would take that from strangers, and anyway it seemed rude.

"The peregrine falcon may be the most advanced avian predator that ever existed, and certainly the fastest," Nancy said.

I drew closer and could tell one wing was different, part of it missing. I got a sudden image of Kyle and wondered if Nancy and Daniel took in injured creatures of all kinds. "Are all your birds rescued?"

"No, but several are. Once I had birds, people knew me as 'The Bird Lady' and started bringing me injured birds. You have to have a permit to keep them, so I joined wildlife rescue." She smiled at the falcon and I could feel the connection between the two of them. "In the summer, the hunting seasons are closed and the birds are molting.

You can't fly the birds, so I started breeding them. I think it's good for their health, to pair up."

That made me think of Mom. I was reading symbolism into everything.

She turned and gestured toward the door but kept talking as she followed us out. "So some are rescued, some were bred here, and a couple were wild caught. Falconry is addictive once you get started." She opened another door a few feet down the outside wall. "In here we have a Harris hawk, Anna. She's an incredible hunter."

This bird was dark brown, with reddish feathers on what I might call the shoulders of her wings, and a white band across the tail. Her coloring wasn't as delicate and pretty as Lucy's, but she was still a lovely bird.

She spread her wings wide and hopped forward. I jerked back, but Nancy was ready for her and held out her arm. The bird landed on Nancy's forearm and seemed to peer curiously at Ricky and me.

"Harris hawks are more social than falcons," Nancy said. "Plus, she's an imprint."

"What's that?" Ricky asked.

"It means she was bred here and she imprinted on me rather than on her mother. She saw me first."

Ricky leaned closer, staring at the bird. "So you're like her mother?"

Nancy nodded. "Some falconers don't like imprints. They'll scream if they're hungry, act out if they're angry. They don't have the aloof nobility of a wild-trapped bird. But I love the chance to see how the birds treat each other. With an imprint bird, you can go in and watch her feed the babies."

Ricky looked at me, his eyes wide. "Isn't that cool?"

It was indeed. I wasn't that excited about the hunting aspect, but it would be something to watch tiny birds growing up.

"How many birds do you have?" Ricky asked Nancy.

"Seven right now, three falcons and four hawks. But I don't fly all of them. You're only allowed to hunt with the ones on your falconry permit. The others are on my breeding permit or rescue permit. I have a falcon I take out in the morning, usually before sunrise, and two Harris hawks I take out in the afternoon to chase after rabbits. But one of those is breeding right now, so we only fly the young one in training."

"It must be a lot of work," I said, eyeing Ricky. I hoped he wasn't getting any serious ideas about this as a hobby.

"Yes, but it keeps me young. I can't imagine sticking to an exercise schedule, but if you have birds that need to be flown, you have to take them out."

She showed us a couple more birds and talked about her work with them. I was just as fascinated as Ricky – so much so that I forgot about rushing the tour. We must've spent forty-five minutes with the birds before Nancy closed the last door and said, "Come into the house and we'll have some tea."

Ricky and I exchanged a look. I think he had forgotten the main purpose of our visit as well. But while I was ready to flee, he nodded with a serious look, as if it was time to get down to business. I knew if I said we had to go, he'd announce that we were on our own all evening. I tried to hold him back a little as Nancy headed for the house. "We need to get out of here," I whispered.

"But we haven't learned anything!"

"I know, but I want to leave before Kyle gets home."

He gestured toward the truck parked behind my car. "I think he's already here."

Drat. I couldn't be sure Kyle had driven the truck, but it hadn't been there when we pulled up. I hesitated, the fluttery feeling in my stomach working overtime. Maybe I could still make an excuse and get away before I had to see him.

Nancy was almost at the door.

"Um, Mrs. Griffin? Nancy?"

She turned, looked past me, and her face lit up. "Well, here's Kyle!"

Twenty-One

I flinched but managed to pull a smile into place as I turned toward the sound of footsteps crunching on the gravel behind me. Kyle's smile looked much more natural and honest than mine felt. "Hi, Audra."

"Hi." My voice sounded a little hoarse. I cleared my throat. "You remember my brother, Ricky?"

He nodded. "Nice to see you again."

Nothing to do now but go along with things. Pretend we were only there to see the birds, that's all.

I felt a pinch on my face and slapped at it. "Mosquitoes," Kyle said. "There's another." He brushed his fingers down the side of my neck and it was all I could do to hold still. I hoped he couldn't feel the flutter of nerves in my pulse. "We'd better get inside," he added. "They don't bother Gran or me much, but they seem to like you."

"That's because she's still a tasty young morsel," Nancy said as she waved us inside. "I'm a tough old bird, and you're a tough young one."

I paused in the cluttered living room. At least the dim lighting would hide my blush until I could find my balance. But Nancy went through a wide archway to the next room. I reluctantly followed into a big kitchen with marble countertops, gorgeous oak cabinetry, and a wonderful smell of baking. This seemed to be the heart of the home.

Daniel Begay was putting cookies onto a pretty pottery plate. "Cookies! Fresh from the oven and still warm."

Kyle took the plate from him. "Gran, the best thing you ever did was bring this man home."

Nancy chuckled. "If not the best, certainly in the top three or four."

"I'm serious," Kyle said. "If you two ever break up, I'm keeping him. You're on your own."

She slid an arm around Daniel. "Guess I'd better stick with him. Audra, Ricky, have a seat. Iced tea okay?"

Ricky said, "Yes, thank you."

I nodded and pulled out a chair, only to find it already occupied by a black and white cat. Kyle put the plate on the table and scooped up the cat, draping it over his shoulder where it settled in, purring loudly. "I hope you're not allergic," he said. "We have five of them."

I shook my head. Ricky asked, "Isn't it bad to have cats and birds both?"

Nancy put a pitcher of iced tea in the middle of the table. "The cats live in this house, the birds live in their own house, and the cage outside the mews ensures the cats mind their manners."

Daniel started filling glasses with iced tea. "Kyle, you share those cookies. I got another batch for you later."

"Well, all right then," he grumbled theatrically. He pushed the plate closer to me.

I picked up a pale rectangle with flecks in it. It smelled heavenly. I tried to identify the scent, which was familiar but unexpected.

"Lavender shortbread," Daniel said. So that's why I couldn't quite place it. I was used to lavender in lotions and potpourri, not food. I took a careful nibble. Daniel watched my face and smiled at my reaction. "Not bad, huh?"

"Amazing." Surprising and different and delightful, just like the people in this house.

"Daniel can make anything," Nancy said. "He built these cabinets." She gestured towards the lovely oak woodwork and then touched the heavy turquoise and silver necklace hanging on her chest. "And this. The Gallery downtown carries his jewelry." Her pride and affection shone through her words, and Daniel's smile showed he felt the same way about her.

No wonder Kyle chose to live here, rather than with his parents. I was glad to know he had a warm and loving home like this. These were wonderful people, all three of them.

And I'd come here to pry into their personal business. The cookie melted in my mouth like butter and settled in my stomach like clay.

Ricky glanced at me and then smiled at Nancy and Daniel. "It was a nice service yesterday."

Nancy, Daniel, and Kyle exchanged looks. Had the comment raised suspicions?

Nancy smiled at Ricky. "That's sweet of you to say."

Daniel said, "Funerals and memorials are for the living, anyway."

When Ricky frowned over that, Nancy explained. "Bethany wouldn't have cared for that service."

"She would have hated it," Kyle said. "She didn't go to my dad's church. Not for years. He used to drag her there – literally drag her out of bed kicking and screaming on Sunday mornings. She moved in with friends when she was sixteen and never went to church again." He scowled at the cookie he was crumbling into little pieces. With his bad arm tucked under the table and a cat draped over his shoulder, he looked young and vulnerable. "Bethany and Dad didn't get along."

"But he was her father." The words came out before I considered whether I should say them. I gave an awkward little shrug as everyone looked at me. "Surely he loved her?"

Kyle shook his head, his lips tight. Before he could speak, Nancy said, "Of course he did, in his way. And in his way, he's hurting a lot."

"His way involves condemning her to hell," Kyle muttered.

Nancy sighed. "People use religion to try to understand loss. Usually they assume God has some greater plan they can't understand but must accept, and the person is better off in Heaven."

"Dad doesn't believe that. To him, she was a sinner."

"He's still using religion to make sense of it all," Nancy said. "If she brought her death on herself through her sins, then he doesn't have to blame himself or God for something that hurts him so badly."

Kyle pushed away from the table and stood. The cat jumped to the chair and then to the floor. "In other words, he's using religion so he doesn't have to feel guilty for pushing her into being the kind of person she was."

"You could look at it that way," Nancy said.

Kyle started to gesture with his bad arm, but he glanced at me and shifted to hide the arm behind his back. Nancy seemed to notice, too. She reached out and took his forearm, drawing him closer. He looked down at her, and the love between them in that moment was so palpable I felt it in my chest.

Nancy looked across at me as if judging my reaction or expecting something. But what?

"Is he your son?" Ricky asked. "Bethany's father?"

I jolted. It was a logical question, but it was hard to imagine.

"No," Nancy said. "Bethany's mother is my daughter." That made more sense, but not much.

She still had Kyle by the arm and was holding him close. "So you see, children always rebel against their parents. It's the way of the world, to want to be something different. I thought I was such a wonderful mother, raising my daughter with so much freedom. But that made her responsible for her own choices, and that scared her, so she married a man who would tell her exactly what rules to follow."

She looked up at Kyle. The overhead kitchen light haloed his bowed head, hiding his expression. Nancy murmured, "Young people choose their own paths. Bethany would have found hers, given time."

I felt a poke in my hip and glanced over at Ricky. With his hand hidden from the others by the table, he motioned in a "keep going" way. Right, we weren't just invading a family's private moment simply by our presence. We were supposed to poke the open wounds.

But it was for a good purpose. It was for Bethany, and they wanted justice for her, too. I took a sip of iced tea and searched for something to say that would be useful and not too offensive. Unless things had been so bad between Bethany and her father that he was somehow responsible for her death, I didn't think we needed to pursue that line of questioning anymore. And even if things had been that bad, I wasn't about to suggest that Kyle's father could be a murderer, when Kyle was already so touchy about the man.

But that got me thinking about the memorial, and the other odd thing that had happened. It wouldn't be too out of line to mention it, would it? "I'm sorry Thomas Bain showed up yesterday. That was awkward."

Kyle ran his hand over his hair and took his seat again. "No kidding. I can't believe he thought we would let him in. Bethany had a restraining order against him!"

Ricky sat up straight, his eyes bright, his detective brain whirring away. "Maybe he knew you wouldn't't!"

"What do you mean?" Kyle asked.

Ricky bit his lip and looked to me for help, but Daniel caught on faster. "You mean he expected to get turned away. It was ..." He spread his hands. "A gesture. He was making a statement."

"He waited until everybody was there!" I said. "We all heard him, even from the front rows. And we saw you turn him away. So ..." I was starting to get the idea, but I wasn't quite there yet.

"You mean he wanted everyone to see me turn him away," Kyle said. "He played the part of the loving former boyfriend who wanted to pay his respects. And I looked like a jerk for kicking him out."

"You didn't," I said softly.

"It was theater," Nancy said. "He was trying to gain sympathy and get people on his side."

"It won't work," Daniel added.

Nancy reached out and touched Kyle's shoulder. "It doesn't mean he killed her. You must let the police decide that."

"There's more," I said. They all gazed at me and I swallowed. "Lia Bain was there. His daughter. Did you know?"

Kyle shook his head. "I've never met her. I know she's his witness, for what that's worth, but I don't know much else about her."

"She came in at the same time he did and slipped into a seat while you were busy throwing him out." I shrugged. "She didn't cause any trouble. I saw her looking at the memory books afterward, but I don't think she stayed long."

Kyle frowned. "Spying for her father?"

"Or wondering about the woman he may have killed," Nancy suggested.

I thought we were onto something with the explanation for Thomas Bain's attendance. But Lia was still a mystery, and I didn't think we were any closer to identifying the killer. "Do you have any idea if she knew Bethany?"

They were silent for a moment, considering. Then Kyle said, "They may have met when Bethany was dating Bain." He shook his head. "I got the impression she doesn't live with Bain. Something the news said, maybe."

"Surely he wouldn't have ..." Nancy glanced at Ricky. "Gotten his teenage daughter involved in the kinds of things Bethany was involved in."

"You mean drugs?" Ricky asked.

"Um, yes."

"Did Thomas Bain get Bethany started on drugs?" I asked. That would be one more horrible strike against him.

Nancy glanced at Kyle, who answered. "Oh no. She was experimenting with anything she could get a hold of in high school. But she might have gotten to know him that way. I think they met at a party."

Thomas Bain, Lia Bain, Bethany, Bethany's father. Drugs, abuse, religion. How did it all fit together? Or did they fit together? Were we missing something else much more important?

One thing was clear. Our pleasant visit had turned somber and edgy. This family had enough trouble without us making it worse. I needed time to think everything through, and Ricky seemed out of questions for the moment.

I rose. "We should get going. Thanks for the tour and the cookies."

Ricky hesitated and then got up, too. I didn't have to prod him to add his thanks. Mom had him well-trained in manners.

"Come back some time," Nancy said. "Kyle can take you out on a hunt."

Ricky looked at me hopefully, so I nodded. "We'd both enjoy that, thanks."

"Let me give you my number," Kyle said. "Call or text me anytime. Nancy or I are out almost every day."

By the time I'd programmed his number into my phone, Daniel had a baggie of cookies for us to take home. As we pulled out of the driveway, I said, "Those are some of the nicest people I've ever met. One thing is certain, none of *them* had anything to do with the murder." Something loosened in my chest as I said those words. Whatever the rumors about Kyle, I couldn't believe he had intentionally hurt another person, let alone his sister.

He'd given me his number. Once this mess was resolved, we could get to know each other. The birds made a perfect excuse. I felt myself smiling despite the flutter of nerves in my chest.

"We learned stuff, though, right?" Ricky said. "I think we should investigate Lia Bain more. Don't you think she's acting weird?"

"I'll agree with that. I don't think it's likely she's the murderer, but she might know something. At the very least, she knows whether her father really has an alibi. Though how we'll get her to tell us, I have no idea."

Ricky got out to open the gate and close it behind me. We turned onto the long dirt road. "What do you think about Bethany's father?" I asked. Fathers were kind of a sensitive subject in our family, but I wanted to give Ricky a chance to talk about the father-child thing if he needed to.

He considered for a while. "He doesn't seem very nice, but I don't think he's the murderer. If he's that religious, he wouldn't kill someone, would he?"

I decided to avoid a discussion of how often people killed despite – or in the name of – their religion. "I don't think he killed his daughter, though I don't think he helped her any. I can start to see why Bethany was kind of messed up." I shot a glance at Ricky and then kept my gaze on the road as I turned onto pavement and headed up the long hill to the plateau. "I'm glad we don't have a father like that."

"Yeah, me too!" He fidgeted in his seat with his usual restless energy, drumming his hands on his thighs. "I wish Nancy and Daniel were my grandparents, though. They're great! I like the birds, too." If he was sensitive about fathers, it was buried more deeply than I was reaching.

At the top of the hill, we headed into town. The first stoplight turned yellow ahead of me. I could almost make it, but to be safe I pressed on the brakes.

The car didn't slow.

I pushed my foot to the floor. My heart stuttered as I clutched the steering wheel and pressed back into my seat. A big white truck sat at the crossroads, ready to pull out into the intersection. We slowed a little since I wasn't on the gas, but the car wasn't stopping.

The light turned red as we hit the edge of the intersection. The white truck started forward.

I jerked my hand from the steering wheel rim and slammed it hard against the center. The horn blared.

The white truck loomed in the passenger-side window. Heading right for Ricky.

Twenty-Two

I jerked the wheel hard to the left. My car swung erratically across the intersection, throwing me to the right. The seat belt scraped against my left shoulder, and I almost lost control of the wheel. An oncoming car I hadn't even noticed jerked to a stop with a screech of tires.

The scene outside the window swam crazily, a blur of color and motion. We bumped off the road onto the sloping gravel alongside. The car tilted and tree branches slapped the windshield. If we rolled, Ricky's side would hit first. If we hit the trees, his side would take the most damage.

I pulled against the wheel and my seatbelt, dragging myself back into place. We bumped back onto the pavement and fishtailed a couple of times before I got the car pointing straight down the road.

I breathed for the first time in what felt like minutes. My breath rasped in and out, loud and ragged. I couldn't tear my gaze from the road, but from the corner of my eye I saw Ricky's hands braced on the dashboard. "You all right?" I gasped.

"Yeah."

The swerving had taken a lot of our speed, but we still coasted. My foot kept pressing on the brake pedal, even though I knew it wasn't doing any good. When we'd slowed to five miles per hour, I eased the car to the side of the road and drove on the shoulder until we stopped. I put the car in park and put on the emergency brake for good measure. Maybe I could have used that earlier. I hadn't thought of it.

Ricky and I sat in the car, catching our breath. My limbs felt numb and my hands lay limply in my lap. I tried to convince myself I didn't need to go to the bathroom. "You're sure you're all right?" I asked.

He nodded. "What happened?"

"No brakes." I noticed a warning light on the dashboard. Great, thanks for the tip.

"That's weird." After a moment, Ricky asked, "What do we do now?" For once in his life, he sounded younger than he really was.

"Call a tow truck, I suppose." Anxiety still skittered along my skin and my hands twitched in my lap. It was an old car, but I took good care of it. Car maintenance was one of those things Mom insisted a woman should know how to do, so you'd never be dependent on a man. I hadn't noticed any trouble with the brakes. Wouldn't they go soft before they went out altogether?

Someone tapped on my window and I jumped, banging my hand on the steering wheel. A man stood beside the car and a glance back showed the big white truck parked behind us. I rolled my window down a couple of inches.

"Are you all right?" He was about fifty, with dark hair and mustache, and a large belly hanging over a giant belt buckle.

I managed a trembling smile. "Yes, thank you. Sorry about that. Brake problems."

"You need an ambulance?"

"No, thanks. So long as no one else was hurt, I guess we're all right." Unless he wanted to report me to the police for running a red light and reckless driving. Wouldn't that make my day.

"Okay. You get help, though. Don't try to drive again. You need a ride somewhere?"

"No." I wanted him to leave so I could think. "I'll call someone. Thanks."

He patted the top of the car and headed back to his truck. I watched as it pulled around us and drove down the road.

"What happened?" Ricky asked.

"I'm not sure." I gripped my hands to control the shaking. "Do you know anything about brake lines? What it takes to cut them?"

His forehead wrinkled. "I read this story." He thought for a moment. "I don't think it's hard if you know what to do. It's a quick snip."

"But they were working when we left Nancy and Daniel's. I stopped when you opened the gate and I slowed down to turn onto the road. We had brakes then."

Ricky nodded, still frowning. "If you cut the lines all the way through, the brakes won't work at all. But I think if you only cut them partway, it takes a while for the stuff to leak out – the brake fluid. I can check." He pulled out his phone.

I put a hand on his arm. "Not now. That can wait until we get home."

"Should we call the police?"

The police. I blew out a breath. I didn't want to see the police again. Bad things happened when they were involved. I knew it wasn't their fault – they were the good guys. But my last encounter with the police was too fresh, and I felt queasy at the thought of men in official uniforms.

But I had to report this to someone. The detective had told me to call if anything unusual happened. This was certainly unusual, and somehow I didn't have the same sick reaction about the detectives. Maybe because they hadn't worn uniforms. Maybe because I'd only seen them at my house, not near the body.

I fumbled in my purse for my phone and found the card for the detective. I left a message on voicemail.

A car drove past us. The sun was low enough that we were in deep shadows from the trees along the road. I put on the emergency blinkers, something I should've done right away. There wasn't much traffic, but I still didn't like sitting in a car at the side of a narrow road. "Okay, the question now is, do we need to call the local police, or can we call a tow truck and get away from here? I don't like sitting practically in the road."

Ricky's voice wavered. "I want to go home."

"Me too." I squeezed his hand. "How about this. We call a tow truck, but we tell them not to work on anything until they hear from us. That way if there are any fingerprints or whatever, it won't mess up the evidence. It's not like the brakes were cut *here*, so we're not exactly disturbing a crime scene."

He nodded, but he still looked doubtful. "Why would someone want to hurt us?"

Sitting on a lonely road with darkness falling was not the time to talk about pissed off murderers seeking revenge. "It's probably just a mechanical problem." I patted my dashboard. "This old thing has been around longer than you have."

Ricky gave me a small smile, but he didn't look convinced. I couldn't blame him. Maybe it was the adrenaline left over from the near-accident, but I felt as if the trees were pressing in on us, and every time a car drove by I tensed, wondering if they would stop – and who would be inside.

"I'll tell you what," I said. "We're ordering pizza for dinner! We deserve a treat."

Maybe it wasn't good to teach Ricky to use food for comfort, but it worked. "Meat Deluxe?" he said, starting to look more like my little brother again.

The detective called back and said he wasn't in town, but he'd have someone look into it. A local officer came by an hour later. So much for avoiding police uniforms. Maybe I was supposed to feel safe and comforted with a large, imposing man in blue dominating the living room. I didn't. Especially when he confirmed that the brakes had been cut.

I answered his questions with my voice wavering and stomach churning. It didn't matter that the police were the good guys; I kept seeing them in unpleasant circumstances and my body made the association. It's a form of killing the messenger, I guess. Once he finished questioning me, he said they'd have a patrol car drive by a couple of times during the night. "You be extra careful for a few days. Make sure the house is locked up, windows too."

Great. He thought the vandal – who was most likely a murderer – might try to break into our house.

He added, "When you get your car back, test the brakes every time you get in, before you go anywhere. Make sure the engine sounds normal. It's too bad you don't have a garage. You might want to get a motion sensor light for the carport."

"Thanks." It was better to know what might happen. It was better to be prepared. But it wasn't pleasant.

Ricky, after finishing half a pizza, started to see the whole thing as an adventure and went off to his room to update our notes. I sank down on the couch, staring at nothing. The police questioning had brought out a few things I'd known in the back of my mind but had avoided admitting.

The brakes had been cut sometime during our visit with Nancy, Daniel, and Kyle. We'd been with Nancy the whole time, but we couldn't vouch for Daniel. And Kyle had been outside when we left the bird building. I tried to imagine him under my car, cutting brake lines. It was all too easy. He seemed like the kind of competent guy who would know cars and be able to handle that simple task. Apparently it only took one hand and some decent clippers.

Then I tried to imagine him sitting at the table eating cookies and bantering with his grandparents, knowing what he'd done. That didn't fit at all. I couldn't believe any of them had tried to hurt – maybe kill – us. But the only other people who knew we would be there were my mother – and Nascha.

Some of the people I liked most had jumped to the top of the suspect list.

Twenty-Three

A few minutes later the door opened and Mom came in. She was wearing a short black skirt and shimmery silver top. I blinked a few times and looked away. It wasn't inappropriate, really – except on my mother.

Mom stopped in front of me, hands on hips, frowning. I sat up straighter and waited for her to complain about the pizza box on the coffee table. Then I'd tell her we'd had a hard day and describe the accident to distract her.

"Lewis Preppard approached me tonight," Mom said.

"Jay's father?" No. Oh, no. Please do not tell me she was starting a romance with him.

Mom nodded. "I don't like that man." Thank goodness. "I never cared for him much. He's a pompous bully." Her nose wrinkled. "He told me to control you. Said you were a troublemaker."

The anonymous phone caller had said something like that – I caused trouble. Could it have been Mr. Preppard? It was hard to imagine a fifty-year-old man making prank phone calls, but I guess some people never grow up.

"He said you were willful," Mom said.

Why couldn't people leave me alone? I sighed. "I suppose you agreed with him."

"Nonsense! You were a reasonably well-behaved child. Until recently, but I suppose I should be glad you're getting some spine. A woman needs to be able to stand up for herself."

I jumped up. "Now you tell me? That's not the message I got growing up."

Mom backed up a step and lifted her chin. "You didn't need to disobey *me*. But that doesn't mean you should give in to everyone else."

I dragged my fingers through my hair, wanting to tear it out. "Thanks for clarifying. So I should be totally obedient to you and stand up to everyone else."

"Is that so unreasonable? I'm your mother. I want what's best for you."

"Oh, right, it's always about what's best for me. Like you never put yourself first."

She edged back another step. I probably looked crazy, hair messed up, dark circles under my eyes, my clothes rumpled and smelling of sweat. But all the exhaustion and fear and frustration of the last few days mixed with the hurt and anger of a lifetime, and something snapped. I couldn't hold back. I didn't want to.

I stepped closer. "You filled my head with so many warnings about men that I could hardly talk to a boy! You didn't teach me how to tell bad from good, which might actually have been useful – you taught me to be afraid. And the one time I started to feel close to a man – the one time I had somebody who might help me understand what it was all about – you ruined it."

She shook her head. "What are you talking about?"

"Gee, maybe Richard? You know, Ricky's father? We could have been happy. We *were* happy, until you drove him away."

She avoided my gaze and grumbled, "I didn't exactly drive him away."

I snorted. "Right. It had nothing to do with the way you nagged him, and all those innuendos. How is a man supposed to put up with those kinds of accusations?" I couldn't stand still. I paced the small open area of floor, two steps and then back. My eyes stung. "Like I would really try to steal your husband, at thirteen."

She gasped. "That had nothing to do with you! He was having an affair with his secretary."

I jerked to a stop. "He was?"

"Absolutely. Of all the clichés women have to suffer! I found sexy messages between them, and then he admitted it. He said they hadn't slept together yet, but what difference does that make? It was still a betrayal. I was going to give him another chance, for Ricky's sake." She looked away and brushed at the corner of her eye with a knuckle. "But I wanted to punish him, too. He had to suffer somehow for what he'd done."

"But you'd say things to him and then stare right at me. I thought you were accusing me of something, too!"

She brushed at her eye again. "I wanted you to understand, to not blame me for what was happening." She clasped her hands at her waist. "I shouldn't have said those things in front of you. No wonder you hate me."

"I don't hate you!" I closed my eyes a second. Then I met her gaze. "Maybe I do hate you sometimes. You have to control everyone. Everything has to be your way."

"I just want what's best for you and Ricky."

I gave a sigh that was almost a groan. "I know. But you can't know exactly what is best for every other person at every moment. I'm an adult now. You have to let me make my own decisions."

Her lips pursed and she didn't say anything for a long time. It was foolish to think she could change after all these years. I sagged, the anger gone, nothing left but exhaustion. I was about to walk away when finally she spoke. "It's hard. Hard to let go."

I touched her arm. "I know. Or at least, I can imagine a little. I want to protect Ricky, too. I guess ..." I searched for understanding. "I guess it's like I want to feel that if he does exactly what I say, and I say the right things, he won't be hurt. Is it like that for you?"

She considered. Nodded once.

"Okay. I'll accept that you want to protect us. But we can't go on like this! Maybe you'll never be able to see me as an equal, but can't you at least try to see me as an adult? You can give me advice as ... as a friend, but you can't give orders anymore."

She blinked rapidly, her eyes moist. Had I finally made a chink in her armor? She gave a kind of half-nod, half-shrug that could have meant anything, but at least she wasn't yelling or storming away. I was tempted to press my advantage, maybe drag an actual promise out of her in her weakened state. But somehow I couldn't make myself do it. It was disturbing to see my mother not entirely in control.

I glanced away. "I do appreciate it all, you know. The fact that you raised me alone. I know it wasn't easy. I wouldn't have wanted to have a child at seventeen."

"Don't." Her voice was low and raw. "Don't start too soon."

I had to smile. "You do realize I'm already five years older than you were then."

She gasped out, "It's still too soon!" She swallowed a couple of times and when she spoke again her voice sounded closer to normal. "Live your life first. The life I didn't get."

I gazed at her, trying not to be hurt by her bitterness. I'd always tried to be a good child. Had life with me really been so hard?

It probably had.

"I'll live my life, and I hope my life will include children. Not right away, but someday. But I won't live the life you wanted. That's for you to do. You're not too old."

She sniffled but managed a smile. "Thanks for that."

I rubbed my hands over my face and finger-combed my hair. "Mom, now that we've sorted that out, I should probably tell you what happened today."

She studied me. "Is this something that needs a pot of tea?"

"Yeah. That would be good."

"Let me change."

"I'll get the water going." I dragged myself to the kitchen and filled the kettle. My phone rang in the living room. I glanced at the clock – nearly ten o'clock. A little late for a weeknight phone call, and I didn't get many calls at any time. I crept toward the phone with caution. Maybe the police had something more to report.

I picked up the phone and saw the caller ID. Nascha. What could she have to say that wouldn't wait until morning? Unless she wanted to see if we'd survived the evening.

Twenty-Four

I took a deep breath and answered.

She spoke before I could. "Audra? Are you all right?"

She knew. She already knew about the accident. "Why wouldn't I be?"

"Kyle said your brakes had been cut!"

"Wait — you said you didn't know Kyle." And how did he know about my brakes? My head pounded.

Mom came into the living room in sweatpants. I covered the phone, whispered, "Ricky will tell you," and headed for my room.

"I don't," Nascha was saying. "Daniel called me, and then he put Kyle on. I guess the police were there, and Kyle was worried about you, but he didn't have your phone number. Daniel thought I might have it."

I sank to my bed. After I sorted through what she'd said, it made sense. I'd taken Kyle's number but hadn't given him mine. Daniel knew that I knew Nascha and knew about her good memory for numbers. And of course the police would go there and ask questions, after what I told them.

"Audra? Are you there? Are you all right?"

"Yeah, I'm all right. We just got a scare."

"It's true then? Someone cut your brakes?"

"Looks that way."

"I can't believe it. I can't believe what's been happening." That made two of us. After a long silence, she said, "It's late. You're probably exhausted. I'll see you tomorrow, but call me if you need anything, any time. About Kyle — I didn't want to give him your number without checking with you first. But he sounded really worried."

Warmth flooded me but quickly turned cool and sluggish. If only I could be sure he really cared about me and wasn't just checking on his sabotage plan. "Okay."

"Do you want me to call them back?"

"No. I'll take care of it. Thanks."

"All right. You take care of yourself, too. Goodnight."

I sat on the bed with the phone in my hand. I could hear Ricky's voice from the kitchen, high-pitched with excitement.

I needed to figure this out. Kyle seemed like the obvious suspect for cutting my brakes. He had the opportunity. He had the – what do they call it – the means, because he no doubt had tools in his truck or at the house. What about motive? That was still open. But if he'd had something to do with his sister's death, maybe through drugs, he might've gotten suspicious about our visit. And decided to do ... what? Get rid of me?

As murder attempts go, it was kind of weak. His house was down in the valley; I was in town up on the plateau. It would have been better to tamper with my car when I was heading down, not up. Besides, with airbags and seatbelts, the chance of a fatal accident dropped. Maybe it was a warning. Maybe he hoped he'd get lucky. The intersection could have gone much worse, and injuries could have stopped our snooping even if they weren't fatal.

Or maybe Kyle had nothing to do with it. The alternatives still didn't fit, but imagining some unknown culprit made more sense than imagining that gentle, hurting man clipping my brake cables, before we'd even asked nosy questions, and then sharing tea and cookies. Or was that wishful thinking?

I lay back on the bed and closed my eyes. Friend or enemy? How did one tell?

If he was a friend, and really worried, I should call him. If he was an enemy, I shouldn't let him know I suspected.

Either way, I should call him. But I didn't think I was up for that phone call. I settled on a text instead. I typed in "Everything okay. No injuries." I sent that and considered following up with, "Thanks for concern."

The phone rang. Kyle. Of course he had my number now from the text, but didn't he get the hint when I texted rather than called? But now he knew I was with my phone, and if I ignored him ... I groaned and answered the phone. "Hello?" I let the exhaustion sound in my voice.

"Audra, you're really okay? And Ricky?"

He thought to ask about my brother. I softened a little. "We're both fine."

"Thank goodness. I'm so sorry."

I tensed. Was that some kind of admission? "For what?"

"When the police came, I could see the stain where your brake fluid started leaking while you were parked. If I'd been paying attention, I could've caught you before you reached the gate." I could hear faint thumps in the background, as if he was pacing in heavy boots. "I was right there! I walked you to your car and stood there watching you – um, making sure you got out of the gate okay. I should have noticed something was wrong."

I felt a smile tugging at my lips. I could see him as a person who felt guilty about something that was in no way his fault, simply because he was a protector at heart. "It's not your fault." I really hoped that was true.

"Gran and Daniel feel terrible, too. Like you haven't been through enough in the last week."

"We all have, I guess."

"Yeah. Well ..."

The silence stretched. I could still hear Ricky talking in the kitchen. He would probably tell me to use this opportunity to get information. Maybe that beat having nothing to say. So far Kyle hadn't seemed upset that I'd sent the police to question him, which seemed a little weird. "Did the police have anything interesting to say?"

"They wanted to know if we had any other trouble. We checked our vehicles, but they're all fine. I hate thinking that somebody was sneaking around the place. We don't usually even lock our doors." Ah, of course he'd assume it was a trespasser, if he was innocent. Or he'd blame an outsider, if he was guilty.

After a pause, he added, "The police wanted to know exactly what we were each doing the whole time your car was parked here. Audra, I hope you don't think we would do anything like this to you. I have no way to prove it, but

I swear we don't want to hurt you or Ricky. You found Bethany's body and reported it – you can't even imagine how grateful we are for that."

I swallowed and found my voice. "Okay. I mean—" I gave a weak laugh. "I'm not sure what I mean. I don't – it's not your fault." I could believe that. I wanted to believe that.

"Are we all right then? I'd still like to take you out with the birds sometime. Or ... we could do something else." His voice held hope and fear, and somehow that gave me confidence. I wasn't the only nervous one.

"Okay." I wanted to see him again. I wanted to look in his eyes and see if I could judge the kind of person he was. Maybe it was stupid to go near someone who might be a murderer, but I had to know the truth. This wasn't just for Bethany anymore – this was for me. "How about tomorrow?"

"Really? Great! We can take the young hawk out after work, if you're interested – and bring your brother, too, of course, if you want."

"We'll see. He might be busy." I'd make sure he was. I wouldn't take chances with Ricky.

"Okay. Can I pick you up?"

My car was in the shop, and I wasn't sure if the police were done with it or how long it would take to get fixed. Mom could drop me off in the morning. "Pick me up at work." I'd have to figure out where to have him drop me off if I didn't want him to know where I lived. Of course, in a town this size, it wouldn't be that hard to find out.

We confirmed time and place and said goodnight. I lay back on my bed, struggling to make sense of my feelings. I had a date. I was pretty sure it was a date. With a fascinating man – who might have something to do with his sister's murder.

Had I done something stupid by agreeing to see Kyle? Maybe the sensible thing would be to avoid seeing Kyle and Nascha, anyone who might be involved with Bethany's murder, until the case was solved.

But what if it never was solved? By refusing to be friends now, I might lose the opportunity later. I had a life to live, and it went beyond being the person who had discovered a dead body. Ultimately, I had to make my own choices about people. If I never went near a man who might be flawed, who might have done something bad in the past or be capable of doing something bad in the future, I couldn't go near men at all. Even Mom, for all her complaints about men, still seemed to want to find one, so she must still believe there were decent ones.

And what about Nascha? Looking at her behavior one way, it seemed suspicious – knowing my phone number, going out of her way to spend time with me, asking questions, and having a connection to the case. But looking at it another way, you had a few coincidences, not uncommon in a small town, and the overtures of someone who could be a very good friend. If I wanted to be the kind of person who deserved a good friend, then I needed to be a good friend. That meant taking some chances and going a little bit on faith.

That didn't mean I had to be careless. When I was out with Kyle, Ricky could be my backup. I'd tell him where I was going and turn on the GPS tracking function on my phone so he could see my location. Not that I expected anything to go wrong ... but just in case.

I gazed around the room at my posters of cute kittens and puppies. A child's room. Never even a teenager's room, since Mom hadn't approved of posters of cute actors and rock stars. I wasn't a child any longer. It was time to take on the responsibilities of being an adult. I hoped to get an apartment of my own before long, after I'd saved up enough money for the security deposit and some furniture. In the meantime, I didn't have to live like this.

I got up and started taking posters off the wall. It was time to take charge of my life. I'd wipe down the walls, vacuum, wash the window – get the place spotless, and then start over and make it mine.

The door pushed open. "Audra, are you okay? Ricky told me—" Mom glanced at the pile of posters on my bed. "What are you doing?"

"Redecorating my room."

"Oh." She studied me for a moment. "I'll help."

Twenty-Five

Mom asked me to drop her off in the morning and said I could take her car. She said she'd walk the two miles home, because she needed the exercise anyway, but I remembered her rule from when I was a teenager – make sure you always have your own way home. Maybe she was looking out for me. If so, she didn't make a fuss about it, so neither did I.

The best thing I could do at work was to learn my job well. I did, however, manage to get some information from Eslinda as we finalized plans for an event the following weekend. Eslinda had no trouble chatting while going over schedules or sketching diagrams, though my head spun from all the details, work and non-work related.

Mrs. Moore had been a nice girl, but timid. Eslinda didn't like Mr. Moore. He was domineering, though not, so far as she knew, physically abusive. Bethany had been rebellious and often in trouble, but she never heard much about Kyle until he joined the military, which had surprised a lot of people but seemed to please his father. Things "had been rough" when Kyle came back with his injury.

When I prodded for any rumors of drug abuse, Eslinda merely looked mysterious and said some things were private. "I wouldn't normally be telling you all this other stuff," she said, "except you're already so involved, and maybe understanding people better will help it all make sense."

She knew less about the Bains, but she confirmed that Thomas wasn't married to Lia's mother – never had been, she thought. Lia lived with her mother and several younger siblings from other fathers. Jay's parents were divorced. Jay's mother had left town with two younger kids, but Jay, then seventeen, had elected to stay with his father to finish high school.

I felt dirty, prying for gossip, especially about unhappy families. Still, I told myself it was better to know. Somehow I had to make sense of everything that had happened.

When Nascha asked if I wanted to grab some lunch, I said, "Sure, if we make it quick. I want to go to the thrift store."

"Looking for anything in particular?"

"I'm redecorating my room." I studied her outfit, a simple but elegant olive-green silk top and slim skirt, with a chunky necklace of silver and dark green stones. "Given that you're the most stylish person I know, maybe you could help?"

She persuaded me to start at the artists' co-op, so I returned from lunch with a framed art print and a quilt with a design of irises that picked up the purple in the painting, each for less than I would have spent on something half as good in a department store. I was going to enjoy having a shopping girlfriend.

I spent the afternoon dealing with one hysterical bride-to-be, a cranky caterer, and a large, loud family planning for their daughter's quinceañera. I knew that the "coming out party" for a Hispanic girl's fifteenth birthday was a big deal, but I didn't realize how fancy and expensive they could get until I was involved in planning one.

And then it was time to meet Kyle. I texted Ricky that I was leaving, turned on my GPS, and checked that he would be able to see me on the mapping program – just in case.

Kyle's truck was screeching again, but this time I knew it must be coming from the bird in the back. I tried to think of conversation as he maneuvered through the parking lot. "Is that a falcon or a hawk?"

"Red-tailed hawk. We take the falcons out in the morning. They're easier to lose, so that gives you all day to find them."

"Lose?" I had an odd image of someone forgetting where they had put down their falcon. Hard to imagine, if they made as much noise as the hawk did.

"They start chasing something and get out of sight, or go where you can't follow, like over a mountain or across the river. All the birds we fly have radio telemetry on so we can track them, but if they hit something hard it can break the telemetry, or it might come off on a fence or something. This is a big state and tends to swallow up birds."

We headed down the hill out of town. I imagined what might have happened if my brakes had gone out on that slope and I'd had to make the sharp turn onto the main highway at high speed, with traffic. I shook the thought away and tried to focus on birds. "That sounds bad. Can they survive on their own after they've been captive?"

"Sure, it happens all the time. One guy in Kansas lost his bird and got a call four years later from Fish and Wildlife. They found a bird with his band number nesting on a building in Milwaukee." He shrugged. "It's good, in a way. Those birds are adding to the wild population. Falconers take birds out of the wild to breed them and hunt with them. Then birds go back into the wild, either intentionally released like the Peregrine Fund did when peregrines were going extinct, or sometimes by accident."

The forest opened up into the dryer lowlands with scrub desert ranchland. I remembered seeing Kyle from up on the ridge. Of course his actions that day made sense now – he was working with the hawk I'd seen soaring above. "I didn't realize they'd been almost extinct," I said. "I thought peregrines were one of the common kind."

"They are now," he said. "They were nearly killed off in the wild because of the pesticide DDT, but falconers came together and bred their birds, and ended up releasing four thousand peregrines in North America. Some people get upset about captive falconry, but it's because of falconry that we still have peregrines today. Falconers are big on conservation. We want to see wild lands preserved and the sky full of birds."

I smiled. "You don't have to convince me. I think it's great."

He glanced over and grinned. "Sorry for the soapbox. Anyway, back to your earlier question; if you've trained the bird right, it can return to the wild, no problem. That's why apprentice falconers can only take two types of birds, red-tails and kestrels, and can only trap them out of the wild. Red-tails and kestrels are very common, and if you trap them wild, they're already hunting, they're not human imprints. If the apprentice loses them, the bird just takes up where it left off."

I thought about that as he pulled off to the edge of the road and got out. Nancy had mentioned that the falcons and hawks weren't exactly pets, they were more like partners. But still, her affection was obvious, and Kyle's, too. It couldn't be that easy to let one of your birds go.

I met Kyle at the back of the truck. "Have you ever lost a bird?"

He shook his head as he opened the back window and lowered the tailgate. "This is the first bird that's really mine, the one we're flying today. I apprenticed in high school, but I've only really been getting into it since I came back. Nancy lost one once, though. It headed over the mountain and then went on to White Sands Missile Range. She had the telemetry signal, but they wouldn't let her go out to pick up the bird. She went every day for a week, hoping it would leave the restricted area, but eventually the battery went out on the telemetry, and she had to give up."

As he talked, he dug through a bag one-handed and pulled out a heavy leather glove – or maybe gauntlet was a better term, as it covered most of his forearm. He pulled it onto his bad arm; the fingers of the glove had been folded over and taped down. He tightened the straps with quick, competent moves and then picked up a leather satchel and hung it across his body from one shoulder to the opposite hip. The whole time, the hawk screeched and ruffled her feathers.

"Should I do anything?" I asked. He didn't seem to need help, but I felt rude just standing around while he took care of everything.

"Almost done." He flipped open the latch on the cage and the bird hopped out, then up onto his leather-covered forearm. The hawk finally stopped screeching, glad to be free, I guess. She peered around with fierce black eyes. I had the urge to run my hand down her feathers, a gorgeous reddish-brown with white mottling. I wasn't sure if it would be okay with Kyle, though – or with the bird. As beautiful as she was, the beady glare and hooked beak didn't exactly invite cuddling.

Kyle stepped back from the truck. "Okay, let's go." He glanced down at my feet. "I should've warned you to wear good shoes."

I would have said these were good shoes, comfortable beige flats that didn't make my feet look huge. But to him, good shoes probably meant something like his hiking boots, which did make more sense for tramping through the desert. "How far are we going?"

"Just a few hundred feet. Is that all right?"

"It's dry, so no problem."

I followed him away from the truck, glancing back once toward the dirt road behind us, and then up to the ridge far behind and above. What if somebody were watching us down here, the way I'd watched Kyle once before? We were farther away than he'd been when I watched him, too far to even identify a person, but if someone had binoculars …

I shivered, turned back, and concentrated on placing my feet carefully to avoid loose rocks and spiky plants. I should've thought to bring jeans and other shoes to change into. Like so many things, it seemed incredibly obvious in retrospect. The flats that were comfortable on carpeted floors didn't offer much protection against the small, sharp rocks littering the sandy field. I couldn't keep up with Kyle's long, brisk strides when I was worried about stubbing my toe or snagging my slacks on a bush.

I caught a glimpse of something rotting and flinched. The memory of death and decay blurred my vision.

I forced myself to take a closer look. It was only a dead cactus, slumped over and yellowed. Not a body. No way would we accidentally stumble on another one. I was just sensitive to decay now.

Kyle had pulled ahead but paused to wait for me. I gave him a quick smile and looked down. There I was again, going off into the wilderness with a guy I barely knew. Was I stupid? Did I *want* to get in trouble?

No. I'd made sure Ricky knew where I was and could track me. Kyle was not Jay. We had a clear reason to be here, and he had the hawk on his arm as a chaperone. This wasn't anything like being with Jay. I wasn't even the same person I'd been then. If anything happened that made me uncomfortable, I'd walk away, I'd call for help. I'd learned my lesson. And hey – I'd stood up to Mom last night. If I could do that, I could stand up to a man.

I looked up at Kyle and smiled.

The hawk spread her wings and flew away, landing on a bush fifty feet ahead. "She'll wait for us there," Kyle said. "What we're doing is trying to flush game. Rabbits in particular. Once we scare up something, she'll go after it."

I pictured the hawk tearing into rabbit flesh. I swallowed and nodded. Nascha had said rabbits could scream. Would we hear it?

Kyle added, "She probably won't catch anything, since she's so young. She's enthusiastic, but kind of clumsy. I'm starting her training now, and by this fall she'll be a serious hunter."

I nodded again, my throat tight and my heart beating a little too fast. He studied my face. I was to his left, and he lifted his arm, the one missing its hand, but quickly dropped it again and shifted so he could reach out with his right hand. He didn't touch me but hovered close enough to catch me if I stumbled or fainted. I didn't think I would, but I felt lightheaded, flushed and cold at the same time.

"Does it bother you?" he asked. "The thought of her killing a rabbit?"

"No ... not exactly." I glanced ahead at the beautiful hawk. "I mean, I know she has to eat. And that's how it happens in the wild. It's only ..."

"You don't want to see it."

"It's not even that." I glanced at the decaying cactus. Just a plant, nothing more. I took a deep breath. "I guess I'm a little sensitive to dead things right now."

He went still. I finally looked at him closely. That had been an awful thing to say. Maybe he'd forgotten, for a few minutes, about his sister. And I'd reminded him.

"I know what you mean," he whispered.

"I'm sorry. I shouldn't have mentioned it."

"No, you should. Believe me, it's better to talk about whatever's bothering you."

"But she was your sister. You don't want to think about her like that."

"Do you think I can ever forget?" He looked down, and I wondered if he was seeing her again – the way she'd been in life, or the way she'd ended up.

I couldn't look away from his face. "That part's been hard," I said. "I haven't had anyone to talk to. I mean, there are people who will listen, but I don't think I can tell them what it was like. I'm not sure I can explain. I'm not sure they want to know." I thought of Ricky, his naïve enthusiasm about hunting a murderer. He didn't understand. But I wasn't sure I wanted him to. Let him be a kid for a little longer.

"You can talk to me," he said. "I know what it's like. When I was deployed, I saw a lot of bad stuff. I can't talk to my parents about it. Mom doesn't want to hear it. Dad doesn't get it. The only thing I ever did to make him proud was join the Army, and he doesn't want to hear anything negative. Gran and Daniel would listen, but I don't want to burden them. They already do so much for me."

I imagined what he must have seen – things far worse than what I had seen. He must think I was weak. I lowered my gaze.

He put his hand lightly on my elbow. "You had a shock, and that makes it worse. I had some idea of what I was getting into in the military, even if the reality was worse than I'd imagined. And after those experiences, I knew what to expect with Bethany. That's why I made sure I was the one to identify her body. I didn't want to put my parents through that."

He knew what he would have to face, and he chose to face it to protect other people, even the father he didn't like very much. While I had let Jay bully me into not calling the police right away. I glanced up and gave him a shaky smile. "I wish I had your strength."

His grip tightened. "You have the strength you need. It will come to you when you need it. But I hope you won't need it often."

He jerked aside quickly and lifted his left arm. The hawk was coming toward us at eye level, gliding on widespread wings. I almost jumped back, but she landed on Kyle's arm and tucked her wings, seeming to glare.

Kyle chuckled. "She was getting bored. Maybe we should skip the hunt, though."

"No." I tossed my hair back and smiled at him. "Let's find her a rabbit."

Twenty-Six

"You're sure?" he asked.

"Yes. No reason she should suffer because I'm squeamish." As he turned and led the way, I muttered, "Maybe it will be good for me." He glanced back and smiled but didn't comment.

We strode across the desert, angling to pass by bushy patches where rabbits might be hiding. The hawk flew ahead again, soaring about twenty feet above the ground before landing on a small tree. She waited until we passed by, then made another hop, farther that time. Kyle raised his left arm to shoulder height. The hawk flew back and landed. Watching her come in sent a strange breathless thrill through my chest. I'd seen owls and eagles fairly close in the zoo, but there they were sitting quietly on perches. This was a glimpse of something wild and beautiful.

After fifteen minutes my feet were hurting even though I was sure Kyle was going slower than usual for him. I tried to hide my limp and wondered how long this usually took.

A jackrabbit bolted out of a bush twenty paces ahead. The hawk took off after it.

Seconds later, she swooped down behind some bushes several hundred feet away. She rose up, made a small loop, and dropped down again. Something shrieked.

Kyle was already running toward the action. I hurried after, though the distance between us quickly stretched. By the time I got there, he had the hawk on his arm again. She had a feather sticking out awkwardly from her wing. I didn't see the rabbit and wondered if Kyle had hidden it to make it easier on me.

"She got beat up," Kyle said. "That rabbit had some moves."

"It got away?"

He nodded and plucked a small tuft of gray fur from the bush. "She made contact. But this time, it looks like the rabbit won." He opened his fingers and the small tuft of fur drifted away on the breeze.

I was smiling. "The rabbit won!"

"It happens sometimes. Fortunately for our girl, she won't starve." He looked into her black eyes. "It's frozen quail for you tonight, my dear."

We turned back toward the truck. "You won't try again?" I asked.

He shook his head. "She's had enough. It was a good training run."

We walked back to the truck in silence. I was still thinking about the rabbit. It might have been injured, but it was not a meal for a hawk tonight. Maybe that shouldn't have pleased me so much. I really did understand that predators needed to eat. But it was nice to know that prey could fight back sometimes.

Had Bethany fought back? If so, it hadn't worked. She'd been a victim, and her predator was still out there. But not, I thought, here with me.

Back at the truck, Kyle efficiently tucked the bird into her cage and stowed the rest of his gear. The whole trip had taken less than an hour. Now what? Would he drop me back at Mom's car and say goodnight? When would I see him again? He might hesitate to invite me out on a hunt after the way I reacted this time.

"Thanks for letting me come along," I said.

"No problem. It's nice having you around. You're ..." He frowned thoughtfully and I held my breath. "Restful."

"Restful." Just what every girl wanted to hear.

"You don't talk all the time. Not that I mind you talking – I'd like to hear you talk more. But you don't babble every thought that comes into your head. You don't complain about every little thing that happens to you, as if there were no bigger problems in the world than a bad parking spot. I get tired of people who can't do anything but complain when they don't have any real problems."

He smiled, looking perfectly at ease. "With you, I feel like I can be myself, say what I really think. I can relax around you."

Oh boy. He thought he could be open with me, when I'd been watching his every move for something suspicious. I couldn't stand it. "There's something I have to tell you." My voice sounded thin and wheezy. He took a step closer, concern in his eyes. I wanted to duck my head, but I forced myself to meet his gaze. "I'm not exactly – it's—" I couldn't think how to explain, so I blurted out, "I've been spying on you."

He looked more confused than angry, though no doubt the anger would come. I rushed on, hoping he might understand a little. "It was Ricky's idea – not that I'm putting the blame on him, I went along with it. What I mean is, he likes mysteries, and thought we should help investigate this one. It's stupid and probably useless, but I got so mad at – at someone else – that I agreed. And anyway, if I didn't, Ricky would do it on his own and maybe get in trouble."

He leaned against the open tailgate of the truck, his head tipped to one side, eyebrows drawn together. His lips twitched in what might have been a smile, or something else.

My face burned. "Anyway, we wanted to learn more about everyone, so when Ricky met Nancy and Daniel at the memorial, he made plans to see the birds. And it was really interesting and everyone was wonderful, but I feel terrible, because we were ... we were there under false pretenses."

"And now?"

I puzzled over that for a moment. "Oh, you mean am I here now for the same reason? Not ... not exactly." I ducked my head a little but kept my face toward his. "Kind of. Partly. But I really did want to come out today with the hawk – and you." My face felt like it would burst into flames. "And I don't think *you* had anything to do with it –

the murder." Not anymore, anyway. He didn't need to know about my earlier doubts.

"That's good."

"We just wanted to learn more about Bethany, and this seemed like the easiest way."

He nodded, frowning, his arms crossed. He didn't speak for what seemed like a long time. Finally he said, "So now what?"

"I ..." What did he mean? "I don't know."

"What's next on your list? How are you going to investigate?"

I gave a helpless shrug. "I'm not sure. Ricky thinks we have an advantage the police don't, because we're local and hear things. But I'm not sure I've heard anything useful, and I don't know how to make sense of what I have heard. Ricky's doing some research into the Bains, but I'm insisting he keep it to online stuff."

Kyle pushed away from the tailgate and took a step closer. "Keep away from Bain. He's dangerous. Whether or not he killed Bethany, and whatever else you believe, trust me on that."

I nodded. He looked ferocious, but I didn't think he was angry at me.

He closed the tailgate and the window and walked around the car without another word. I got in, too, and shot a cautious glance at him. He seemed to be in his own world as he started the truck and pulled back onto the road. I kept my hands clasped in my lap and my mouth shut. I hoped I hadn't ruined any chance we might have had of becoming friends.

A few minutes later, he said, "Do you mind if I drop the bird off first?"

"No, of course not. Oh, you don't have to take me home – I borrowed my mother's car. It's at the resort."

"Okay." He turned toward his house. I was going to open the gate, but before I could even undo my seatbelt, he put the truck in park and jumped out. I hesitated and then got out, too. "I'll close it behind you."

"Don't bother. We're coming right back out again."

Right. "Then I'll wait here and get it when you come out." That way I could avoid Nancy and Daniel. I wasn't ready for another confession. Maybe Kyle would tell them so I didn't have to. Cowardly, perhaps, but I hated confrontation and I'd already had more in the last week than in nearly my entire previous life.

"Okay." He hopped back in the truck and pulled away. I leaned against the gatepost. I tried to remember the confidence I'd felt the night before, the sense that I was in control of my own fate. Mostly I felt foolish. So much for being an adult. Although, thinking of some of the adults I'd met lately, like Jay and his father, maybe I wasn't so far off. But that wasn't the kind of adult I wanted to be.

I hadn't seen Jay since Saturday. Maybe he'd decided to give up on his harassment. Maybe yelling at him had actually worked – he'd looked astonished.

Or maybe he had whined to his father and now the older Preppard would keep causing trouble.

I wondered what Ricky was up to. I needed to give him the warning about Bain. I started to pull out my phone, but the truck was already heading back. I closed the gate after it passed through, and then I got in. Kyle barely glanced at me, and he seemed lost in thought as we drove up into town.

He finally gave me a smile as we neared the resort. "There's no need to look like that. I can understand what you did. I don't like it because it's dangerous for you. But I won't tell you to stop, because that's not my place, and because you need to do whatever it takes to deal with your feelings about this."

I could only stare at him. I'd never heard support like that from anyone, not even my own mother. Actually, especially not my own mother.

He turned in at the resort and paused in the parking lot, looking at me. Finally he said, "Where are you parked?"

"Oh! Employee parking area." I pointed. "That silver one on this end." With the daytime employees gone, that section was more than half empty. Kyle pulled in near Mom's car, with an empty space between the vehicles.

We got out, and he came around the truck to join me. I tried to think of something to say. Something that would make him believe I wanted to see him again, not because of Bethany, but for himself.

He glanced at my car and frowned. "Uh oh."

I followed his gaze. The back tire was flat, with a gash in it. And the front one looked the same.

Twenty-Seven

Kyle stepped around to the other side of the car. "These tires are okay." He looked toward the resort. "Too much in view, maybe. Or someone was coming. That's a bit of luck, or else you might have needed four new tires." He came back around and stopped a couple of feet from me. "Are you all right?"

I nodded rapidly. "It's not a coincidence, is it?"

He gazed at me for half a minute. "I guess it could be, but more likely ..."

I swallowed and spoke through a tight throat. "You don't have to be delicate. This was a threat, or warning. Or revenge." I sniffled. The tires themselves were only an inconvenience, an annoying expense, but a whole lot better than the cut brake lines. But the ongoing malice had a cold knot settling in my stomach.

Kyle rubbed my arm gently. "Somebody is definitely annoyed with you. Bain, I suppose, because you brought his crime to light, although ..." He trailed off and shook his head. "I would've thought he'd be more direct."

I sighed and tried to make light of it. "At least I already have the tow truck number in my phone."

I pulled out my phone and saw a couple of text messages from Ricky. "Bain taken in for questioning this morning!" and then from only fifteen minutes ago, "Still there. Has a lawyer."

"It wasn't Bain." My voice seemed to come from a distance.

"What?"

"Ricky says Bain was taken in for questioning this morning and is still there." I frowned, thinking back. "I took my car out at lunch. The tires definitely weren't slashed then. Bain couldn't have done it."

Kyle looked baffled. "How many people could want to hurt you?"

"You'd be surprised," I grumbled. Jay seemed the most likely culprit. But would he have recognized my mother's car? Maybe, if he'd seen me pull up in it, though I hadn't noticed him at all that day. This had his kind of pettiness, not actually dangerous, but an annoyance. The brake lines had been potentially dangerous, so slashed tires weren't an escalation of violence, but the opposite. In fact, if the vandal had done any real damage – cutting these brake lines, or tampering with the engine – he'd also ensured I wouldn't drive the car in that state. The actions of two different people? Someone who knew how to damage my older car, but not Mom's newer one? Or simply someone who took out their annoyance on cars, in whatever way seemed convenient?

I shook my head, giving up on the problem for the moment. I called a tow truck and the cops. I didn't think the police would normally get involved with slashed tires, but given everything else that had happened, I thought I should let them know. I also called my mother to let her know the bad news, so she could make plans for a ride the next morning, in case we couldn't get new tires in time.

Kyle crouched and examined the tires while I was on the phone. When I hung up, he rose. "It looks like it was a fairly small knife. He had to saw a bit to make that gash." He shrugged. "Not that that helps a lot, but I guess I feel better knowing that if you have an enemy, he only carries something like a pocketknife. It would have to be a strong one, though, to get through that rubber."

I didn't point out that I could also have an enemy who went around carrying a huge dagger – just not this enemy. Or the person could have had a gun, but not wanted to use it on the tires because it would be too loud. I wondered again how Bethany had been killed. Gunshot? Stabbed? Strangled or hit over the head? Not that any of those options would make me feel better.

I was thinking too much. I drew in a deep breath and tried to blink away the spots flickering before my eyes.

Kyle edged closer, lifted his right arm, and hesitantly put it around my shoulders. "I'm sorry you got caught up in things. You shouldn't have to deal with any of this."

I agreed with him there.

But what if it had never happened? If Jay and I hadn't taken that particular turn, Bethany could still be lying in the woods. She might not have been found for weeks or months – or ever. And without that evidence, her murderer would likely go free.

What would have happened between Jay and me if we hadn't had the interruption to his plans? How long would it have taken me to understand the kind of man he was? How much might I have been hurt first?

And if I hadn't taken that path, I wouldn't have met Nancy and Daniel, or seen the beautiful hawks and falcons, or met Kyle. I gazed into his eyes and said, "I'm not sorry."

His hand tightened on my shoulder. I wanted to turn to him, lean my head on his shoulder, feel his arm slide around me in more than a brotherly gesture. We gazed at each other a long time. Was that the same longing I felt echoed in his face, or just my wishful thinking?

He drew me fractionally closer. Was he going to kiss me?

An engine growled behind us. Kyle glanced over and dropped his arm. I turned to see the tow truck. Darn small towns with prompt service.

Kyle smiled. "I guess I get to take you home after all. Unless – I was thinking we could go somewhere. Get some dinner. Finish talking about ... stuff."

"Sure, I suppose." I imagined gazing across the table at Kyle in some quiet little bistro, his understanding gray eyes on me as we talked about anything and everything.

"The best place for private conversation is someplace noisy. How about the pizza parlor?"

The dream image shifted, but the alternative wasn't worse. "Okay." I grinned. "My brother will be jealous, though. I think Mom's making a vegetable casserole tonight."

"We'll bring him the leftovers." He winked.

A police car pulled up a minute later and an officer took a report.

"Do you think there's any chance of fingerprints?" I asked.

He chuckled. "Yeah, we'll get the CSI team right on that."

I took that as a no.

The tow truck hooked up my car, and Kyle and I climbed back into his truck. By the time we walked into the pizza parlor, the dinner rush was over and my stomach was grumbling.

We found a tiny table in the corner, and the waitress came over with a basket of breadsticks. Kyle looked across the table at me. "Do you want a glass of wine, a beer?"

"Um, amber ale, I guess." I reached for a breadstick and took a nibble.

"Iced tea for me," Kyle said.

If I'd known he wasn't going to order alcohol, I wouldn't have either. But it would look silly to take back the order now. As the waitress walked away, I tried to make a joke of it. "You're going to let me drink alone?"

"I don't drink anymore."

The rumors came back. Gail at the festival saying Kyle had a drug problem. Eslinda refusing to confirm or deny. I felt my face warming and hoped Kyle couldn't read my thoughts.

"Guess I might as well get this out of the way." He looked down and sighed, then lifted his gaze to mine. "After I lost my hand, I was on some really strong painkillers."

"I would hope so."

He grinned. "Maybe, but I stayed on longer than I should have. Then I got some anxiety medication, because I was having trouble dealing with it. And then I found out that alcohol made it even better."

I kept my gaze on his face, but it didn't escape me that the arm in question was tucked out of sight under the table, while his remaining hand rested on the table, playing idly with his napkin.

"My mother is an alcoholic. Bethany was an alcoholic and addict. So it's not like I didn't have those warnings." He shrugged, but I sensed tension in the set of his shoulders and the tight skin around his eyes. "I never drank in high school, because I hated what it did to my mother and sister. It wasn't easy to get alcohol in

Afghanistan, so I didn't bother. But when I came back, I went kind of crazy with it. I knew better, but I did it anyway."

"It must have been hard." I couldn't think of anything better to say.

He shrugged. "Life often is. Anyway, I don't drink anymore. Or take drugs except over the counter stuff when I really need it."

I nodded and opened my mouth, still not sure what I wanted to say. The waitress came back and dropped off our drinks. I looked at the golden liquid in my glass and wished I hadn't ordered it.

"Don't worry," Kyle said. "I don't mind if you drink. In fact, I'd mind a lot more if you avoided it because of me."

"It doesn't make you feel ..." I waved my hand vaguely.

Kyle grinned. "I have a beautiful woman to look at. I'm not going to pay any attention to what she's drinking."

I ducked my head, smiling through my blush. I couldn't think of a response to that, so I fumbled for something else to say. "It must be hard, though, when there's so much alcohol around."

"Gran and Daniel don't keep alcohol in the house, which makes it easier. I can't give in to a moment's temptation when it would take half an hour to get to a bar. But really, I figured out that the alcohol was a way of dealing with stress. So when I feel the urge for a drink, it means I need to deal with some stress."

I looked across at him. "You've had a lot lately."

"Life again. It happens. I can't use it as an excuse."

Had he grown handsomer since I'd met him? His face no longer seemed ordinary, but full of wisdom and character. "I think you're the strongest person I've ever met."

He laughed and shook his head. "Don't make me into some kind of a hero. I'm really pretty messed up. I just do what has to be done, no more."

"That's more than a lot of people do." I hesitated, remembering his parents at the memorial, how they had dealt with the stress. Had Kyle ushered his mother out not only because of her despair, but because she'd been drinking? "Your mother. You didn't use the past tense when you said she was an alcoholic."

"She still drinks. More than ever lately, despite the fact my father bans alcohol from the house. I want to get her help, but my counselor says I need to focus on myself first. I can't allow myself to think I should be responsible for someone else, or I really will have too much stress. And Mom isn't ready to change. You have to want it."

"Your dad is trying to help her?"

He made a face. "He's trying to control her. Not the same thing."

"You actually make me grateful for my own mother."

He grinned. "That's something. Now, before we order the pizza, I wanted to give you a chance to talk about everything *you've* been going through lately. The stuff you said you hadn't told anyone yet. You can tell me."

I thought about the details the police had dragged out of me, the way her skin had been green and her hand had lain curled on her chest. I covered my nose and mouth with my hand as the memory of the stench rose up. He wanted to talk about that *here*?

I glanced around at the busy tables, full of laughing families. Teenagers clustered around the videogames in the background, the beeps and shouts mixing with the general roar of conversation. I dropped my hand and took a deep breath. The rich smell of pizza filled my nose and mouth, wiping away that other scent. Maybe this was the right place.

What I'd seen wasn't the most important part anyway, not now, not to me. The hardest things I hadn't even told the police – the nightmares, the anxiety I felt whenever I looked at the woods, the way Bethany had become important to me even though I'd never met her.

I looked across at Kyle. "I think you're right. I think I can tell you." And I wanted to hear about his experiences as well. If we shared our burdens, maybe they'd feel a little lighter.

Twenty-Eight

Eventually we ordered dinner and by the time it came I was so famished that not even the unpleasant topic could dampen my appetite. We talked about other things as we ate, his time in the service, my time at college, the future. He was getting some of the fundamentals out of the way at the community college while he adjusted to his new situation. He was still figuring out what he wanted to do and what he could do with one hand. He talked about his missing hand easily enough, though after a while I realized he wouldn't look directly at me when he mentioned it, and he kept the injury hidden under the table.

Family came up eventually, which led us back to Bethany and the frustration of not knowing the truth about her death.

At one point I said, "You seem kind of resigned about the whole thing."

"Justice works slowly. Even if they make an arrest soon, it could be a year before they get a conviction. I'm determined to see justice done, but in the meantime the rest of us have to live our lives."

I thought about waiting a year for real resolution. Even if you were convinced the police had the right person, you couldn't be satisfied until you knew the killer was going to be properly punished. If there was any such thing as a proper punishment. Nothing could undo what was done. And what if he only got a few years, or got off on a technicality or because his lawyer was better than the prosecutor?

"I'll still be relieved when they make an arrest," I said. At least then I wouldn't have to worry so much about someone stalking me and sabotaging my car – assuming the killer and the saboteur were the same person. "I don't like knowing that a killer is wandering around loose."

"I know. It bothers me that someone is harassing you. Why aren't they going after my family, if this is about Bethany? Is it because you're young and female, like Bethany was?"

I shivered. I focused on my glass of water as I lifted it and took a slow sip, trying not to imagine what had happened to Bethany at the end.

Kyle shifted forward in his seat. "I'm sorry, I didn't mean – I shouldn't have said that. Maybe they're getting closer to an arrest, if they took Bain in for questioning. The police won't say much about the case, but I know they've been keeping an eye on him."

I hesitated. The image of Bethany was fresh in my mind, and there was something I wanted to know, even though I was afraid to find out. But if I didn't ask, it would keep haunting me. I took another sip of water and glanced up at Kyle, fighting the urge to look away as I asked an uncomfortable question. "Have they told you how she died? I mean what exactly killed her?"

He looked at me a while. "Why do you want to know?"

"I just ..." I looked away. I wanted to say never mind, forget it. But we'd been honest with each other so far, more honest than I'd been with nearly anyone. I needed to know something, and he had a right to know why I was asking.

I forced myself to meet his gaze. "I remember the way she looked. Of course some of that was ... time. How long she'd been out there. But there was something wrong with her face, and I've been trying not to think about it, but I keep thinking about it." I broke off and put a hand over my mouth, swallowing back the acid taste.

Kyle glanced around the room and finally leaned forward, dropping his voice. "She was shot in the back of the head. They haven't released that information publicly, so don't tell anyone. They're keeping some things secret so they can judge the authenticity of tips that come in."

I nodded. That explained the damage to her lower face. But I wasn't sure knowing was actually better. I kept picturing Bethany kneeling in a ditch while a killer stood behind her with a gun to her head. I didn't like guns. I pictured the shot, her falling.

I forced myself to breathe and tried to think logically. "Wait, if she was shot from the back, wouldn't she have fallen facedown?"

"They don't think it happened there. They haven't figured out where she was killed, but they think she was moved to the woods afterward."

The scenes in my head shifted. No one had been killed in the woods, which made the trees seem a little less threatening. But the idea of somebody shooting a woman in the back of the head and then calmly carrying her into the woods to hide her body was equally chilling. That suggested a lot of planning. And strength. From her pictures, Bethany had been plump. I couldn't imagine tiny Lia Bain or even Nascha carrying a body that distance.

The waitress brought the check and Kyle put a twenty on the little tray. I wondered if I should offer to pay half, but he said, "I got it."

"Thanks. And thanks for letting me talk." He rose, so I did too. As we walked out I said, "You said the police are keeping an eye on Bain. Do you mean they're watching him constantly? Or just checking in once in a while?" Were the police spying on us when Bain talked to me and Ricky at the festival? I hadn't noticed them, but maybe that was the point. I wasn't sure if it was comforting or creepy to think somebody might have been secretly watching us then.

"I'm not sure. They only said they're watching him. I assume so he doesn't try to run."

That could mean anything. Bain couldn't have slashed my tires, if he was at the police station, but he could have cut my brake lines if he'd followed me to Kyle's. That was an unnerving thought. I imagined Bain sneaking around behind me, and the police sneaking around behind him, like some crazy spy movie. It wasn't as funny as it should have been.

What about the prank phone calls? Had they tapped his phone line? That seemed like something the police would do with a suspect, but didn't they have to have a warrant for that? I didn't know much about the rules, or how hard it was to get a warrant, or anything. I'd never much cared before.

Kyle opened the door for me, and I climbed into his truck. It smelled slightly musty, of straw and dirt and old leather from the cracked seats. When Kyle got in, he added a spicy scent, pleasantly male.

He drove me home and I wondered how to say goodnight. What were we, exactly? Friends? Comrades in arms against Bethany's killer? Was this simply "misery loves company," or the start of something more?

Or was he trying to get information from me, keep track of me, the way Ricky and I had been investigating him?

That was an uncomfortable thought. I put it aside. I had decided to trust him, which didn't have to mean complete and total trust, but it did mean I should hope for and expect the best. I liked him more all the time, and I wasn't going to blow it by acting like my mother and assuming the worst.

He pulled up in front of my house. I debated asking him in, but that meant dealing with Mom, and I wasn't sure I wanted to add that to the mix yet. "Thanks again," I said. "I really did enjoy seeing the hawk at work." I hesitated, then took a chance. "I'd love to do it again sometime."

I couldn't see much in the dark interior of the cab, but he was turned toward me and I thought he was smiling. "Any time. You should come out some morning when I take the falcon after pigeons. He hardly ever catches one. Pigeons are really tough prey."

Who would have guessed? His pigeons must have been a different species from the mourning doves that stood on our birdfeeder trying to figure out how to get down to the opening. Those had not impressed me with their intelligence. "I'd like that."

"I usually go out at sunrise, around six right now. I know it's early, especially on the weekends when you could sleep in, but if you want to go out during the week, I could get you back to work in plenty of time." He leaned closer and spoke in a seductive murmur. "I'd even bring coffee and some of Daniel's muffins."

I laughed. "I'd love that."

"You've had a hard few days, so I don't want to drag you out of bed early, but if you happen to be up some morning, call or text and I'll pick you up. Or we can meet somewhere after you get your car back."

"Okay. Thanks again for everything."

I slipped out of the car and dashed up the front walk. At the door, I waved and went inside. He didn't pull away until I was closing the door behind me.

Mom glanced up from the couch. "Hey, how was your dinner?"

"Very nice." I braced for probing questions and critical comments.

"Good, I'm glad." Mom's gaze drifted back to the TV. I glanced at the screen and saw famous people dancing. She was a sucker for celebrities and reality talent shows, so the combination was a winner. "Want to join me?" she asked.

"Maybe in a few minutes."

She nodded, her attention on the TV, and I had to smile. I dropped my purse in my room, remembering with a pang of disappointment that my new quilt and art print were still in the trunk of my car. At least the garage had said they'd have the tires on Mom's car in the morning and should have my brakes fixed in the afternoon. I needed to give her that update.

First I headed to Ricky's room, where music was playing from behind his closed door, and knocked. Ten seconds later the door opened a few inches and Ricky peered out. He opened the door wider. "Oh good, it's you!"

"Who were you expecting?"

Ricky backed into his room and went around his desk. He leaned down to look at the screen. "It's all right, it's Audra." He glanced up at me. "Come in and close the door!"

I did and started around the desk. "Who are you ..." I trailed off when I saw the face on the screen. Richard. Ricky's father.

Twenty-Nine

"Hi Audra," Richard said. "Is that really you? I can only see your elbow."

I noticed the small camera on top of the screen. Ricky was having a video chat with his father.

"Who ... how long ..." I sat on Ricky's bed, where I could still see the screen but Richard probably couldn't get a good look at me gaping at him.

Ricky sat in the desk chair and looked back at me. "Mom doesn't know, okay?"

"How long has this been going on?"

"I tracked Dad down a few years ago. We try to talk every week when Mom is busy."

"Why didn't you tell me?"

He shrugged and looked away. "I wasn't sure if you'd tell Mom."

Richard spoke from the screen. "Audra? Can you come closer so I can see you? I've missed you. Ricky tells me all about you, but it's not the same."

I shook myself as if coming out of a trance. All this time, I'd been worried about Ricky growing up without a father. And the little brat had taken matters into his own hands and found his. I shot him a glance, half amused and half disbelieving, and he gave me a lopsided grin. I stood and leaned down so I was in the camera's view.

"You look great!" Richard said. "And hey, congratulations on the new job. Ricky's been telling me about this murder. Audra, I don't like it."

"I'm not so crazy about it myself." It was strange seeing him again after ten years. He looked older, a little heavier, his hair going gray. I remembered what Mom said about Richard having an affair. Did Ricky know? Had Richard explained why he'd left without trying to get shared custody, or even visitation rights?

"I want you two to be careful. I wish you'd drop this whole investigation."

I stiffened. He might be Ricky's father. He might even be right about the investigation. But that didn't mean he could scold me after ignoring me for ten years. "We're not the ones causing trouble."

He frowned. "I know I don't have the right – I can't make you – look, please careful. For your own sake."

"I'm always careful." If he'd stuck around, he would know that. I put a hand on Ricky's shoulder. "And I'll look after my brother, too."

He gazed at me, sadness in his eyes. I wanted to cry. I wanted to hit him, or hug him, or both.

"I hope we can talk again," he said. "Ricky knows how to reach me."

Yes, Ricky did. It was selfish of me to feel hurt. Richard wasn't my father. And I had never bothered to track him down, had never even considered it. I pushed down the feelings and said goodbye with as much of a smile as I could manage. As Ricky said his goodbyes, I sat back on the bed and rubbed my stomach, right below the rib cage, where it ached.

Ricky turned toward me. "Audra? Is it okay?"

I forced the smile back on my face. "I'm glad you found him. I'm glad you two have a relationship."

"We wanted to tell you. But you know you're not good at keeping secrets from Mom, and if she found out ..."

I stared at him. "I can't believe you hid this from her! For years?"

"I think I was eight when I found his address online. It took a while to get to video chats."

I started to laugh. "Come here." I pulled him into a hug, and if a few tears mixed in with the laughter, who cared?

Eventually I told him about the hawk hunting trip, the slashed tires, and everything I'd learned from Kyle. When I told Ricky that I'd admitted we were spying on Kyle's family, he rolled his eyes. "See, I said you couldn't keep a secret."

"Yeah, well. It's done now, and I feel better. But I won't tell Mom about Richard. That's between the three of you."

I studied him, seeing a lot of his father in his face. "Is that why you wanted your own computer so badly for your tenth birthday?"

"Yeah, before that I sent him messages from the library computers, and sometimes he called me, but I couldn't call him because Mom would see it on the bill."

"You haven't seen him in person?"

He shook his head. "He's in Denver. But now that you know, maybe we could meet him in Albuquerque sometime? He said he'd come down."

"Yeah, maybe." I rubbed my hands over my face, suddenly weak with exhaustion. I needed an early night and preferably no nightmares. "I'm going to bed. Update our notes, will you?"

"So we're not going to stop investigating?"

I glanced up at his grin. He might have his father now, but I could still be the cool sister. Besides, I was pretty sure he'd keep going without me. "We've hardly done a thing, and someone's attacked two of our cars. So long as we're careful and smart, I don't see how we can make things worse. But I want you to keep it to online research. I don't want anyone else knowing what we're doing, so no following people or anything like that."

"Okay." He said it too easily. I narrowed my eyes at him, but he went on innocently, "I can tell you what I found out about the Bains."

I sat back on the bed with a sigh. "All right."

He looked down at some papers on his desk. "Lia Bain is eighteen years old. Her parents weren't married. She lives with her mother and three younger kids. She's the only one with the last name Bain." He looked up at me. "That makes the others half-siblings, right, like us?"

I nodded. And she was the oldest. I didn't really want to have anything in common with Lia Bain. One difference, though – she knew her father. Given what I'd heard about him, I didn't think that made her luckier.

"She doesn't do very well in school," Ricky went on. "And she's kind of a troublemaker. She got suspended for fighting once."

"You got all this online?"

Ricky hesitated. "Mostly. You should see some of her profile pictures. They're kind of ... um ... Mom would say she doesn't respect herself." He looked away, blushing.

"I'll bet. What do you mean about mostly online?"

"You know my friend Josh? No, I guess you haven't met him 'cause we've only been hanging out this year. Anyway, his mom is kind of a gossip, so I heard some stuff there."

That wasn't so bad. I'd been prodding Eslinda for gossip, too. So long as the gossips didn't gossip about us gossiping about – I was too tired to think about it. "Okay, so Lia is an apple that didn't fall far from the tree. So what?"

"So she's Thomas Bain's alibi. Which means that he's *her* alibi, too, if they're claiming they were together the weekend she disappeared. You said you didn't think she could carry Bethany's body alone. But what if they did it together?"

I trembled, suddenly queasy. A father-daughter murder team? The image of Bethany in the ditch flashed through my mind, and I had to close my eyes for a second. Surely no father would drag a daughter into something like that. But what did I know about fathers? And what if it was the other way around – what if Lia had killed Bethany, maybe by accident, and her father had helped cover it up?

Surely not. And yet ...

I stared at my brother. "I want you to stay away from them."

"Sure."

"I mean it. If you see them, run the other direction. Go someplace safe or call the police."

"Now you sound like Mom."

"Ricky!"

"Okay, okay, I'm kidding." He sat at his desk. "I guess I'll poke around online some more, since that's all I'm allowed to do."

I gazed at the back of his head. Seeing his father for four years without telling Mom or me proved that he got away with a lot more than he was "allowed" to do. And he was hitting that age where rebellion was its own reward.

I stood and put my hands on his shoulders. "Remember how horrible it was when the car was out of control yesterday? Someone doesn't like us. Or me, anyway, but that puts you in danger as well. I want you to be safe. Please promise me that you'll be safe."

He twisted his head to look up at me. "Yeah, okay. Don't worry. I'm not stupid."

I squeezed his shoulders. "No, you're definitely not." Maybe too smart for his own good, though. "I love you, kid."

He looked embarrassed but mumbled, "Love you too."

I headed for my room. I definitely needed a good night's sleep. Maybe if I woke early enough I could call Kyle. Was it too soon? It was probably too soon. But I remembered the beauty and thrill of the hawk soaring toward us, and the comfort of Kyle's arm around my shoulders. Maybe I needed moments like those even more than I needed a good sleep.

When I entered my room, my phone was ringing. The number was blocked. I watched it go to voicemail. When I finally got up the nerve to check the message, the voice was low and unfamiliar. "You'll pay for what you did. I swear you'll pay."

Thirty

I got through the night with the help of Mom's sleeping pills, but I did not wake early enough to call Kyle. The day passed in a blur of work, retrieving cars, reviewing the articles on Bethany when I had a few minutes free, and looking over my shoulder. Jay seemed to be keeping a low profile, which suited me fine. Mr. Preppard glared when I passed him in the hall, but he didn't start anything.

At home, it was my turn to make dinner. While we ate, Mom finally got around to prying into my sort-of-date with Kyle, but she kept her advice to a manageable level. In fact, she said, "He sounds like a decent man," which was about the best compliment she'd ever give a man.

I gave a weak laugh. "He's darn near perfect. It's intimidating."

She studied me for a minute. I braced for the lecture about how no man could be trusted. Finally she said, "No man is perfect. No woman either. But don't sell yourself short. If he's a good man, you're worthy of him, and he'd be a fool not to realize that."

I stared while she dug back into her chicken, ignoring the fact it was dry from overcooking. Maybe we really would be able to develop a new relationship.

After dinner we left Mom watching TV, and I dragged Ricky back to his bedroom. "We need to do something," I said. "I'm going crazy waiting and not knowing what the police are doing and wondering if someone's watching me and—" I decided not to go into detail about what might happen if Bethany's murderer decided to take revenge on me for finding the body.

"Do you have any ideas?" Ricky asked.

I sat on his bed. "One thing came to me when I was reviewing the news articles. The police have been looking for Bethany's car ever since she was reported missing. They haven't found it."

"You think it will help solve the crime?" Ricky asked. "If the murderer used it to move her body, maybe he left something behind! A clue, like a hair or some blood."

I made a face. "Right. I don't know if the police are still looking for it, since she's been found. I guess they must be, but now they know she's not with her car, so maybe they're not worrying about it. The question is, if they haven't found her car, how could we?"

Ricky squinted in concentration. "What would the police have done? They must have put out an alert."

"Probably. But that would mostly work if the car got left someplace where it would be towed or ticketed. Maybe a police officer would notice it driving down the street, but it was a white Toyota Corolla, not exactly something that would stand out in a crowd. Since obviously Bethany didn't leave town in it, the car could still be around somewhere."

"It's not near the resort, is it?"

"No. I looked around the parking lot when I left today, but it's not there. It's possible the police found it, towed it, and didn't let the paper report it. But surely one of the employees would have noticed, and I haven't heard any rumors about that."

"Okay," Ricky said. "She didn't leave her car anywhere obvious, like her house or where she worked, or the police would have found it."

"Either she left her car someplace else, or someone moved it afterward. If the police haven't found the car yet, maybe the murderer hid it somewhere. But where?"

The door opened and Mom came in. "What are you two doing?"

Ricky and I exchanged a guilty glance as I tried to think of an excuse. But did we really have to keep this a secret? We weren't doing anything except thinking. And Mom, who usually assumed the worst about people, might have insight into sneaky behavior. "We're trying to figure out where someone might hide a car."

Her eyebrows went up. "Any particular car?"

"Bethany Moore's car, which is missing. We wonder if the murderer might have hidden it someplace, either to hide evidence or to make it look like Bethany left town."

Mom sat beside me on the bed. "That makes sense. He might have hidden it in a remote corner, pushed it into a ravine in the mountains, or drove it down some wash outside of town. That's hard to track. Have you checked Google maps?"

I glanced at Ricky's computer, where the screensaver was a mesmerizing kaleidoscope. "They're not updated that often, are they? Even if you could identify a car from the air like that, I don't think you're seeing what's out there right now."

"Not to actually find the car," Mom said. "To find places where it might be – back roads and so on."

I looked at Ricky. "That's not a bad idea."

Mom sniffed. "What did you expect?"

Ricky got on the computer and brought up a map of our town and the surrounding area while Mom and I leaned over his shoulders. "Of course, her car could be in Mexico by now," Mom said. "But we can't do anything about that, so we might as well start with what's possible for us."

"If I really wanted to hide a car, I'd drive way back into the mountains," Ricky said. "I bet you could lose a car for years."

"How would you get home?" Mom asked. "You'd have to have somebody pick you up in another car, and if the murderer was working alone, he wouldn't want that. Even hitchhiking would be dangerous, because someone might remember you."

"Right," I said. I sometimes forgot how clever Mom was when she focused on solving problems rather than complaining about them. "More likely he'd drive the car someplace where he could walk back home." All of our known suspects lived in or near town, so that narrowed down the area. We didn't have local bus service, so that wasn't an option. Still, the question remained – *was* the murderer working alone?

I studied the map of the roads in and around town. "There are an awful lot of back roads and remote corners around here," I said. "It will take forever to check them out." I didn't like the idea of driving out into those lonely places alone, or with Ricky and Mom. The murderer must have better things to do than keep an eye on a hidden car, but what if someone really were following me?

"It's definitely a needle in a haystack." Mom took over the mouse and started sliding the map around. "Eight thousand people in town. You have to figure several thousand cars, plus tourists passing through. That's a big haystack."

There had to be a couple dozen white Toyota Corollas, not to mention all the other similar white cars. I had a hard enough time picking my own small blue car out in a crowded parking lot, especially when parked between two larger cars.

I straightened. "Wait a minute." Maybe that was it!

Mom and Ricky turned to look at me. I glanced at the computer screen again, at the streets and buildings and parking lots that looked vaguely familiar but so different from above. "If you wanted to hide a car, why not hide it among a bunch of other cars? Say, in a large parking lot?"

Ricky's eyes widened. "Like hiding the real jewels in a bunch of cheap fakes!"

Mom nodded slowly. "Where then? A shopping center? There aren't many places open overnight, though. A car would stand out if it was the last one left, and it was parked in the same place for a month."

I bent over the desk and shifted the map around some more. There had to be someplace in town. "There."

"The college?" Ricky said.

"Yep." I straightened. "Lots of cars, and with student housing, people are there twenty-four hours a day. Plus, I bet lots of students leave their cars in one spot for weeks and only drive if they're going shopping or skiing or something. That's how it was at UNM. Especially during the semester, I don't think anyone would notice."

We looked at each other and the air tingled with excitement. Mom said, "Let's go find out."

"Really?" Ricky grinned.

Mom nodded. "I don't like the idea of that murderer going free, and I really don't like the fact that he's harassing Audra by damaging our cars. I don't see any danger in looking for Bethany's car. And I don't trust the police to follow up on our advice. So let's see what we can find. Maybe we'll help catch the bastard."

We scrambled for the door and piled into Mom's car. Ricky chattered as we drove across town, comparing this idea to mystery stories he'd read. But the closer we got to the college, the more my idea seemed naïve. As we turned through the college campus gates, I said, "Do you really think it could be here? Wouldn't the police have found it?"

Mom said, "Depends on whether they were really looking for it, or only sort of looking for it. When the girl was reported missing, they might have assumed she left on her own, especially given her history. In that case, the police wouldn't have driven all around town looking for a parked car. So the question is whether or not they've thought to do so since her body was discovered."

The detectives who'd interviewed me might think of something like that, but I wasn't so sure about the local police. And the detectives had other cases and weren't based here in town. Since they wouldn't be familiar with the town, they might have simply asked the local police to look around. The college was on the opposite side of town from the resort and in no way associated with the case, so the local police might not have looked carefully there. It seemed that we had at least a chance of being a step ahead of them.

And then what?

Then we reported the car to the police and let them do their job. And hoped for an arrest soon, so I could get back to building my life. Finding the car wasn't the answer to everything, but it was an answer to one of the questions. That was a start.

We drove to the main parking area near the large school buildings. The lots were only about a quarter full, since daytime classes had ended, and that made our job easier as we drove up and down the rows. Every time I saw a white car my heart raced. None of them had Bethany's license plate, which we knew from a news article. Most weren't even Toyota Corollas.

We finally found a Corolla and paused behind it, peering out our windows. "Wrong license plate," I said. "But what if he changed it? We'd never find the right car."

Mom frowned over that for half a minute. "I was going to say that would suggest premeditation, but since it's been a month since she disappeared, he could've come back any time since then. A bit risky, but not impossible. I don't know how we can deal with that. Tell the police our idea, I guess, and let them check the vehicle identification numbers."

That made sense, but I didn't want to wait for the police or to wonder if they'd actually done anything, since they probably wouldn't tell me. I swallowed hard and got out of the car. Across the parking lot, a young guy was getting in his car. A few people were walking along the sidewalk between the parking area and buildings. A car drove slowly past on the street. No one seemed to be paying attention to me.

I ducked and looked through the window of the white Corolla. I heard a door close and Ricky moved around the other side of the car. After we'd studied it for a minute, I glanced across at him. "Okay, hotshot detective. What do you deduce?"

"That's a chemistry textbook on the front passenger seat. I don't think Bethany ever went to college. And that gym bag in the back is partway open, I can see a pair of shoes. They look like men's."

I moved around to his side of the car. "Good spot on the shoes, I couldn't see them from my angle. I also noticed a crumpled bag from Sonic and a drink in the cup holder. The window's cracked open and I can smell French fries. If the car had been sitting here in the sun for a month, the smell would have faded – or gotten a lot worse, I'm not sure which, but this smells pretty fresh. Conclusion?"

"It's not the right car."

"I agree. Nice work, detective." I put my arm around him and we headed back to our car. Ricky grinned at me as we got in. I wished I could think of it as just an intellectual challenge, the way he seemed to. It would be fun to play detective together. But this was no game. I was torn between wanting Ricky to understand that, too, for his own safety, and wanting to protect his innocence a little longer.

The best way to keep him safe *and* protect his innocence was to expose the killer and get him behind bars.

Mom pulled out onto the road that circled through campus. Our headlights cut through the dusk. This would have been easier during the day, when we could easily see any cars parked down the side streets or in the few smaller lots.

"We should look by student housing," I said. "That's the one place where parking will be as full at night." I knew from my own experiences at UNM that many students liked to hold onto a parking spot once they'd gotten it. It wasn't surprising to see a car in the same place for a week or more.

We found the upperclassman apartments first and then the two-story dorms for underclassmen. We went through the parking lot on one side and moved around to the other. At a glance, I didn't see any white cars at all.

We pulled past a big SUV that seemed far too fancy for a community college student. Tucked in on the other side was a white car, and by now I was fairly certain I recognized a Corolla.

It was backed in, the front facing us, so we couldn't see the license plate. Before I could do or say anything, Ricky jumped out of the car and squeezed between the Corolla and the SUV. The car was backed close to a waist-high wall, so Ricky had to duck down to see the license plate. I held my breath while he studied it for about five seconds, looked at the article he was holding, and peered at the license plate again.

He ran back to our car grinning. "That's it!"

I let out a gasp. We had actually done it!

Ricky got in and leaned over the seat for a high five. I slapped his hand, but I was trembling. The relief, the joy at the success, was tempered by the knowledge that I was in this even deeper now. What would happen next? Would the car help break the case, or just complicate things further, or do nothing at all?

"I could barely get a good look with it against the wall and the streetlight so far away," Ricky said. "But that's the right car."

"Whoever left it there isn't dumb, backing it in like that," Mom said. "If New Mexico used front license plates, it wouldn't matter. But like this, I can see why no one noticed it." Mom pulled forward and parked illegally at the end of the lot. She pulled out her phone and called the police.

I glanced back toward Bethany's car, which was almost hidden from this angle. A perfect hiding spot, really. But not quite perfect enough.

Another car, a dark sedan, drove slowly past the entrance of the parking lot, maybe trying to spot empty parking spaces. The headlights pulled around the building and disappeared. I imagined some student going home for the night, with no idea that something strange was going on over here.

The police arrived ten minutes later. We pointed out the car and explained how we found it. I let Mom and Ricky do most of the talking. The sight of police uniforms still made me breathless. I didn't want to embarrass myself, so I turned away and rubbed my arms against the cooling night air.

A dark car sped past the entrance to the parking lot with its headlights off. It could've been the same sedan I'd seen a few minutes earlier – or not. Maybe they couldn't find a parking spot after all. Maybe they'd finished their business and left. But they shouldn't drive without headlights, especially with the police right there. Or were they trying to go unnoticed?

A hand clamped my arm. I gasped and jumped.

"Miss Needham? I'd like to talk to you privately." The officer led me away from his partner, Mom, and Ricky. "First you find the body and now her car. A pretty big coincidence, isn't it?"

Thirty-One

"And they sounded suspicious of *me*!" I told Kyle the next morning. Somehow the whole story poured out minutes after we met up.

I'd left my car at his place and rode with him into the valley, talking the whole time until he pulled off a back road and parked. He sat with his forearms resting on the steering wheel, frowning out the front window. "I guess I can see their point."

I gasped. He turned to me with a crooked smile. "Sorry, let me put that another way. They're complete idiots. Anyone with an ounce of sense could tell you're just an innocent bystander."

"Thanks, I guess."

"I only meant I can see how it looks like an unlikely coincidence. It's not a coincidence," he quickly added. "You have a reason to be interested, to look, and you were smart and lucky to find the car. But I suppose criminals sometimes come to the police with evidence or information, trying to throw a false trail."

He glanced toward the back of the truck, where the falcon was screeching like a rusty swing. "Junior's restless." We got out and met at the back of the truck. "Nobody could seriously consider you a suspect, though," Kyle said. "You didn't know Bethany. You have no reason to wish her harm. You weren't even living here when she disappeared. The police are trained to sound suspicious so people get nervous and talk more, but I doubt they're really focused on you."

I leaned my hip on the tailgate as he got out equipment. "I hope you're right, but it's insulting. I never had a problem with the police before, but I'm starting to hate the sight of them."

"Try to remember they're doing their job. It can't be easy for them, when people only see the police if they're in trouble or getting bad news." He pulled the leather glove over his arm. "I learned something interesting after Bethany disappeared, when I was prodding the police to find her. A lot of times people uncover crime scenes, even find bodies like you did, but they don't report it."

I thought of Jay. "I should be shocked, but I'm not."

He opened the cage and the falcon hopped out and up onto his arm. "I was shocked at first. Why on earth wouldn't someone report something like that? But then I thought of all the reasons people might not want to talk to the cops. People who were doing something wrong, even if it's only teenagers drinking or cutting school. Illegal immigrants. Anyone with a police record could be afraid they'd be seen as a suspect. Lots of reasons someone might not want police attention."

"I guess so." I tried to remember Jay's reasons. That whole experience was a blur – except for the horribly vivid memory of the body itself – but I didn't think he'd given any real reason. The joint, of course, but he could've hidden that. He'd said something about me not knowing what was going on. I'd almost forgotten that. Was Jay the kind of person who never wanted to get involved, or was his wariness more suspicious?

Kyle turned to face me, the morning sun glowing golden on his skin and highlighting his hair. He looked healthier than when I'd met him a few days before. Maybe knowing for sure that Bethany was gone had lifted some burden. Or maybe it was the wide-open desert background, the vivid blue sky, and the gorgeous young falcon on his arm. Something about holding a bird of prey a foot from one's face had to make anyone look rugged and manly.

Of course, his grandmother also worked with the falcons and hawks, and I doubted she'd appreciate being called manly. Though given what I'd seen of Nancy, she might get a kick out of it.

"You're smiling," Kyle said. "Good." He removed the bird's hood. It peered around with fierce eyes. The falcon had a lovely brown and white mottled pattern on the breast, a brown back, and a white and brown face. "Gran might have mentioned that we don't hunt a lot of the birds at this time of year, because they're molting and breeding. But this is one of the earliest of this year's chicks, so we'll get him started. The juveniles have tons of energy so it's fun to get them out there and give them some confidence."

He hefted a small animal carrying case in his hand. Pigeons cooed inside. "Ready to go?"

He led the way across a grassy field, sexy in the jeans that hung low on his hips. I was wearing jeans and hiking boots myself, with my work clothes in the car. I can learn.

Kyle stopped and put the carrying case on the ground. He raised his other arm, holding the falcon above his head. The bird spread its wings and took off, and I got that same flutter in the chest at seeing a spectacular creature in action. It made a low loop and then kept circling higher. Within a couple of minutes, it was a speck in the sky.

Kyle bent to the carrying case, opened the door, and a moment later stood up clutching a pigeon against his stomach. "You're sure you're okay with this?"

"I'm sure it's prejudiced of me, but I find I can't care that much about a pigeon. Rabbits are cute; pigeons poop on park benches."

"Fair enough." He checked the falcon's progress and then tossed the pigeon into the air. It fluttered erratically before speeding away. "This isn't really falconry," Kyle said. "With real falconry, a trained bird hunts wild animals. Releasing pigeons is only a training technique, but it'll give our guy some exercise."

I glanced up to find the falcon, and when I looked for the pigeon again, it had disappeared. The falcon must have spotted it, though. It arrowed down from the sky.

My heart raced and I tensed, holding my breath. Would the pigeon escape or would the young falcon make a kill? This time I was rooting for the falcon.

I couldn't tell what happened at that distance, but Kyle said, "Nope. He got close, but the pigeon got away." The falcon rose higher in the sky.

"Will it try again?"

"Not with that bird. Homing pigeons are a challenging quarry. We breed them for boldness, so they dodge and swoop and try to get up above the falcon. After a couple of tries, the falcon will say, all right, it's easier to wait for another pigeon than to chase this one to the ends of the earth."

Kyle pulled something out of his shoulder bag, a crescent-shaped piece of leather eight or ten inches across. He started swinging it into the air by a long cord.

As the falcon flew toward us, Kyle tossed the leather thing onto the ground. The bird landed beside it and plucked a piece of meat out of the bag.

"So he gets rewarded for trying," I said. "What happens to the pigeon?"

"It goes back home, ready for another day."

"Why are you feeding the falcon, instead of releasing another pigeon?"

"We don't want him wandering off, getting interested in something else. I use the lure to get him in the habit of coming back."

"Food as a reward seems to work on my brother, too. I haven't tried getting him to exercise that way, but maybe I'll start."

He laughed. Then he somehow managed to interrupt the bird's meal and get the falcon back on his wrist. I didn't think I'd want to come between something with a beak like that and its breakfast.

Kyle held the bird and they seemed to lock gazes for a moment. The falcon gave a soft cry. Kyle pulled a hood out of his bag and slipped it over the bird's head, murmuring softly.

"You really seem to have a connection with it," I said.

"I love working with raptors. It's this wonderful window into the life of a wild creature, and it helps keep me sane."

We headed back to the car. The whole experience hadn't taken long, and the sun was barely rising above the distant treetops. The warmth and the faint breeze felt good on my skin. We were far enough off the main road that we couldn't even see it or any sign of civilization. It felt like we were the only people in the entire world. I wanted to get up early every day, to start by doing something special like this instead of the typical rush to get ready for work.

"Thanks for letting me share this," I said. "I don't think I'm ready for the work and commitment of having my own falcon, but this was wonderful. I feel ready to tackle anything, even though you and the bird did all the work."

"Anytime. I mean that." He slid the pigeon carrying case into the truck and nudged the falcon back in its cage. After all the gear was stowed, he pulled out some disinfectant wipes and cleaned his hands. "I almost forgot. I promised you breakfast."

I shook my head. "I should be bringing you breakfast, as a thank you. Of course," I added as he pulled out a plastic tub and opened the lid to show scones crammed with dried fruit, "I'm not going to turn down those."

We leaned on the tailgate and shared a thermos of coffee and some of the best scones I'd ever tasted. I brushed crumbs off my hands and sighed. "I think this is the most perfect morning ever."

"Good." He took a deep breath. "Because there's something I have to ask you. I think I know the answer, but I want to be sure." He pushed away from the tailgate and took a couple of steps before swinging back toward me. His nerves were contagious; I found myself breathing faster, tensing in preparation.

Was he suspicious of my involvement in Bethany's murder after all? Had something new happened? What could fluster a man like Kyle?

Thirty-Two

"Do you have a boyfriend?" Kyle asked.

I stared, trying to process a question that wasn't at all what I'd expected. "Um ... no."

He blew out a breath. "Good. I mean that's what I thought, but ... I wanted to be sure." Was he turning red?

I had to smile. It was empowering to realize that *he* was nervous around *me*. My own nerves settled. I figured I'd better take advantage of that before I froze up again and let him know a few things that could be important if this was going the way I thought it was. "I haven't had a lot of relationships. I was pretty quiet in high school." Yeah, like I wasn't now. "In college, I came home every month to see my brother. That put a damper on getting involved with anyone too seriously."

It made a good excuse, anyway. The truth was I rarely felt comfortable around men, even when I liked them. Between Mom's warnings and my own natural shyness, I'd grown up thinking men were scary. I wasn't entirely comfortable around Kyle, despite his gentleness and compassion. But he was worth the extra effort.

"You really care about your brother."

"I'm all he has. Well, me and my mother. But ..." And Ricky had his father, too, but I hadn't known that.

"Parents can sometimes do as much harm as good."

"You do understand."

His smile grew and something sparked in his eyes. "I understand a lot of things."

I gazed at his face, not handsome or cute exactly, but good-looking and comfortable. This was what a man could be, both strong and safe. "It would be good for Ricky to know you. That is – not that I'm saying you should—"

"I'm flattered." He had a great smile, slow but worth the wait. I felt myself leaning forward, my body asking to be closer to him. He had to know how I felt, he had to see it in my eyes, as our gazes held and time spun out. But he didn't move.

He was leaning forward, too, our bodies calling to each other while our minds held back. I thought I read longing in his gaze, but also hesitation and some indefinable pain.

"I like you," I blurted out. My heart pounded and my chest felt like someone was ripping it apart, but I needed him to know. I couldn't bear to walk away from this.

His gaze softened. "I like you, too." And yet he held back.

"Then why ..." I dropped my gaze as my face heated. "Your sister. You can't be thinking of romance now."

He leaned against the tailgate beside me. "It's hard. There are feelings I still have to deal with. But it's not new."

I forced myself to look at his face again, trying to understand.

"My parents wanted to believe she ran away. They said they couldn't expect any better of Bethany. But I knew she wouldn't do that."

He gave a short laugh. "Not because she wouldn't want to hurt or scare us, but because she didn't have that kind of nerve. She wouldn't leave on her own, maybe with a man, but if she left with a man she'd just met ..." He shook his head. "Either way, I've been mourning for my sister for a long time. Even before she disappeared."

I eased my weight off the tailgate and turned toward him so our knees were almost brushing. I wanted to offer comfort but wasn't sure what would be welcomed.

"You're so lovely," he whispered. "So sweet and ... oh, I know it's laughed at these days, but wholesome, innocent. It's a wonderful thing, that innocence. Getting involved in my family's mess won't damage you, not in the long run." He closed his eyes and the lines etched on his face made him look older and world-weary. He opened his eyes and sighed. "It's been a long time since I was innocent. I won't ever be innocent again."

I swallowed past the lump in my throat.

He lifted his hand as if he was going to touch me, but let it drop. "You deserve a complete man. I'm trying to get my act together. Go to school, find a job I can do well, stay clean, so that someday I might deserve ..." He lifted his stump a few inches. "But this won't ever change."

With my gaze still on his face, I reached for his damaged arm. I ran my fingers down his forearm and then over the shiny skin on the stump. His breathing grew louder, raspy. "Does it hurt?" I asked.

"Not when you do that. But I wish I had fingers so I could hold your hand. Touch your skin. Stroke your hair."

Without letting go of his forearm, I reached for his other hand. I brought it to my face so it cupped my cheek and laid my hand over his.

His palm was warm against my skin, his hand broader and stronger than mine. His thumb, pleasantly rough, stroked across my cheekbone.

I let out a breath with his name on it. "Kyle." I shifted closer, easing myself between his knees. With his weight back on the tailgate, we were near the same height.

His hand slipped into my hair and held the back of my head. My eyes fluttered shut, but I opened them again so I wouldn't miss anything.

His lips caressed my cheek, my jaw. They passed lightly over my mouth and across my other cheek. My arms went around his shoulders and his arm pressed against my lower back, pulling me closer.

Our bodies brushed, our lips met, and something broke free in me and soared, like the falcon taking flight. It rose up and up, close enough to touch the sun.

I trembled and nestled against his shoulder with a sigh. He stroked his hand down my back and his breath warmed my ear. "I guess that means you're willing to take a chance with me."

"Yes." I pressed a kiss to his neck and breathed in the scent of him, warm and earthy and male. I wanted to burrow close and never leave.

He kissed my cheek, my neck, my mouth. After a while, he took a deep breath. "I have to ask—you said you hadn't dated much. Does that mean you've never ..." He gave a half laugh and shook his head. "It doesn't matter either way, I just figure I should know."

My face must have been flaming, but it was a fair question. If we couldn't talk about sex, we shouldn't have it. "No. I mean, I have. But not with anyone important." I put my hands on my hot cheeks. "That sounds terrible. What I mean is, I dated a couple of guys, and I'm not good at saying no, so ... stuff happened. With two guys."

He scowled and I wondered if he had expected better of me. He took my arms. "You can always say no to me. About anything. You have the right to say no."

I couldn't take my eyes off his face. I said softly, "With you, I don't think I'll want to."

He shifted his weight off the tailgate, turned, and before I was quite sure what had happened, I found myself sitting on the tailgate with him standing between my spread knees. He kissed me again, deep and slow, until I felt like I was flying and falling all at once.

He leaned his forehead against mine and our breath mingled, smelling faintly of piñon coffee. He stroked his hand down my face, along my neck, and across my collarbone. He kissed his way down my cheek and the side of my neck, up my throat, and to my mouth again. His kiss seared into me like a brand. I felt like part of him. No, part of something new and bigger that we were creating between us. I hooked my arm behind his neck, opening to him, making promises.

He eased back, his breathing harsh.

I blinked, trying to focus. "Are we stopping?"

"Unless you really want me to take you on my tailgate in the middle of an empty field."

"Well, when you put it like that." I smiled. "Actually, the idea is surprisingly tempting."

He chuckled. "Not that I'm exactly opposed to it, but I didn't bring protection, and anyway maybe we could be a little more conventional our first time. Say, dinner and conversation? Whatever night you're free." He ran his fingers lightly down the side of my face. "And then, if you still want to, I'll be glad to take you to bed."

"Pretty sure I'll want to."

The bird screeched behind us. I wondered if it had been screaming this whole time, and I hadn't noticed.

"We should get Junior home." Kyle stroked the back of a finger down my cheek.

I smiled at him, so full of joy I could hardly contain it. I took his face in my hands and pressed my lips to his, hoping to convey some of what I couldn't put into words. When I finished, he gave a lazy sigh, and I thought another shadow had left his eyes.

He pulled me off the tailgate and nestled me close, pressing his cheek against my hair. We stood like that for a minute, just being together.

We got into the truck and he started it up. I noticed how competent he seemed one-handed. I decided to start practicing not being embarrassed.

"Were you right-handed or left-handed – before?"

"Right-handed, fortunately. That made things easier, though I never realized how much I used the other hand until I couldn't."

"Have you thought about getting a ..." I opened and closed my hand, trying to remember the right word. "Prosthetic?"

"Sure, I have a simple one with a hook, actually. It's handy, no pun intended, but it doesn't exactly attract less attention or make me feel more normal. I'm being fitted for a high-tech one that looks like a hand. It will read signals from my muscles, and when I get the hang of it, I'll be able to grab things, hold things. But after the accident happened, I needed time to heal enough that it wasn't so painful having anything on my wrist. And then I wanted to get used to being this way. To come to terms with it – own it."

He leaned forward as he eased the truck onto the paved road. "That's not quite true. At first I wanted to hide it. I wouldn't go out in public. After I gave up the drugs and spent more time with a counselor, I realized I'd never come to terms with it unless I could live out in the open like this."

He grinned at me. "And it's nice knowing I don't have to figure out when to tell you about it, or worry about how you'll react."

"If you'd asked me a week ago, I might have said it would bother me," I admitted. "But for some reason it doesn't."

He didn't say anything, just smiled. I wondered about the accident where he'd lost his hand. I'd ask him about it sometime, give him a chance to talk about the things he'd been through, the way he'd given me a chance to talk. But not yet. I didn't want to break the peace of this moment.

After a comfortably quiet drive, we pulled up in front of his house. "Thanks again for an amazing morning – all of it." I looked down and added, "I hope we can get together soon for that dinner and conversation and … whatever."

"I've changed my mind about one thing."

I looked up and he laughed at my expression. "Not about wanting you," he added. "About you saying no."

"Um … oh?"

He leaned closer. "It's not enough that you don't say no. I want you to say yes. I want you to look me in the eyes and tell me exactly what you want."

I half laughed. "I'm not sure I can do that."

His slow grin curled my toes. "I bet you can, if you want something badly enough. And that's my job – to make you want me enough."

"Ah. Okay." That should be interesting. The storm of the last week hadn't blown over, but the clouds sure had one heck of a silver lining.

Thirty-Three

I hurried into work carrying my good clothes. If I changed quickly in my office I could be ready to start work at eight. I passed through the lobby thinking of Kyle, wondering what I'd gotten myself into, and hoping my passionate morning didn't show on my face.

I heard a sharp, excited voice from the check-in desk, and then the room went silent. Even the people milling around the lobby seemed to pause in sudden awareness. I faltered, glancing toward reception.

Gina and another woman behind the counter were staring at me. A familiar figure leaned against the counter. He turned his head and smiled slowly. Jay.

I kept moving. Something was wrong, but I didn't know what. My only defense was to pretend I hadn't noticed. I made it around the corner to the hall before I started to tremble. Jay. Just when I thought he'd backed off, that he'd realized his best bet was to keep quiet, he was stirring up trouble again. But what?

First things first. I went into my office and closed the door. Got into my office clothes. Touched up my makeup. Turned on my computer. Tried not to think.

I glanced over my schedule. I had an initial meeting for a wedding at ten. Final planning for Saturday's "big game hunt" event with Eslinda and the catering team in the afternoon. E-mails and calls to answer and paperwork to prepare or review in between the meetings. A full day.

I did not want to deal with Jay. It was tempting to pretend I hadn't noticed him, to go about my business and hope that whatever trouble he was stirring up would fade if I ignored it. But I had a feeling Jay was not a problem that would quietly go away.

I reminded myself that he was a coward and a bully. The one time I'd yelled at him, he'd backed down, at least for a while. It was better to deal with someone like that head on.

My stomach hurt.

Before I faced Jay directly, I wanted to know what I was dealing with. Eslinda had promised to protect me if Jay's father tried to fire me. And Nascha had offered her help. I didn't have to face this alone. I could gather my posse.

Twenty minutes later we sat in Eslinda's office. Nascha reported what she'd learned on a quick reconnaissance. "Jay is saying you found Bethany Moore's car."

"That's right. With my mother and brother's help."

Nascha hesitated. "He's saying you knew where it was all along. That it proves you were involved in her death."

Leave it to Jay to latch onto that. I tried to keep my voice steady. "The police suggested something like that."

"That's ridiculous!" Eslinda said.

"I certainly think so."

Nascha leaned forward. "Here's the thing. I read in this morning's paper that the car had been found. But it didn't say anything about who found it. So how did Jay know it was you?"

How indeed? I remembered the dark sedan driving with its lights off while the police were interviewing us. "What kind of car does Jay drive?"

Nascha said, "You mean you haven't seen the flashy red sports car he always parks across two spaces so no one will park too close? He couldn't afford something like that on a groundskeeper's salary, so I assume it was a gift from Daddy."

"And Lewis drives a silver BMW," Eslinda said.

So much for that idea. I still had a feeling someone was keeping an eye on me. I remembered what I'd been doing with Kyle, and my stomach churned at the thought of someone witnessing our private moment, but we'd been in the middle of nowhere, without a single car or person around.

I had to focus. The first problem was Jay and this rumor. "Maybe he has friends at the police station."

"Maybe," Nascha admitted.

"Does Jay have a grudge against you for some reason?" Eslinda asked. "Other than the fact that you reported the body when he didn't want to, that is."

"I would've said he barely knew who I was until a week ago. We didn't run in the same circles." I rubbed my hands over my face. "Back in high school, he was such a sports hotshot. He was going to play college basketball, maybe go all the way to the NBA. But he didn't even go to college, did he? What happened?"

Nascha and I looked to Eslinda for the answer. She tapped her pen on her desk and squinted as if peering into her memories. "I seem to recall Lewis saying that Jay had gotten a scholarship, but they turned it down because it wasn't good enough, or wasn't a big enough school. They were holding out for something better. I guess it never came."

That was kind of sad. I might have felt sorry for him if it was someone else.

Eslinda sighed. "That boy is spoiled and sneaky, but I can't believe he's involved in a murder."

I considered the idea, as I had before, and once again put it aside with some regret. "I have to agree. And not only because it makes me sick to think I might've been out there in the woods alone with a murderer and his victim. It doesn't make sense. Why would he take me out there to discover the body and then refuse to report it? Why would he keep harassing me?"

Nascha frowned. "Maybe he's trying to set you up for the murder."

I gripped the arms of my chair as the world blurred for a moment. Nascha added, "But why you? You're about the least likely person. Why not pick on one of Bethany's friends or boyfriends or let the police focus on that other guy, Thomas Bain?"

"I don't know, but this is ridiculous. I have enough to deal with without fighting off rumors." I was glad I'd told Kyle about finding the car, so he didn't hear Jay's version first, even though I didn't think Kyle would be swayed by gossip. What about Nancy and Daniel? I didn't want to put it to the test when they barely knew me. And as for

Bethany and Kyle's parents, and the people at work, and the rest of town –

"This has to stop." I stood. "I need to know how Jay is involved in all this, if he is. If he had anything to do with Bethany's murder, he needs to go to jail. If he didn't, I need to figure out what else is going on and stop it."

Eslinda blinked up at me. "Are you sure that's wise? Rumors can't really hurt you, and if you ignore them people will get interested in something else. The police will catch the murderer."

"The police are taking too long." I wanted to do my job without my coworkers wondering if I was a dangerous criminal. I didn't want to make Eslinda and Nascha choose sides in defending me. I wanted to be part of Kyle's life and to be welcomed in his home with no questions or suspicions.

"I've got a life and I'm ready to get on with it," I said. "I'm going after Jay."

Thirty-Four

"How?" Nascha asked.

I stared at her and let out a weak laugh. "You would have to ask that. Here I am ready for battle, and you have to mess it up with sensible questions?"

She smiled. "I'm not trying to discourage you. Jay has to go down, and I'll hold him while you kick him if that's what it takes. I just want to know what you have in mind."

I sank back into my chair. "I have no idea. Snoop, I guess." I frowned over that. "What am I looking for? What could help?"

"I doubt he keeps a journal about his crimes and plans," Eslinda said.

"No, but maybe there's other evidence?" I thought over everything that had happened. "The knife that punctured my tires – maybe it would still have rubber on it? A tool to cut brake lines?"

"He might keep a tool kit in his car, but it has an alarm system," Nascha said. "I've heard it go off. But he might carry a knife with him, or leave it in his office – come to think of it, he probably has all kinds of tools in the greenhouse. Knives, clippers and things for working with the plants. Maybe even the murder weapon!"

I shivered and rubbed my forearms. I couldn't tell them what I knew about the murder weapon, but a gun could certainly be evidence. I'd have no way of knowing if it was the right gun, but if I found one, I could tip off the police. That seemed like wishful thinking, though. "I wouldn't recognize evidence unless it's pretty obvious. It's not like we have access to a forensics lab." I wasn't even sure the local police did.

"You don't want to mess with evidence anyway," Eslinda said. "That would ruin it for the police."

I groaned. "This is hopeless!" I remembered Jay saying I didn't know what was going on. He was all too right. I straightened. "I don't care. I have to do something. If I look, maybe I'll find something, even if I don't know what I'm looking for yet. Maybe there's something to connect him to Bethany – e-mails or phone messages. She's a few years older, but not that much. Jay smokes pot and Bethany did drugs. They could be connected. If I can get on Jay's computer, look around his office ..." I shrugged. "Or am I crazy to even think about this?"

"A little crazy," Eslinda confirmed. "But desperate times, desperate measures and all that. I'm not saying I approve, but I don't have a better idea."

"When will you try?" Nascha asked.

"Some time when Jay isn't in the greenhouse. Or that other guy, Rodrigo. Can't forget about him. I suppose they lock it at night. I'm not quite up for breaking and entering."

"I can call a meeting." Eslinda peered at her calendar. "It will have to be at four o'clock. Let's see, we don't need any greenery for the big game hunt, but maybe ... the Martinez fiftieth anniversary. I'll say they're looking for something unusual and different, with some live plants." She looked across at me. "I'll insist they both come. I can buy you half an hour. Maybe longer, but no guarantees. And I know *nothing* about this."

"You're the best."

"I'll go with you," Nascha said. "I might be able to help with the computer. In fact, give me five minutes alone with Marty the computer guy, and I bet I can get Jay's password."

I grinned. "You're both the best!"

Eslinda put her hands over her ears. "I didn't hear any of that. I hope you two realize what you're getting into. At least I'm retiring soon, so if this all blows up they can't fire me." She brightened. "Or if they did, I could collect unemployment for a while. Ha! Now let's get back to work. This conversation never happened."

I struggled to concentrate with all the stuff going through my head – my new relationship with Kyle, the nerve-racking plan to stop Jay, my discomfort at being the center of gossip. I hid in my office until four o'clock and waited for the e-mail from Eslinda letting me know that Jay and Rodrigo were safely trapped in her office. When the message came, I slipped down the hall and picked up Nascha.

As we passed the entryway to the lobby, something caught my eye. I paused and took a closer look.

Ricky.

"Hang on." I detoured into the lobby, but as soon as Ricky saw me he got up and walked toward the front doors. I almost called out, but the receptionist was watching me and I didn't need the extra attention.

I blinked in the bright sun outside and glanced around. No Ricky.

"Hey," he hissed, and I spotted him pressed against the wall. He waved me toward the corner of the building.

Nascha came out behind me. I glanced at her, shrugged, and followed Ricky.

We clustered around the corner. "Nascha, my brother Ricky," I said. "What are you doing here?"

"Waiting for you to get off work." At my look, he added, "And poking around." Eying Nascha, he held up a notebook. "I wanted to get a map of the place and figure out when all the workers would be here. I was pretending to be a guest. I thought you were going to give me away in front of everyone! What are you doing?"

I closed my eyes for a moment. If I told Ricky what we had planned, he'd want to help, and I didn't want to drag him deeper into this. But I didn't want Ricky snooping around on his own either. And we only had half an hour to get to the greenhouse, conduct our search, and get out of sight again. It might take that long to persuade Ricky to leave. Better to keep him close.

I sighed and gestured them to come with me to the greenhouse. I explained during the two-minute walk around to the back of the main resort.

"You can be a lookout," I said. "Stay outside the door and knock if you see anyone coming." That would keep him out of the worst of it, and it would be a help. Eslinda was supposed to call us when the guys left her office, but it would only take them a couple of minutes to get out of the building, and I liked the security of an extra warning. So far as I knew, Jay wouldn't recognize Ricky.

"Okay." Ricky kept glancing at Nascha, seeming more interested in her than in my instructions.

I paused at the greenhouse door and put a hand on his shoulder to get him to look at me. "Ricky, pay attention."

"I got it, I'm not a baby!"

I opened my mouth and shut it again. I would not point out that he *was* a child. I would not become my mother.

I looked around to make sure no one was watching. Other than a few distant golfers, I didn't see anyone. Nascha pushed open the greenhouse door, scanned the room, and motioned me through. We left Ricky leaning against the wall with his arms crossed.

I paused to let my eyes adjust to the dimmer green light. The scent of earth and growing things enveloped me. The sweetness of blooming flowers drifted on the heavy air. It was hard to believe that someone who spent his life growing things could be such a jerk, and maybe a murderer.

We passed between rows of plants. The door to Jay's office was closed. I tried to turn the handle. "Locked," I murmured. "We should've expected that."

Before I could turn away, Nascha had a set of keys in her hand. One went into the lock, and a moment later the door opened.

"Where did you get those?"

"I have the master keys, for inventory. But I doubt Jay knows that." She gave me a quick smile. "And don't worry, it's not even breaking and entering. I'm allowed to go anywhere on resort property."

She led the way into the office and sat at Jay's desk, flexing her fingers. "All right, Mr. Former Basketball Star Who Thinks He's Still a Hotshot. Let's see if we can uncover your secrets."

While she tapped away, I looked around the office. A set of golf clubs leaned against the wall, reminding me of the near miss with the golf ball. It didn't prove anything; a lot of resort employees kept golf clubs handy so they could play nine holes after work. But given the timing of the "accident" – I had just left Jay angry in the greenhouse – Jay was at the top of my suspect list.

I turned to the file cabinet, putting my shirt over my hand to pull out the drawer so I wouldn't leave fingerprints. Probably pointless, but Ricky would approve. Nothing was locked, so it seemed unlikely Jay would hide anything in the drawers, but at least looking made me feel somewhat useful. Everything seemed legitimate – one drawer of purchase orders, one full of notes on plant health, and one with catalogs for gardening companies. Jay seemed to know his job.

I checked the time. It was already 4:20. I glanced around the cluttered office. Jay could have something hidden in one of the boxes stacked against the wall, but we didn't have time to shift things around. I started glancing in the boxes on top. "Anything yet?" I asked Nascha.

"I searched his e-mail for Bethany or Moore and didn't find anything. I'm looking through some of his files. He keeps excellent records. The guy isn't an idiot. Nothing suspicious so far, though this is a little peculiar. He has a huge folder of documents tracking tomato growth. I know he grows some of the food for the restaurant, but nothing else gets that much attention."

"Odd, but not really relevant. I'll go search the main room, maybe look at his tools." I didn't really expect to be able to tell if one of them had been used to damage my car. But if we didn't learn something fast, I'd have to put up with Jay's harassment. Even if we uncovered a minor infraction of resort rules, I'd have something to hold over him in return for his silence. So far his only shortcoming seemed a tendency to clutter.

I stepped out into the greenhouse. A head popped up from between the rows.

I yelped and stumbled back against the office doorframe. "Ricky! You're supposed to be waiting outside."

"I want to help search. This investigation was my idea."

"And you were helping – as lookout."

He rolled his eyes. "You were trying to keep me out of here. I told you, I'm not a little kid. I can help for real."

What was this sudden obsession with how old he was? Then his gaze went past me and he straightened, a strange look on his face. I glanced back to see Nascha behind me. Oh great – was my little brother really trying to impress my grown-up friend?

Nascha and Ricky said at the same time, "I think I found something."

Thirty-Five

I looked from one to the other. Nascha nodded at Ricky. "You first."

"Okay. You see how these other tables are open underneath, with storage for pots and bags of soil and things? Well, in this row, the bottom is covered with these pieces of plastic, but it looks like you can take them off."

Nascha and I joined him. He was right; most of the long tables had open storage underneath, but the row of tables set against this far wall had the undersides blocked off with thin panels of three-by-six-foot plastic. "See, it's just hanging on these hooks," Ricky said. "There's an extension cord going under the bottom, that's why I noticed."

I helped him lift the panel away, and we crouched to look underneath the table. "More plants," I said.

Nascha reached past me and flipped a switch on a grow light mounted to the underside of the table. The long tube flickered on, lighting up the lush plants in hydroponic containers. Something about the long, serrated leaves made me pause. "Wait a minute."

"Not just any plants," Nascha said. She leaned under the table to look down the length of the row. "Jay is growing a very nice crop of marijuana."

I sat back on my heels. "Of course! He works with plants. He smokes pot. It makes sense that he'd grow his own, and if he's used to managing a greenhouse, why wouldn't he grow marijuana for sale? No wonder he didn't want to attract any attention from the police."

Nascha nodded. "That's what I suspected from his records. I finally remembered something about tomatoes. That's a code word growers use for pot, I think because the plants have similar requirements. Jay has been running a huge operation right here, where he can order lights and soil and fertilizer without anyone suspecting anything."

She stood and brushed her hands on her slacks. "His assistant must be involved as well."

I rose, still trying to wrap my brain around what we'd discovered. My phone vibrated in my pocket and I jumped. I fumbled for it. "It's Eslinda! Hello?"

"They're leaving, hurry!"

I almost dropped the phone. "They're coming!" Ricky grabbed the plastic cover and pushed it against the table. Nascha ran for the office door with her keys jingling.

"They're already down the hall," Eslinda hissed. "They're using the side door. They'll be out on the lawn in a second!"

"Okay, bye." I shoved the phone back in my pocket and helped Ricky attach the cover. Once the men were out on the lawn, they'd have a decent view of the greenhouse. "Hurry." I pushed Ricky toward the door.

Nascha was already there. She opened the door a crack and peered out. "Too late. They'll see us if we leave."

My head spun. I wasn't ready to confront Jay yet, and who knew what the two men would do if they realized we'd discovered their secret. We didn't have time to call the police and explain things before being discovered. And there was no other exit.

"Hide," Nascha said. We scrambled away from the door and hid in the farthest row, near the marijuana.

My heart thumped as I tried to control my breathing so they wouldn't hear the rasping. The seconds ticked away slowly and my thighs started to burn from crouching. Maybe they weren't coming back after all. It was nearly five; maybe they'd head home for the day. Or maybe they were standing outside, having a smoke. Maybe they were almost at the door, and if we went to check they'd open it in our faces.

My calves felt uncomfortably stretched. I needed to shift into another position, especially if we'd be stuck for a while. Ricky was on his hands and knees. Nascha sat cross-legged, which looked more comfortable. I shifted my weight back.

The door creaked open. I sat down hard and bit back a grunt that was fortunately covered by Jay's voice. "... why they can't just send an e-mail. Let's shut down and get out of here."

Through the gaps between boxes, pots, and bags stored under the tables, I saw his legs turn toward the office. The other set of legs went in the opposite direction, toward the big racks of equipment. I knew from the previous time I'd snuck in that someone back there wouldn't have a clear view of the room or the door. But could we get out before either of them came back?

If we waited, they might leave without ever seeing us. Or they might check the whole room before leaving. I glanced back and saw switches on the wall behind us, probably for lights or water systems. Jay had said, "shut down."

I gestured Ricky toward the door. He nodded, his face pale and oddly tinged in the greenish light, and started crawling.

My hands came down on loose dirt and stray woodchips. The cement floor was painful under my knees. My shoes dragged across the floor with a faint scraping sound.

I shifted into a crouch and shuffled forward, bent over, right behind Ricky. I could barely hear Nascha's soft breathing behind us.

As we passed between the last rows, I glanced to the right and saw Rodrigo, turned away from us and half hidden among the equipment racks. My heart jumped and I wanted to leap forward, but with Ricky right in front of me I could only keep waddling. A second later Ricky was at the door. Escape was in reach.

I heard a door close to our left and then the sound of a handle turning as someone checked to be sure the door was locked. Ricky glanced back at me with huge eyes, one hand resting on our exit. To our right I heard the shuffle of feet on cement. Nascha crowded close behind me.

I waved Ricky forward. He pushed past the door on hands and knees. I shoved through after him and tried to haul him up with me as I stood. Nascha squeezed out behind us, and before the door swung shut we were running.

"Left!" Nascha gasped as we neared the corner of the greenhouse. I glanced back as we swung around it and thought I saw the greenhouse door opening, though I couldn't be sure from that brief, blurred glimpse. Nascha pointed at a door in the back of the resort. She sorted through her keys as we cut across the lawn at an angle. I looked back as she unlocked the door and thought I saw a shadow through the translucent plastic panes on the corner of the greenhouse. Then we tumbled through the door and pulled it shut behind us.

We paused, gasping. I'd never used this door before so it took me a few seconds to recognize the hallway that led past the employee break room and then connected to the hall with our offices. "That was close," Nascha said.

"I don't think they saw us."

Sweat beaded Ricky's flushed face, but he grinned. "That was great!"

I leaned against the door, waiting for the trembling to stop, and shook my head. "I don't agree with your idea of fun. But at least we did find something. I can't believe he would run that operation from here!"

Nascha pushed her hair back from her face. "It's crazy, but smart, too. What place is better than this? We live in the mountains, with snow in winter and not enough rain in summer, so he can't simply pick a remote spot in the wilderness. He has everything he needs here, and he doesn't have to keep the pot in his house. Even now, it will be hard to prove he's the one responsible. No one will believe he didn't know about it, but a good lawyer could make the case for circumstantial evidence."

I sighed. "Well, at least it should keep him distracted for a while."

"You're right. But Audra, let me report this. You've attracted enough attention, and enough trouble from Jay's father."

"I won't argue with that, but Mr. Preppard will be after you if you get his son in trouble."

She shrugged. "I do excellent work and I have friends here. And if I do lose this job, it's not the end of the world.

I can go somewhere else. You want to stay here with your family."

I looked at Ricky. "All right. But you know the police will ask how you found this. It's hard to explain without telling everything. I learned that when I tried to report the body and leave Jay out of it."

"I won't lie, and no doubt they'll want to talk to you. But we can try to keep your part quiet around here. I'll make sure the police understand why that's important."

"Thank you."

Nascha tried to brush the dirt off her backside. "So what, if anything, does this have to do with Bethany Moore's death?"

I thought a moment and then let out a long sigh. "Probably nothing," I admitted. "If Jay had killed her, he surely wouldn't lead me to her body when he had this to hide. But I guess the police can decide for sure. They have a good excuse to investigate him now. Maybe they'll find something to tie him to Bethany."

The police might try to tie the two cases together. That would be easy and neat. But I found it hard to believe Jay had anything to do with the murder. That meant the killer was still out there, walking free.

Thirty-Six

The next morning, the rumors were all about Jay. Neither he nor his father showed up to work. A police officer was stationed at the greenhouse. The media moved in, but security guards tried to keep the cameras contained in the parking lot. With Mr. Preppard absent, Eslinda took over as spokesperson, expressing shock and dismay that such a thing could happen on resort property, laying the blame on a rogue employee – because of course such a thing would never be tolerated by management – and vowing complete cooperation with the police.

When things finally settled down, she came into my office and collapsed in the guest chair. "I know you wanted to stop Jay, but really? Turning the resort into a circus is a bit extreme."

I winced. "I'm sorry. We had no idea we'd find—"

She waved me to silence. "Not your fault. It might have been nice to handle this quietly – fire Jay and Rodrigo, remove the evidence, pretend nothing happened – but that would make us all accessories to a crime." She sighed. "They want to know if this had anything to do with the murder."

I looked down at the paper on my desk, where I'd been absently drawing curlicues in the margin. "What did you say?"

She sat up straight, opened her eyes wide, and somehow managed to look young and a bit silly. "I put on my best innocent look and said *I* didn't see any connection." She slumped down again and closed her eyes.

"I'm sorry I got you and the resort involved in this. I'm sorry it's making us all look bad."

She didn't open her eyes. "Oh well. You can't buy publicity like this. That's what I'm telling the directors." She settled deeper in the chair and yawned. "Maybe we can set up a crime tour package. Could be good business."

"I think I want to be like you when I grow up."

She gave a sly smile. "Oh honey, you can wish." She sat up and clapped her hands. "Back to work. What have I missed?"

I glanced at my notes. "The caterers are worked up because they don't know if they'll have access to salad greens and herbs from the greenhouse. I told them to make other arrangements for the rest of this week."

"Good."

"At least it doesn't matter for the big game hunt event, because we have the outside vendors."

"Not like that crowd would be eating organic greens and fresh herbs anyway." Eslinda sighed. "I wish that wasn't this weekend. All those macho men in fatigues, guns, the idea of violence – it's bad timing. I wish we had something nice and sophisticated, like a wine tasting, or a family-friendly day of magicians and jugglers."

"I'm not crazy about hunting anyway." Okay, technically I'd been hunting with Kyle, but that was different. "But at least they won't actually be hunting during the event."

"No, just playing with guns."

The hunting season wouldn't start until August, with a brief window for bears, and then it picked up in October for elk hunting. The resort set up packages on the Reservation with Native guides and provided lodging, meals, and transportation. They even had people to pack out the meat, dress it, and mail it to the hunters' homes.

With limited hunting licenses available for the big animals, and the deadline for applications coming up soon, the "big game hunt" event that Saturday was more of a fair, with displays, safety training, talks by the guides, and carnival-style games for the kids. Still, I could see what Eslinda meant about bad timing. The big game hunts had a high profit margin, but they were a small part of our business, and given the resort's recent association with drugs and murder, any suggestion of violence might hurt the reputation.

"I don't see what we can do about it," I said.

"No. Except make it as family-friendly as possible. Promote the games for kids and encourage women to participate as well, so we can't be accused of encouraging male violence. Invite any women you know. How about your mother?"

"That could be interesting."

My phone beeped, signaling an incoming text. I glanced at it and saw a message from Kyle. "Baby falcon born this morning. Come see after work? Bring Ricky."

I smiled. A baby falcon had to be adorable. I looked across at Eslinda. "Hey, I have an idea. I know this really neat lady who keeps falcons and hawks. Maybe she'd bring one of them to the event and talk about it. She could focus on how the falconers are helping preserve wild lands and how they saved the peregrine from extinction."

"Hmm, play up the conservation angle. And it's a woman? That could help balance out the testosterone." She stood. "See if she'll do it."

"I'll talk to her after work." As Eslinda left, I started texting Kyle. Of course I wanted to see the baby, and Ricky would be thrilled. Bringing him meant this wouldn't turn into a real date, but it was nice that Kyle wasn't solely focused on getting me alone. I could ask Nancy about Saturday. She'd make a better spokesperson for falconry than Kyle under these circumstances, but maybe he'd come as well. And maybe afterward we could spend some time alone together.

And see if I could answer his challenge to letting him know what I wanted.

Ricky couldn't keep still as we drove out after work. "I want to take pictures. And video." He bounced and fidgeted in his seat. "Do you think she'll let me?"

"Probably. But make sure you ask permission before you share anything online."

He jumped out to open the gate. As he closed it behind us, I watched him in the rearview mirror, smiled, and started pulling ahead. He ran after the car, laughing. I parked down by the house and got out as he came panting up. "I thought you needed to burn off some energy," I said.

He tried to poke me in the side but I dodged, slung an arm around his shoulders, and turned him toward the house. The door opened and Nancy waved to us. "Well if it isn't two of my new favorite people! Come in, come in." Her beaming smile suggested she had a good idea of my developing relationship with Kyle. I wasn't sure whether to be embarrassed, or flattered that she obviously approved.

My heart speeded up as I looked for Kyle, but Daniel was the only one in the kitchen. I suspected he was responsible for the mouthwatering smell of chocolate chip cookies, which was enough to make anyone feel welcome. I could hardly blame him for my disappointment.

Nancy said, "Kyle will be home any minute." Obviously he'd inherited his ability to read my mind from his grandmother. "Which first," she asked, "cookies or falcon chick?"

Ricky hesitated, eyeing the plate of oversized cookies on the table, but finally said, "The falcon chick, please."

I expected Nancy to head back outside, to the building where the birds lived, but instead she led the way down the hall and into a small room that had the same zoo-like mustiness as the bird building, though fainter. She crouched by a rubber tub, lifted the lid, and pulled out something. She set the thing down on a towel. It was a scraggly bit of white fuzz about four inches long.

Ricky and I knelt beside her. The thing twitched, proving it was alive, but it looked more like something you would sweep out from under the bed than a living creature. When it shifted I finally spotted a tiny beak. This little thing would eventually take to the skies as a powerful hunter?

"Born this morning," Nancy said proudly. "We'll keep it in here for three days, to make sure its insides are working properly, and then take it back to its mother. It's time for a feeding. They get fed five times a day." She rummaged in a mini fridge and came out with a dish of chopped meat. She scooped up the falcon baby in one hand, holding it in a loose fist so the little head poked up. She took metal forceps in her other hand, plucked a tiny piece of meat, and held it over the chick.

"What does it eat?" Ricky asked.

"Quail meat. You have to keep it sterile because they don't have an immune system yet." She leaned closer and made a repetitive keening sound.

The little falcon gave a faint, high screech and opened its miniature beak. Nancy dropped in the meat. "Falcons use sound to attract the baby to food, so I do the same. Hawks use motion, so you wave the meat over its head."

"Can I take pictures?" Ricky asked.

"Of course!"

He started taking photos with his phone. I wouldn't have called the little thing cute, exactly, but it was certainly fascinating, especially when you knew how it would grow up.

I caught motion out of the corner of my eye and glanced over to see Kyle. My heart bumped, and a quick flush warmed my body. I rose and crossed behind Nancy and Ricky to him. "Hi," I whispered.

"Hi." He glanced at Nancy and Ricky and then motioned down the hall. Halfway down, he pulled me into a room and closed the door behind us. I barely had time to recognize the room as a bedroom before he backed me against the wall. "Hi," he said again, his voice rougher. His arms enclosed me and we kissed.

I leaned against the wall as my legs went weak. His hand slid around the back of my head as he deepened the kiss.

Some time later he leaned his forehead against mine with a sigh. "I need you. I didn't realize how much I need—" He broke off and stepped away. "I'm sorry, that's not fair."

"What – what isn't?"

He sank into a chair. "Putting that burden on you. Making you responsible for my happiness. You were good enough to accept me as I am, to give me a chance, and I want more. I'm demanding too much, too soon." He gave a long sigh. "I know I have to find happiness and peace inside myself. I want you in my life, but I don't expect you to make everything better. I'll take what you're ready to give, and I won't ask for more."

I watched him as he cradled his arm against his stomach, covering his stump with his other hand. His impairment obviously bothered him more than he sometimes let on.

Something shifted in my heart. He was right when he said he wasn't a hero. He was a man, and that was better.

If he thought I pitied him, that would make matters worse. But I couldn't let him back away from the fragile bond we had out of some mistaken sense that he was making things easier on me.

I took a step closer. "You said I needed to practice saying no. How can I if you won't ask for anything?" He looked up and I held his gaze. "I'd rather you ask, or tell me what you want, than make me guess. I'm no good at guessing." I took another step.

I read longing in his face, but the hesitation lingered, too, and his voice came out low and raw. "You make me want to be the best man I can be."

I eased myself down onto his lap. "I'm glad. But I don't want to wait until you get there. I'd rather help you along the way." I pressed a kiss to his temple and felt him relax. But I couldn't stop yet.

"You once told me not to make you a hero. Don't make me a saint. I'm as flawed and messed up as you are. Maybe more. I'm trying to figure out how to be an adult, how to handle my mother, how to help my brother. When to do things on my own and when to ask for help. Who to trust. I don't have the answers, just a lot of questions. But maybe we can figure things out together?"

"Yes." He put his arms around me and rested his head against my shoulder. "I'm sorry. I'm in some pain today. It makes me cranky and discouraged. It makes me doubt myself and the people around me."

He nestled me close with a sigh. "But being with you makes me feel like I'm home." He gave a short laugh. "Maybe I should clarify that, since you've met my parents. It's the feeling I had when I got back to American soil. When I flew into Albuquerque and saw the mountains and desert spread out below before we landed. When I got back to town and knew this is where I belong, after trying so hard to get away. It's how I feel here, with Gran and Daniel."

I rubbed my hand over his chest and shoulder, needing to touch. "I'm flattered. But ..."

He shifted so we could see each other better. "What?"

I glanced away and then met his eyes. "You do realize that may be why you like me. The girl next door, so to speak. A memory of home." I stopped myself from adding, "nothing more" and prayed it wasn't true. I forced myself to hold his gaze. I could feel my heart beat, but I couldn't breathe.

Finally he spoke. "It might have started like that. But there's always been something about you that called to me, even in high school. A sweetness, an honesty. Your face shows everything you're thinking." A smile tugged at the corners of his mouth. "I bet you're a terrible liar."

I made a face. "So I'm told."

He chuckled. "I like that. I'm tired of secrets and being careful of what I can say and how I can say it."

"You mean the military?"

"Yes, and before that, my parents, and high school. I'm tired of trying to fit in, keeping things buried, pretending everything is okay when it's not. I can't do that anymore if I'm going to stay sober. I have to be honest with myself, so I need someone who will be honest with me."

I brushed my fingers down his cheek. "Apparently I'm not capable of being dishonest, at least for long, so I guess that works. And I need someone who will encourage me to talk, to say what I really think. Otherwise I tend to freeze up and keep quiet." I cradled his cheek in my hand, enjoying the faint rough stubble against my palm. "You do that for me."

"Then maybe we can make this work." He squeezed me tighter and a glint lit his eyes. "And besides, you're really pretty. Plus, breasts. Can't go wrong there."

I chuckled and leaned in to nuzzle his neck. "And you smell really good. That drives me wild."

"What more could we ask for? It sounds like the perfect basis for a relationship."

Thirty-Seven

Everybody went to the big game hunt day. Mom and Ricky, Nancy, Daniel, and Kyle, Eslinda and Nascha, and a good portion of the town.

Well, maybe not everyone. I didn't see Jay, his father, or Rodrigo. When I asked Eslinda if she'd heard anything, she said Jay and Rodrigo had officially been fired, and Jay's father was taking vacation time. Nascha added that Jay and Rodrigo had been arrested but Jay at least had been released on bail.

I scanned the crowd again, glad that Jay was tall and would stand out. "Great, now I'll be looking over my shoulder all the time." I wanted to believe that Jay would back off, but his prior behavior made it equally likely he would try to get revenge.

"He can't afford to harass you," Nascha said. "Not with the police keeping an eye on him."

"I hope he realizes that," I muttered.

"Don't worry. When I reported the drugs, I told the police that Jay had been bothering you. They promised to warn him to keep his distance. He knows he has to be a model citizen to have any chance of avoiding jail. Plus, they'll be asking questions about cut brake lines and Bethany Moore. That should keep him busy. And it's the same with Rodrigo. *His* best chance is to pretend he was following Jay's orders and either didn't know the plants were marijuana, or didn't know about them at all."

I relaxed a little, though my shoulders still felt tight. "So I only have to deal with Jay's father."

Eslinda put her hands on her hips. "Lewis Preppard will be busy trying to hold onto his job and keep his son out of jail. It won't be easy to do both. If Lewis defends Jay too strongly, people are going to wonder if he was involved, too. The directors are already hinting that an early retirement might be appropriate."

My shoulders dropped a little more. It wasn't over, but at least I had friends – and the law – on my side. "I hope you're both right. But I still can't quite figure out how I got into all this. Each step seemed logical enough at the time, but when combined with what other people were doing and some random events, suddenly I've uncovered a murder and a drug ring."

Eslinda frowned. "Is it a ring if there were only two of them?" She came across as a little flaky, but I'd seen how she orchestrated big events, keeping on top of a thousand details and handling glitches with a smile.

"I bet people underestimate you all the time."

She giggled. "It makes it easier to get what you want. Anyway, this whole thing. Murder and drugs and getting involved. You do what you have to do. You can't do more, you shouldn't do less."

She smiled, her round face cheerful and comforting "It reminds me of a song I like. 'Did you stand up for what's right? Can you sleep at night? To your own heart be true, or regret what you failed to do.' I think of that when I'm tempted to be lazy or take the easy way out." She put her hand on my arm. "You didn't back away from trouble. You don't have to regret the things you didn't do – which is often harder than regretting the things you did."

I'd have to think about that. For the moment, I gave in to impulse and hugged her. "Thanks."

"You'll be all right," she said. "Now on to more important things. I want to meet that interesting lady with the bird."

We wove our way through the growing crowd. The fair looked like the summer festival the week before, with lots of food stands smelling of hot grease and cooking meat. Kids lined up for the duck shooting carnival game. A big tent provided shade for vendors advertising guns, ammo, and tour packages, and nonprofit groups or government representatives giving out information on wildlife conservation and hunting regulations.

Tribal members from the Reservation answered questions about their displays of traditional weapons, animal pelts, and blankets woven from turkey feathers. A wall of hay bales had been set up along the trees, and volunteers were helping kids and a few adults attempt to use atlatls, ancient spear throwers.

All in all, the event had a nice family-friendly feel, more educational than "let's go kill things." Nancy had set up under a small shade tent, and she had a crowd of admirers taking pictures of her beautiful rescued falcon.

Kyle kept a low profile but always seemed to be where he was needed, fetching an icy water bottle or answering visitors' questions while I took Nancy into the side entrance of the resort so she wouldn't have to use the portable toilets.

He joined Mom, Ricky, and me for a lunch of buffalo burgers and withstood Mom's probing with a quiet humor that didn't escape her notice. When we finished eating and rose to join the fray again, Mom turned to me and nodded once. I took that as a sign of approval. Disapproval wouldn't have stopped me from dating Kyle, but this made it easier.

Kyle and I stole a moment together while Nancy let Ricky try on the falconer's glove and Mom watched. "You're probably going to be exhausted tonight," Kyle said, stroking his hand lightly down my arm.

I leaned closer instinctively, even though I wanted to avoid obvious public displays of affection while on the job. "Yes. But I'd still like to see you. Just don't expect brilliant conversation." I could think of a few things we could do that didn't involve talking at all.

"How about a quiet dinner at my place, followed by some quiet cuddling?"

The energy sparked between us. "I have a feeling that might not stay so quiet. And that wasn't a complaint." I glanced at Mom, Ricky, and Nancy. Daniel had wandered off to talk to friends. As much as I cared for all of them, I wanted to be alone with Kyle that night – completely alone. They might suspect we were fooling around, but that didn't mean I wanted to advertise it.

I took a deep breath. "I know it's impossible to keep our relationship a secret, and I don't want to. But it strikes me as a bit awkward, conducting the, um, physical parts of that relationship when we're both living with other people." Maybe that wasn't the most coherent sentence ever, but at least I was sharing my concerns rather than fretting over them alone.

Kyle's eyebrows rose. "Didn't I tell you? Gran has an RV out behind the house. That's where I live, mostly. When I first got back I needed more help and didn't want to be alone a lot, so I used the guest bedroom in the house. I still sleep there sometimes if I'm having a bad night."

Somehow we'd shifted closer, so our bodies were almost touching. His wonderful spicy scent filled my senses, and the rest of the world seemed to recede. His voice was low and caressing. "They'll know you're there, unless we sneak you in, which could be entertaining. But at least we won't have to worry about, you know, being quiet."

I was breathing fast, my heart lightly hammering. "I'm usually pretty quiet anyway."

He dipped his head closer to murmur in my ear. "We'll see about that."

I gasped and he backed up with a grin. "Anyway," he said, "Sunday morning Daniel makes waffles, so I hope you'll stay the night. But if you don't want to do that, you can come back in the morning."

I glanced again at Mom. Things like this would be easier when I had my own place, but I couldn't wait until then to think and act like an adult. For me, that meant being honest about what I wanted and what I was doing. It might be awkward at times, but we'd work it out.

My gaze paused on Ricky. I understood why he'd kept his connection with his father a secret, and it might have been the right decision at the time, when Mom had the power to interfere. But I'd encourage him to be honest about it in the future. I thought Mom would tolerate the communication and maybe even think better of Richard for wanting it. Anyway, Ricky was old enough to demand his right to visit his father. It was better for Ricky to learn to ask for what he needed openly and not get too used to keeping secrets.

I looked back at Kyle, who was watching me solemnly. I looked into those sober gray eyes and knew the humor and the heartache behind them. My heart gave a little tremble. "I'll stay tonight."

His lips curved as he bent down to kiss me. It was a brief kiss, but warm and full of promise.

I eased back as Mom strode over to us. "Go relieve your grandmother," she told Kyle. "It's hot and I'm going to take her into the restaurant where she can relax with some iced tea."

"Good idea." He winked at me and went to take the falcon from Nancy.

"Keep an eye on your brother," Mom told me.

"Of course."

It looked as if Kyle would be busy for a while, so when Ricky wandered over, wanting to try some of the carnival games, I grabbed my tote bag and went with him. After trying a couple, we paused in the sliver of shade at the corner of the big display tent and I scanned the crowd, still half on the lookout for Jay. "So which game do you ..."

I trailed off as I spotted a figure standing alone near the path to the woods. The path that led to where Bethany Moore's body had been found.

Ricky must have followed my gaze. "Hey, it's that girl. Lia Bain."

Even at this distance, I was pretty sure he was right. She was short and curvy, in a tank top, miniskirt, and sneakers. Black hair hung down past her shoulders. She seemed to be staring at the path into the woods.

She turned. I ducked back so the corner of the tent offered some cover, but she seemed to scan the crowd without really looking in our direction. Something in her posture looked tight, hunched. Then she turned back toward the path, straightened like a soldier preparing for battle, and disappeared into the woods.

Ricky hurried forward. I scrambled to catch up. "What are you doing?"

"We have to follow her! She was acting really weird. They say criminals return to the scene of the crime!"

I grabbed his arm and hauled him to a stop. "We are not going into those woods."

He huffed out an impatient breath. "But this could be a clue! We could break the case."

"It's not safe."

He looked toward the path. "She was alone. And it didn't look like she was carrying a weapon."

He was right about that. She might have had a pocketknife, but her clothes were too revealing to hide much else. "If there's any chance she was involved in a murder, we are not going near her."

"Don't you want to solve this? Remember the car accident. We won't be safe until we catch the murderer."

Also true. "*We* don't have to catch anyone. We'll tell the police what we saw."

He rolled his eyes. "What good will that do? If she's removing evidence or something, she'll be long gone before we can get the police here."

I hesitated. He was making some good points, but it had to be a bad idea to go after someone who might be involved in a crime, even if she was a petite, eighteen-year-old girl in a miniskirt. Besides, I hadn't been near the woods in over a week and didn't want to start now. Even the thought of going back there made my stomach ache and sweat break out on my forehead. The memories and nightmares were bad enough without facing the reality.

"I'll go alone if you're afraid," Ricky said.

Given his mutinous expression, he would go whether or not I agreed. And I wasn't about to let him go in there alone. Whatever else happened, I needed to keep him away from danger. "No, I'll go."

Before he could argue, I held up a hand. "I need you to get Kyle. Tell him what's going on. And then find one of the security guards or the police." We might look foolish if it turned out Lia Bain was simply meeting a boyfriend, but I didn't want to take chances. Kyle would be easy to find and would understand the situation immediately. He could come after me while Ricky kept busy finding other help and explaining.

"You'll really go after her. You promise." His narrowed gaze said he didn't quite trust me.

I took a deep breath. "I promise. Now go get reinforcements."

"Use that recording app I put on your phone." He trotted away, but after a few steps looked back at me. I nodded and moved toward the woods. It looked as if I would have to face my nightmares, whether I wanted to or not.

Thirty-Eight

I turned down the path but stopped after a few feet. The trees seemed to close in, even though I knew I was steps away from open sky, green grass, and hundreds of people. I concentrated on breathing. The smells of the woods filled my nose, earth and grass and the sickly sweet scent of some wildflower, and under it all, the faint odor of decay.

Life and death. Perfectly natural there. Leaves fell, crumbled, and became dirt.

But the scent of smoke and cooking meat drifted from the fair and mixed with the earthy scents. I thought of all the death in the woods, animals, birds, insects, hunting and eating, or if something was lucky enough to survive to a natural death, lying on the forest floor while the insects took advantage of the free meal. My stomach churned.

Ricky wouldn't be able to see me where I was. I could wait for Kyle. He would be there in a moment, and then we could figure out what to do together. It wasn't cowardly to wait for help. It wasn't depending on a man to not want to face danger alone.

So maybe I didn't just want help. Maybe I wanted Kyle and the police to take over, to send me back to safety. Better to be a coward than to end up like Bethany Moore.

I took a couple of steps back and peered out at the crowds while still screened by the trees. The shrieks of children on the waterslide didn't quite cover the *pop-pop-pop* from the carnival-style shooting gallery.

I didn't see Kyle. What if Nancy had come back already, and Kyle had wandered off? What if he'd decided to take the falcon home, out of the heat? I pulled out my phone and sent a quick text. That way Kyle could be on the lookout for Ricky.

I turned back and stared down the path. Lia was probably only two or three minutes ahead of me. What was she doing? Was this really a clue to solving the murder? Whatever was happening, I was missing it.

I crept down the path. I had promised Ricky. And I wanted to know what Lia was doing. She was one unarmed girl, and I had at least six inches and a few pounds on her. Plus help on the way. I didn't even need to get close to her, just close enough to figure out what she was doing.

I sucked in a deep breath and let it out, trying to ignore the smells around me, trying to forget that other smell from my last trip down this path. The woods seemed strange, large and looming and silent, despite the faint sounds from the fair behind me. The trees seemed to be waiting, as I was.

"They're only trees," I whispered. My voice offered some measure of comfort, of company. I straightened my shoulders. "These are the same woods you've known your whole life. What are you going to do, avoid trees forever?"

I checked my phone. No answering text from Kyle. And no sound of people hurrying toward me, to the rescue. But they would be there any minute. Kyle and probably Ricky, if I knew my brother. If they found me here, ten feet in, they'd know how frightened I was. I would let Ricky down. Maybe Kyle, too – his sister had been murdered. Who could blame him for being upset if I was too cowardly to follow up on a clue that might expose the murderer? If he were here, he'd be running after Lia.

Or maybe sneaking. Sneaking was better. See what she was up to without being seen.

I took another deep breath and started forward, gripping the shoulder strap of my bag like a lifeline. I could sneak after Lia. She didn't even have to know I was there. Eslinda's words echoed in my mind. You do what you have to do. I couldn't let one unpleasant experience keep me from doing what I needed to do.

The path seemed to stretch forever. Had Jay and I really walked this far? We must have, because I hadn't come to the clearing yet. But somehow, with all my senses on high alert, the journey seemed much longer.

Finally the path got brighter up ahead, and I glimpsed the tall yellow grasses of the clearing. I glanced back down the path behind me. I didn't see anyone coming, but a curve in the path would hide them. They had to be on their way.

I edged forward, listening for the sound of anyone ahead. If Lia really had gone to the "scene of the crime," she'd be out of sight on the side path by now. And if she'd kept going along the main path, she could be far ahead, given my dawdling. But I still crept toward the clearing with my heart hammering. I tried to tell myself it was only that the clearing would feel more exposed, and not because I was getting closer to a lot of bad memories.

Finally I took the last step that brought me barely into the clearing. Something dark caught my eye. I turned my head and looked straight at Lia Bain.

We stared at each other, neither of us moving or speaking. I wasn't even breathing. I wanted to flee back down the path, but my legs felt numb. I should have acted surprised to see her, but it quickly became too late for that. And my brain couldn't come up with any excuse.

Lia lifted her chin. I saw the muscles work in her throat. "Is this where she was?"

"What?"

"Was she here?" Her voice trembled. "Bethany?" She looked very young despite – or maybe because of – the heavy makeup and revealing clothes. At eighteen she was legally an adult, but I remembered how young I'd been at eighteen.

I didn't know what she was doing there, what she really wanted, but I played along. "Not quite." I gestured into the woods. "Over there."

She pressed her lips together. Her chin rose another notch. "Show me."

I stared at her. I couldn't imagine why she wanted to see the spot where Bethany's body had been dumped. But I believed that she didn't already know. She hadn't been there. And for all her attempt at tough pride, she looked like she was about to cry. Something was bothering her greatly. If she knew something about the murder, or suspected something, she was ready to break.

I looked back down the path. Still no sign of Kyle or anyone else. And no sign of anyone else in the clearing or beyond, anyone that Lia might have been meeting.

I looked back at her and nodded. "Down that little path. You go first." Seeing her up close, I doubted she even had room for a pocketknife in her clothes, but I didn't want her behind me where she could pick up a branch or something and hit me before I knew she had it. While she had her back to me, I slipped my phone out of my bag and turned on the recording app. I stuck the phone in the breast pocket of my shirt. If Lia said anything important, I'd have it recorded.

When she came out into the smaller clearing with the fallen log, she stopped and looked around. "Here?"

I didn't look in the direction I pointed. "Over there. In that ditch."

She turned with a wary look, as if she was afraid something was going to jump out of the bushes at her. She hunched her shoulders, ducked her head, and stomped over there.

I lowered myself to the log, trembling. The clearing seemed to blur and dance in my vision. I concentrated on my breathing. I had to pull myself together if I was going to stay alert. I wished I had a mint or hard candy, something strong enough to overpower all the other smells and distract my senses.

Lia turned back. I glanced at her and caught a flutter of yellow behind the trees, police tape marking the crime scene. I looked away and tried not to see a memory.

After a moment Lia crossed the clearing and sat on the other end of the log. When she finally spoke, her voice was a whisper. "You found her."

I nodded.

"What was it like?"

I looked at her. "Horrible."

She made an impatient gesture with her hands. "What was *she* like." When I didn't answer right away, she said in a low, broken voice, "I have to know!"

I turned so I was focused on Lia, not the woods. "I smelled her first. Like rotting garbage left in the sun too long, like spoiled meat."

She flinched. But she'd wanted to know. It was important for some reason I didn't quite understand.

"She didn't look human. There were clothes and hair. Her hand curled on her chest, but wrong somehow. Her skin was green." I swallowed and told myself I would not throw up. "Something ... something wrong with her face," I whispered. I touched my chin. "The lower part of it missing."

Tears ran down Lia's face, smearing her eyeliner. "He did it," she choked out.

My body went numb, hot and then cold. "Who?"

She took a shuddering breath. "My father!"

The world tilted and spun. So it had been him all along. The obvious suspect. "You knew?"

She shook her head vigorously. "I didn't know! But I knew he lied about the night she disappeared. I wasn't with him. He said I had to say I was, or everyone would suspect him, because he dated her, and hit her a couple of times. He said it wasn't fair ..." She broke off, her chest heaving, her voice ragged.

It wasn't proof. But the pieces seemed to be slipping into place. Bain might have taken his daughter to the memorial so people could see him pretending to grieve, but she'd stayed to learn more about the dead woman. The woman she suspected her father had murdered.

I remembered the first time I'd seen her, at the summer festival – angry, defiant, blaming me for causing trouble. A daughter who didn't want to believe the worst of her father.

She was wiping at her eyes with the backs of her hands, smearing her makeup further. I hated to think what I would have done in her place. Would I have lied to protect someone I loved, even when I suspected he was a killer?

I hardened myself against sympathy. We needed answers, and this was the time to get them. "So how does Jay fit into all of this?"

"I don't know. He called and asked me to meet him at the festival. He said he had information that would help my father. I was worried that he was going to try to blackmail us or something, but he just wanted to talk about you. He was angry." She paused to sniff. "He's kind of a jerk."

I gave a choked half-laugh. "Yeah." I dug into my tote bag for a pack of tissues. I took one for myself and handed the rest to her.

She wiped at her face and whispered, "I don't know what to do."

I said, as gently as I could, "You have to tell the truth."

"But what if it wasn't him! What if I put him in jail, and it wasn't him after all?"

"But you think it was."

She nodded miserably

"Are there other reasons besides that he asked you to lie about that one night?"

"I think he was seeing her again. And he's been acting weird for a month. At first, right after she disappeared, kind of high strung. I thought it was the drugs."

She took a deep breath and let it out in a sigh. "After we knew she was dead ... He wasn't grieving over her, like he should, even if they hadn't been dating lately. More like ... I don't know, like he's proud of himself. My mom would say cocky, like he got away with something. And then Monday he made me help him sneak away, because he said the cops were watching him, and he took my car. He said he was going to spy on Bethany's brother, but I was so scared he'd do something terrible. He kept hinting that Kyle must've killed Bethany, and he got mad when no one took him seriously."

Monday. When my brake lines had been cut. Bain must have been spying on Kyle's house and taken the opportunity to cause me some trouble. Maybe he hoped Kyle would be blamed.

"Was that the only time he snuck away from the police?"

"Yeah, so far as I know, but he had me follow you some. I told him you went driving around the college and then called the cops. I didn't know why you did, but he got angry about it. Then I heard her car had been found there. That's suspicious, right?"

"Right." It was looking bad for Thomas Bain. At least if Lia could be convinced to testify in court. She obviously felt guilty, but would that be enough to make her betray her father? What if she denied all of this once we were out of here?

At least I would have the recording. I had to get as much evidence as possible, in case she refused to talk to the police. I had to keep things friendly, though, so it wouldn't feel like an interrogation. "It must be awful to think your father could have done something like that." It was hard for me to imagine, since I only had a shadowy ideal where the image of Father should be. Would I be strong enough to turn mine in for murder? Or would I defend my family at all cost? Which form of honor was right?

Of course, Thomas Bain was a horrible person, but did Lia think that?

She hadn't answered, so I tried again. "You knew Bethany."

She nodded. "She was all right. She didn't mind if I came by when she was there. We'd hang out sometimes." Her breathing and voice sounded more normal, though she still sniffled and dabbed at her eyes.

This was really hard. I didn't know what to say to her, for her sake, or to get her to confess on the recording.

I heard a murmur and rustle in the trees from the path behind me. A wave of relief washed over me. Maybe Lia wouldn't be so talkative around Kyle and Ricky, but at least I didn't have to handle this alone. I hurried to get in one last question, one that would let Kyle and Ricky know everything was under control. "So will you tell the police the truth? Bethany deserves it."

Lia sighed and looked up at me. "I guess I have to ..." Her gaze went past me and her eyes widened.

I turned with a smile, ready to offer Kyle the gift of this witness, ready to see the pride in Ricky's eyes.

Ricky stumbled into the clearing. But the man who had a hold of his shirt, who held a gun in his other hand, wasn't Kyle.

It was Thomas Bain.

Thirty-Nine

Lia jumped up. My own legs were too weak to move me. The scene blurred and then focused again. I stared into Ricky's eyes but couldn't offer any hope. I'd brought him into this.

Lia stood with her hands fisted at her sides. "Daddy, what are you doing?"

"Finding out my daughter is betraying me. Just like a woman. I never should've trusted you."

She looked toward the gun. "It doesn't look like you did." Her voice trembled but her chin went up. "What are you going to do now?"

"Get rid of these two." He looked at me. "It's your own fault. You shouldn't have gotten involved."

I couldn't have spoken even if I had an answer.

"Daddy, you can't," Lia said.

"I can't help it," Bain said. "I didn't mean to kill Bethany."

"It was an accident?" Lia asked.

His face twitched. "I didn't plan it. She drove me to it. She made me so mad. I was getting away with it, but her brother kept making noise, and then this bitch interfered."

I wanted to tell him finding Bethany's body hadn't been my choice. I struggled to get words out. "You won't get away with this either. How can you?"

"You'll have a little accident during this hunting thing." He looked at Lia. "And you'll help me."

"I won't!" she cried. "You can't do this! It's crazy."

She was right. He had to be insane. He'd never be able to stage an accident to take out both Ricky and me and get away with it. He'd be caught for sure. But that wouldn't help us.

How did one fight madness? He came closer, pushing Ricky before him. Bain was sweating, and his hand holding the gun twitched. His eyes looked glassy, the pupils tiny black points in washed-out blue. Maybe not crazy. Maybe on drugs that made him stupid and overconfident. But that didn't make him less dangerous.

Time seemed to slow and the scene receded, like a dream where I was watching from far away, a hawk soaring on lazy wings. This couldn't be happening to me, to us. I'd wake up soon.

I met Ricky's gaze and snapped back to reality. I wasn't the hawk, I was the rabbit. I'd darted into the open when I should have stayed hidden. Bain meant to kill us.

Was my phone capturing all of this? Would someone find it and know what happened? Or would Bain find the phone and destroy it, and hide our bodies, to decay like Bethany's had? Would someone stumble across us weeks or months from now, and have nightmares?

Lia stepped closer to her father, hands out in a pleading gesture. "Please, Daddy, stop it."

"You'll help," he growled, "and with your fingerprints on the gun, you'll keep quiet. No one will believe you weren't part of it all along." He added almost gently, "It's better that way, so I don't have to kill you, too."

Bain shoved Ricky forward, and he fell into me. I clutched at him as I sprawled back on the log. As Ricky scrambled for balance, my bag shifted and spilled onto the ground.

Ricky pulled back, out of my hold. Bain grabbed Lia and dragged her in front of his chest. The gun jerked around the clearing, pointing at the trees, swinging back to us.

I had to get up. I had to protect Ricky.

I had to fight.

I twisted and rolled off the log, landing on my hands and knees. The contents of my bag lay scattered before me. I seized the closest thing to a weapon.

I scrambled to my feet and turned. Lia was wrestling with her father. She pushed his arm to the side, while he tried to force her hand onto the gun. Ricky jumped forward and grabbed Bain's arm.

Lia screamed, "Run!"

The gun went off. The explosion rocked the clearing and an acrid scent joined the smell of fear.

I popped the top off my canister of bug spray. My legs wobbled as I took two steps forward, reached past Ricky and Lia, and sprayed it into Bain's eyes.

He shrieked and jerked back. The gun went off again. Ricky and Lia crumpled in a heap.

Bain staggered back, no longer holding the gun, scrubbing at his eyes. I stumbled forward, reached out a hand, and pushed.

Bain fell against a tree. The leaves shuddered and he tangled in the lower branches.

I swung toward Ricky and Lia, tears blurring my vision.

Ricky was already scrambling to his feet. No blood. My legs almost gave out in my relief.

Lia sat up and shook her head, tossing the hair out of her eyes. She glanced toward her father and then snatched the gun from the ground beside her.

I reached out a hand for Ricky. "Come on, let's go!"

He came to me but glanced back at Lia. She stood, holding the gun, and said, "Get help. I'll stay here."

I hesitated. Would she keep her father under guard until the police came – or help him escape? Despite everything he'd done, he was her father.

I didn't care; I wanted us out of there. I grabbed Ricky's arm and turned toward the path, already running.

I smacked into a broad chest. I jerked back and stared at a man I'd never seen before. Ricky stumbled into me from behind and I swayed.

The man stepped back and raised a gun.

I still had the bug spray in my hand. I lifted it with a sob.

"Police, nobody move!" he said.

My vision blurred again, and when it cleared I was trembling, but this time it was relief as I focused on the badge he held up. He wore jeans and a long-sleeved shirt open over a T-shirt, so he must have been either undercover or off duty. I took a deep breath and tried to think of something to say.

The man sidestepped, looking past Ricky and me. I glanced back. Lia still held the gun, but down at her side.

She looked at the man, squinted at his badge, and then bent to place the gun on the ground. She hesitated as she stood back up and then raised her hands, palms out, to shoulder level.

I wondered if we were supposed to do the same. I settled for putting my arm around my brother's shoulders and drawing him off to the side as the police officer retrieved Bain's gun.

"How did you find us?" Ricky asked.

The man tucked his gun in a shoulder holster hidden by his long-sleeved shirt and slid the second gun into his waistband at the back. Bain was still whimpering and rubbing at his bloodshot eyes. I wondered if he'd realized what had happened yet. "We've been keeping an eye on Bain for over a week. When I saw him grab the boy—"

My voice went shrill. "You've been here the whole time?"

He had the grace to look guilty as he flipped Bain onto his stomach and cuffed him. "I was waiting for backup. And hoping Bain would say something to hang himself – which he did. And then I didn't want to make things worse when he had the gun on all of you. But I was about to interfere when all he broke loose. Nice work with the bug spray, by the way. You can probably take your finger off the trigger now."

He nodded toward my arm, and I realized I was still holding the bug spray. Before I could put it down, I heard voices in the woods. I jerked and sprayed insect repellent down my leg.

"That should be backup," the cop said. He raised his voice to call out, "Over here. Situation under control."

A uniformed officer came down the path with his gun drawn, but he relaxed and put it away when he saw Bain on the ground. This guy I recognized; he'd responded to our call about finding Bethany's car. "Everyone all right?" he asked.

We looked at each other and nodded. Wherever the bullets had gone, they hadn't hit any of us. I tightened my grip on Ricky, and if it was partly to hold myself upright, no one had to know.

The uniformed officer looked at me. "Your mother and her friends are back there, and it was all I could do to make them wait while I checked out the situation. You'd better go let them know you're okay while we secure the scene."

Kyle was already sneaking down the path. I grinned and pulled Ricky with me. When we reached Kyle, I let my brother go, and he headed for the larger clearing. Before I could speak, Kyle pulled me into his arms. I clung to him, shaking all over again. He rubbed his cheek against mine and kissed my neck. I burrowed close, letting his scent fill my senses and wipe out the smells of the woods and the gun smoke and fear.

"You're all right?" he whispered.

I nodded against his neck, refusing to back up an inch.

"When I heard the shots – I've never been more frightened in my life."

"Me either."

"We'd better go let your mom know you're okay." We moved down the path still snugly arm in arm.

"Why are you here?" I asked. "How did you know?"

"I got your text, so I was keeping an eye out for Ricky. When your mom and Gran got back, I was going to go look for him. You didn't explain what was wrong, but it made me nervous. Then I saw the cop hurrying through the crowd and had a feeling there was trouble, so I took off after him." We stepped out into the larger clearing. Kyle gestured at the group in front of us. "And everyone else followed."

Mom was squeezing Ricky, who looked half embarrassed and half pleased. She saw me, gave a cry, and reached one arm out without letting go of my brother. I slipped away from Kyle to join them in a hug. Over Mom's head, I saw Nancy, with the falcon still on her gloved arm, and Daniel. I grinned at them and they beamed back.

I eased away from Mom and went to stand beside Kyle. Mom watched with a slight frown, but then she met my eyes and gave a resigned smile.

"Well?" Nancy's gruff voice rumbled. "Is anyone going to tell us what happened? Who got shot?"

"No one," I said. "Except Thomas Bain with bug spray in the eyes. But I think it's safe to say that we know who killed Bethany, and we can prove it."

A moment of silence followed. The victory was bittersweet. It wouldn't bring back Bethany. But maybe those who cared for her could take comfort that some kind of justice would be found.

"Oh!" I suddenly remembered the phone still in my front pocket. I pulled it out and checked – still recording. I ended the recording with a grin at Ricky. "Nice trick. I got it all on tape."

Kyle laughed and pulled me closer to his side. "That's my girl!"

Movement caught my eye, and I turned to see Lia Bain hesitating where the side path entered the clearing. She ducked her head and started to skirt our group.

"Wait!" I said.

She pressed her lips together and her chin trembled, but she managed to lift it in that little act of defiance as she looked up.

"Thank you," I said. "You probably saved our lives."

She blinked rapidly, her eyes shiny with tears. Had she really thought we would blame her? Maybe she'd lied at first, and had accidentally led me into danger, but she'd been willing to stand against her own father when she knew he was wrong. She'd done what had to be done.

Nancy and Daniel converged on the girl. "Then we owe you our thanks as well," Nancy said. Daniel, give her your handkerchief." Lia cringed away from the falcon, but Nancy soon had her talking about it, and Lia even ran a finger lightly down the bird's wing.

I leaned into Kyle. "Maybe Nancy will take her hunting some time. It might be good for her. I know it's been good for me."

His arm tightened. "We'll do whatever you want."

I turned to face him and put my hands on his shoulders. "Does that offer last until tonight?"

His eyes gleamed. "At least."

I brushed my cheek against his to whisper in his ear. "Good. Because I'm starting to figure out what I want. And I'm ready to go after it."

Dear Readers,

Several years ago I was hiking in the wilderness with two friends when we stumbled on a dead body. Of course we reported it at once. I then took pages of notes on all the thoughts and feelings that went through our minds in the days that followed. (I didn't know when or how I would use these notes, but for a writer, all of life is research.)

I heard later that many people do not report crime scenes. How could someone simply ignore a sight like that? That question and the powerful experience of uncovering the death of a murdered stranger inspired this book. All the characters in *What We Found* are fictional, however.

I am grateful to falconer Matt Mitchell for his kindness and generosity in introducing me to the world of falconry. The scenes with falcons and hawks are based on my experiences interviewing or observing him at work, though any mistakes are mine alone, of course. If you would like to see photos of falcons and hawks, including baby pictures, please visit my website page for *What We Found*.

You can also learn about my other books and read sample chapters on my website, www.krisbock.com, or on my Amazon page.

I hope you'll keep an eye out for my future books. Visit my website at www.krisbock.com to sign up for a newsletter announcing new releases.

Kris Bock

About The Author

Ordinary Women, Extraordinary Adventures

Kris Bock writes action-packed romantic suspense, often involving outdoor adventures and Southwestern landscapes. Her stories will interest fans of Terry Odell, Mary Stewart, Lillian Stewart Carl, and Barbara Michaels. Books include *The Mad Monk's Treasure, The Dead Man's Treasure, Counterfeits, What We Found,* and *Whispers in the Dark*. Read excerpts at www.krisbock.com or visit her Amazon page. You can also sign up for the Kris Bock newsletter announcing new releases.

Sign up for the Kris Bock newsletter for new releases and special offers:

http://eepurl.com/5Dd_f

You can also learn about my other books and read sample chapters at www.krisbock.com or on the Kris Bock Amazon page.

What We Found

22-year-old Audra Needham is back in her small New Mexico hometown. She just wants to fit in, work hard, and help her younger brother. Going for a walk in the woods with her former crush, Jay, is a harmless distraction.

Until they stumble on a body.

Jay, who has secrets of his own to protect, insists they walk away and keep quiet. But Audra can't forget what she's seen. The woman deserves to be found, and her story deserves to be told.

More than one person isn't happy about Audra bringing a crime to life. The dead woman was murdered, and Audra could be next on the vengeful killer's list. She'll have to stand up for herself in order to stand up for the murder victim. It's a risk, and so is reaching out to the mysterious young man who works with deadly birds of prey. With her 12-year-old brother determined to play detective, and romance budding in the last place she expected, Audra learns that some risks are worth taking – no matter the danger, to her body or her heart.

Praise for *What We Found*:

"Another action-packed suspense novel by Kris Bock, perhaps her best to date. The author weaves an intriguing tale with appealing characters. Watching Audra, the main character, evolve into an emotionally-mature and independent young woman is gratifying."

"This book had me guessing to the end. Well written characters drive the story. Good romance. Exceptional and believable plot twists and turns. I loved it!"

"This is a nonstop suspense. Love the characters and how real they seem with every episode played out. This is a love story and suspense all in one."

Whispers in the Dark

Young archeologist Kylie Hafford heads to the remote Puebloan ruins of Lost Valley, in the Four Corners area, to excavate. Her first exploration of the crumbling ruins ends in a confrontation with a gorgeous, angry man who looks like a warrior from the Pueblo's ancient past. If only Danesh weren't so aggravating . . . and fascinating. Then she literally stumbles across Sean, a charming, playful tourist. His attentions feel safer, until she glimpses secrets he'd rather keep hidden.

The summer heats up as two sexy men pursue her. She finds mysteries – and surprising friendships – among the other campground residents. Could the wide-eyed woman and her silent children be in the kind of danger all too familiar to Kylie?

Mysterious lights, murmuring voices, and equipment gone missing plague her dig. A midnight encounter sends Kylie plummeting into a deep canyon. She'll need all her strength and wits to survive. Everything becomes clear – if she wants to save the man she's come to love and see the villains brought to justice, she must face her demons and fight.

Whispers in the Dark is action-packed romantic suspense set in the Four Corners region of the Southwest.

Praise for *Whispers in the Dark*:

"This book was a delight from start to finish!"

"*Whispers in the Dark* has a hefty dose of adventure and mystery, as well as a strong main character."

"This book kept me turning pages until the end. The plot was full of twists and turns, always keeping the reader rooting for the heroine. Excellent read!"

Counterfeits

Counterfeits
Kris Bock

Painter Jenny Kinley has spent the last decade struggling in the New York art world. Her grandmother's sudden death brings her home to New Mexico, but inheriting the children's art camp her grandmother ran is more of a burden than a gift. How can she give up her lifelong dreams of showing her work in galleries and museums?

Rob Caruso, the camp cook and all-around handyman, would be happy to run the camp with Jenny. Dare he even dream of that, when his past holds dark secrets that he can never share? When Jenny's father reappears after a decade-long absence, only Rob knows where he's been and what danger he's brought with him.

Jenny and Rob face midnight break-ins and make desperate escapes, but the biggest danger may come from the secrets that don't want to stay buried. In the end, they must decide whether their dreams will bring them together or force them apart.

Praise for *Counterfeits*:

"*Counterfeits* is the kind of romantic suspense novel I have enjoyed since I first read Mary Stewart's *Moonspinners*, and Kris Bock used all the things I love about this genre. Appealing lead characters, careful development of the mysterious danger facing one or both of those characters, a great location that is virtually a character on its own, interesting secondary characters who might or might not be involved or threatened, and many surprises building up to the climax." 5 Stars – Roberta at Sensuous Reviews blog

"Counterfeits actually kept me guessing! ... I love when a writer manages to do that to me. Grab *Counterfeits* and keep trying to guess. Be surprised like I was." – Rochelle Weber, Roses & Thorns Reviews

KRIS BOCK

the MAD MONK'S
TREASURE

The Mad Monk's Treasure

The lost Victorio Peak treasure is the stuff of legends—a heretic Spanish priest's gold mine, made richer by the spoils of bandits and an Apache raider. When Erin, a quiet history professor, uncovers a clue that may pinpoint the lost treasure cave, she prepares for adventure.

But when a hit and run driver nearly kills her, she realizes she's not the only one after the treasure. And is Drew, the handsome helicopter pilot who found her bleeding in a ditch, really a hero, or one of the enemy?

Erin isn't sure she can trust Drew with her heart, but she'll need his help to track down the treasure. She heads into the New Mexico wilderness with her brainy best friend Camie and a feisty orange cat. The wilderness holds its own dangers, from wild animals to sudden storms. Plus, the sinister men hunting Erin are determined to follow her all the way to the treasure, no matter where the twisted trail leads.

Erin won't give up an important historical find without a fight, but is she ready to risk her life—and her heart?

[originally published as *Rattled.*]

Praise for *The Mad Monk's Treasure*:

"This book kept me turning its pages until I finished it. The action never stopped and I just had to know what happened next. I really cared what happened to the heroine. I loved the sexy helicopter pilot and enjoyed the romance even when I was on the edge of my chair with the action. It was adventure and romance at its best."

"The story has it all – action, romance, danger, intrigue, lost treasure, not to mention a sizzling relationship ..."

KRIS BOCK

the DEAD MAN'S
TREASURE

The Dead Man's Treasure

Rebecca Westin is shocked to learn the grandfather she never knew has left her a bona fide buried treasure – but only if she can decipher a complex series of clues leading to it. The hunt would be challenging enough without interference from her half-siblings, who are determined to find the treasure first and keep it for themselves. Good thing Rebecca has recruited some help.

Sam is determined to show Rebecca that a desert adventure can be sexy and fun. But there's a treacherous wildcard in the mix, a man willing to do anything to get that treasure – and revenge.

Action and romance combine in this lively Southwestern adventure, complete with riddles the reader is invited to solve to identify historical and cultural sites around New Mexico. See the "Books" page of my website for a printable list of the clues and recipes from the book.

"*The Dead Man's Treasure* is fast-paced and a perfect read for the weekend. I highly recommend this one."

"I can't say enough how much I loved this book! It has mystery, adventure, danger, romance, and above it all family remains a huge theme."

The Mad Monk's Treasure is the first of the Southwest Treasure Hunters novels. *The Dead Man's Treasure* is book 2 and *The Skeleton Canyon Treasure* is book 3. Each novel stands alone and is complete, with no cliffhangers. This series mixes action and adventure with romance. The stories explore the Southwest, especially New Mexico.

Ms. Bock also writes for young people as **Chris Eboch**. Her novels are appropriate for ages nine and up.

The Eyes of Pharaoh is a mystery set in ancient Egypt. This story of drama and intrigue brings an ancient world to life as three friends investigate a plot against the Pharaoh.

In *The Well of Sacrifice*, a Mayan girl in ninth-century Guatemala rebels against the High Priest who sacrifices anyone challenging his power.

Kirkus Reviews said, "[An] engrossing first novel ... Eboch crafts an exciting narrative with a richly textured depiction of ancient Mayan society ... The novel shines not only for a faithful recreation of an unfamiliar, ancient world, but also for the introduction of a brave, likable and determined heroine."

The Genie's Gift is a lighthearted action novel that draws on the mythology of The Arabian Nights. Shy and timid Anise determines to find the Genie Shakayak and claim the Gift of Sweet Speech. But the way is barred by a series of challenges, both ordinary and magical. How will Anise get past a vicious she-ghoul, a sorceress who turns people to stone, and mysterious sea monsters, when she can't even speak in front of strangers?

The Haunted series follows a brother and sister who travel with their parents' ghost hunter TV show and try to help the ghosts.

In *The Ghost on the Stairs*, an 1880s ghost bride haunts a Colorado hotel, waiting for her missing husband to return.

The Riverboat Phantom features a steamboat pilot still trying to prevent a long-ago disaster. In *The Knight in the Shadows*, a Renaissance French squire protects a sword on display at a New York City museum.

During *The Ghost Miner's Treasure*, Jon and Tania help a dead man find his lost gold mine—but they're not the only ones looking for it.

Bandits Peak

While hiking in the mountains, Jesse meets a strange trio. He befriends Maria, but he's suspicious of the men with her. Still, charmed by Maria, Jesse promises not to tell anyone that he met them. But his new friends have deadly secrets, and Jesse uncovers them. It will take all his wilderness skills, and all his courage, to survive.

Readers who enjoyed Gary Paulsen's *Hatchet* will love *Bandits Peak*. This heart-pounding adventure tale is full of danger and excitement.

Learn more or read excerpts at www.chriseboch.com.

Cover art by Alan Erickson.

This is a work of fiction. Names, characters, places, and incidents are the product of the author's imagination. Any resemblance to actual persons, living or dead, is entirely coincidental.